Praise

“With balances [illegible] of speech with a lyric sensibility … The heightened language and the influence of native mythology are incorporated seamlessly into the narration, and deepen the novel without undermining the plausibility of Trista’s voice … The emotional force of this novel is undeniable.”

—*Quill & Quire*

“Shines in expressiveness.” —*The StarPhoenix* (Saskatoon)

“Enduring Trista’s trials along with her can be daunting, but … within the grim confines of the prison there are acts of kindness on the part of the staff and Trista’s fellow detainees, there is the thrill of Trista’s illicit romance, the memories of her mother, her best friend, and times spent with the Snow Nanuks, elder women who live according to Inuit tradition. These make the tragic elements of Trista’s story that much more affecting … With offers a fully realized and authentic narrator beset with tremendous personal and cultural obstacles. Trista’s deftly portrayed sense of delusion, despair and hope is ultimately both moving and unsettling.” —*National Post*

Praise for *Skids*

“[An] impressive debut collection … We lose characters, then find them again, usually no better off—but more familiar, and more worth knowing.” —*The Globe and Mail*

“This is fiction that shines a unique light into our common darkness. *Skids* is filled with brilliant, powerful and compassionate voices. If ever I need a guide on the dark side of the moon, I want it to be Cathleen With.” —Bill Gaston

"Original, fresh, and authentic. With inhabits her characters from the inside out, and presents them to us with a clear, unblinking gaze. These stories feel lived rather than imagined." —*Quill & Quire*

"A nervy and powerful tour de force, written with wit and honesty in an entirely original voice. Unforgettable." —Helen Humphreys

PENGUIN CANADA

HAVING FAITH IN THE POLAR GIRLS' PRISON

CATHLEEN WITH, author of the short story collection *Skids*, worked as a teacher in Inuvik and Seoul. She now lives in Vancouver. *Having Faith in the Polar Girls' Prison* is her first novel.

ALSO BY CATHLEEN WITH

Skids

HAVING FAITH IN THE POLAR GIRLS' PRISON

CATHLEEN WITH

PENGUIN
CANADA

PENGUIN CANADA

Published by the Penguin Group

Penguin Group (Canada), 90 Eglinton Avenue East, Suite 700, Toronto, Ontario, Canada M4P 2Y3
(a division of Pearson Canada Inc.)

Penguin Group (USA) Inc., 375 Hudson Street, New York, New York 10014, U.S.A.
Penguin Books Ltd, 80 Strand, London WC2R 0RL, England
Penguin Ireland, 25 St Stephen's Green, Dublin 2, Ireland (a division of Penguin Books Ltd)
Penguin Group (Australia), 250 Camberwell Road, Camberwell, Victoria 3124, Australia
(a division of Pearson Australia Group Pty Ltd)
Penguin Books India Pvt Ltd, 11 Community Centre, Panchsheel Park, New Delhi – 110 017, India
Penguin Group (NZ), 67 Apollo Drive, Rosedale, North Shore 0745, Auckland, New Zealand
(a division of Pearson New Zealand Ltd)
Penguin Books (South Africa) (Pty) Ltd, 24 Sturdee Avenue, Rosebank, Johannesburg 2196, South Africa

Penguin Books Ltd, Registered Offices: 80 Strand, London WC2R 0RL, England

First published in Viking Canada hardcover by Penguin Group (Canada),
a division of Pearson Canada Inc., 2009
Published in this edition, 2010

1 2 3 4 5 6 7 8 9 10 (WEB)

Manufactured in Canada.

LIBRARY AND ARCHIVES CANADA CATALOGUING IN PUBLICATION

With, Cathleen, 1967-
Having Faith in the Polar Girls' Prison / Cathleen With.

ISBN 978-0-14-316907-9

I. Title.

PS8645.I84H39 2010 jC813'.6 C2009-906561-4

For the children

of the Mackenzie Delta

one

It's early morning and Faith is fussing again, hardly got the sleep out of my eyes. I tell the worker that comes in that sometimes Faith can't get her mouth to seal around my nipple. She leans over us both, gently smoothes her finger over Faith's upper lip. Faith flutters her little lashes like she's trying to wake up more and I shift her closer in to my nipple. The worker reminds me that preemies get tired easily from the sucking and maybe too used to the bottles. She looks at me like she's gonna say something more, but then she goes and leaves us alone. Faith is snuffling a bit against my breast, starting to latch on, and I feel relieved she's finally sucking proper. I'm thinking this is the best feeling ever, makes all the outside shit go away, the other girls in here, some of the staff looking at me with needles in their eyes. I never know who's related to that woman from the Aurora Store. I mean, in Jackfish Bay everyone is related to everyone. Hell, I think even I was related to her.

Through the sliver of a window I got in here I can see some of the Iceroad down the hill, the white headlights of one or two cars making their way north to Tuk or maybe south to Inuvik, hook up with the Dempster Highway and away from here. The Iceroad's not just one road; you got the oxbows of the east channel going to Tuk and out to the Arctic Sea, then a windy road going west to Aklavik. Lots of kettle lakes and channels connect up, and though maintenance rigs patrol it, with sensors even to check the ice, still a blizzard come up and it's easy to go off the road. Or just get lost in the loneliness of the dark and the ice, let the green ghosties of the northern lights come dancing, lead you astray.

Even though it's early morning, there's no bit of light anywhere near the Iceroad. Sun won't really touch our town until January, just some dusky skies around noon, sun squeeze up for a little peek maybe 11 a.m., then right back down to shine on them in the south. November and dark days here in the Mackenzie Delta.

Saturdays are sometimes bad. Even though I get to spend the day with Faith, and not have to give her to the workers while they make me go into the classroom and learn my language arts and math, I still spend the whole day thinking about Tyler, what he's doing down there in Yellowknife, if he's thinking about Faith, or me. Would he even have wanted us, once she got born and her being the way she is?

Some workers say maybe even foster care can't take her, she's so retarded. Don't think Auntie or Nanuk come to take her; been here three weeks now and they're not come in to see me, too ashamed, only Keely been to see me. And the Snow Nanuks are too old and almost gone out of their house, most of them at the Elder Hospital. If Faith could have the Snow Nanuks who looked after all us kids, maybe things could be okay. Simple and sweet, like when we was real little. Me and my best friend Keely dreamed of being like them when we grown, like they all good and looked out for their little ones, and then their kids' little ones, us coming from the back roads of Jackfish Bay. The Snow Nanuks always had their door unlocked and something hot to drink on their stove. Maybe they won't let me in now, what I done, where I am going and maybe for life. No one to look after Faithy now, maybe just strangers. Mom would of taken her, she been here, Mom would of taken her right up, not scared of any retarded kids, not my mom. But that Iceroad taken her long ago. That worker says maybe I got two more months with Faith in here, then they're thinking about what to do with her.

On a good day, when the snow is flaking down soft I'm in my small room, watching it flutter onto the scrub trees, some kids zipping by on Ski-Doos, can see the flash of their faces under the facility lights, their cheeks red and chafed, mouths open and laughing. Me and Faith inside, warm, and Faith at my breast, sucking proper, I think of her all-normal future, running to her new mom. Her hair in pigtails, her feet have on the beaded slippers Nanuk sent her, and me watching her on the webcam here. Don't know how long they're keeping me inside for what I done. I forget all the good I keep trying to remember, how we're calling our grandmothers Nanuk, and trying to get some old spirits talking to me in here, like Nanuk says to me: "Trista, remember your Snow Nanuks, we all who are loving you. Remember the good they learned in you." Who is going to save me and Faith but those northern spirits long gone? Who is going to look at me—quarter Eskimo, three-quarters rig-pig, and who knows what else—and my fucked-up baby?

Faithy starts to gurgle a bit, this hum she makes when she's done feeding. I swear she's looking at me with those dreamy eyes, lips pushed together with her tiny mouth humming, and I put her up to my shoulder, pat her bum. Her hand brushes against my ulu necklace, the one Mom gave me when I was five. Then the red light goes on, and the bell goes off. My door snicks open, free from its electric lock.

"Trista. You coming?" Deanne says. Her eyebrows pointed up like they do when she knows I'm in my head, just mooning over Faithy and not paying attention.

"Yeeah. Let me put her in the rolly crib." That Deanne's always out and getting to breakfast or going to Group the minute the door opens, but I hate to leave the warm of my bed.

We got Group Saturdays after breakfast and it sucks because the weekend float staff's on instead of Linda and Deb. They got names, but none that we care to remember. Maybe they're not as committed to it or something, being they're on weekends. Maybe they got other work they do all week. I know I worked with one over at the Northmart, but she's okay.

It's the Bitch we have to look out for. The Bitch's got her concentrated look on, with her plain black pants she probably irons right before work and then takes a cab here so she doesn't mess them up pulling snowpants over them. Her hair is near perfect and I think she might even get blonde highlights done in her brown hair. Pay big money for that, only place they do it is Inuvik. She's yapping something at Megan, and Megan is fiddling in her seat none too happy about it. Aimee's picking at the chair's arm, not looking at anyone, and Deanne's just sitting there grinning. Deanne's almost always good for coming up with something because most of us hate Group, feels like we're on camera or being studied like some science project.

"I'm reading that book on addictions," says Deanne.

The Bitch looks over at her and nods, asks her, "So what are you getting out of it?"

"Just … Stuff. Like how you gotta get away from triggers and that. Thinking Yellowknife was a big trigger for me," says Deanne.

Me and Aimee's looking at her, but then real quick we look down because you never know when the Bitch is going to start on someone else, she whips it around quick, her talk. Group is better with Linda or Deb because even though I only been here three weeks, easier to know them, know what's coming up.

Deanne's older than us, she's sixteen and from Yellowknife and been here already three months or so. She's skinny, but skinny tall, like a model with her black hair long and straight, she's got straight-across bangs too, makes her eyes bigger underneath her bangs, glow kind of.

Then there's Megan, who's been here maybe a month and she's the youngest, thirteen, but you wouldn't know it because she's funny, brave, hyper, and real outgoing-like, electric. She's dyed her hair orange and it don't look too bad, more like a red fox, just lights up the room, can't help but see her, fiery.

Me and Aimee are new, I come in, then Aimee a week later and we're both fifteen, Aimee's real small for her age though, not skinny like Deanne but more skinny sick. She's got beautiful long hair too, down her back, it's got a kind of dark brown horsetail colour to it. Makes my heart hurt for her hair, kind of looked like mine except mine is black, hers just straight and long everywhere, no bangs. I miss my long hair, could brush it and brush it, tie it in a knot even and it was strong, soft against my cheek when I slept, my own built-in pillow. Mine's the shortest now, in a bob that's kind of below my ears like a little kid's. Used to be down to my bum, before that night.

Deanne's going to Yellowknife again soon, she can't be in the facility much longer because she needs to be in the youth detention there past sixteen. But she had to get out of Yellowknife, bad shit at that youth facility she got into. Not like she tells it, but like the workers say to her.

"I'm thinking I can go to meetings, you know, Narcotics Anonymous, and then maybe hook up with that one family took me in when I was ten, maybe they can take me in again," Deanne says. She's all confident-looking, but I can tell she's nervous just by the way her hand's rubbing at her jeans.

"Be careful not to get your hopes up," the Bitch says. She's looking down at her clipboard, writing something we can't see.

"Yeeah, I know, it's not like it would be a big deal, just would be nice to know someone," Deanne says.

Deanne looks over at me and winks, and I know she's just stalling for us all again. She's good at that, getting the attention off us, then making herself look all good and healthy. Most times Linda and Deb don't fall for it. I don't think the Bitch is gonna either because she says, "So, Aimee, you have some visitors coming today?" Megan sucks her breath in and Aimee just starts chewing at her hair nervous, because we all know Aimee don't ever have visitors and what's that Bitch doing bringing it up like that? But then I think maybe the Bitch doesn't know, because she says in a more gentle voice: "Aimee, you want to talk about the letter you got yesterday?"

"No," Aimee whispers, and we can see her closing up right then and there. And I think the Bitch's gonna go into her, but she just leaves it, starts going on about chore allocation for the week, how we might have to do more upkeep stuff around the facility because there's only four of us right now and usually in winter there's eight or nine.

The girls are sweet on me and Faithy. They like to see a baby in here, makes them remember and miss their little sisters some. With Aimee it's because of the letter too. Her own baby died of SIDS and she showed me that letter. The official death certificate. Linda let her come into my room yesterday to open it, and after she didn't cry or nothing, just asked if she could hold Faith some. On the CBC we know they calling us the babies who having the babies up north; we're not stupid to how those people from down south see us. We got them workers come up from down south at first, they been telling us that they going to university, hearing about us all huffing paint. Then they come up and stay a while and know we're not all like that of course. Yeeah, you got some of the boys try huffing on a dare. But it's not like we can just go into the hardware store and get it. They know we're kids and the town tries hard not to get us paint, even booze. Okay but maybe not at the house parties, but the town people try anyways. Drugs are easy though. People drive them up the Iceroad, or over the Dempster come summers, weed, heroin, coke, even meth. Sometimes easier to get that shit than to get some old drunk to buy you a mickey at the liquor store.

We're not like other northern jails you hear about, how Nunavut's getting all with their culture and shit, trying to rehabilitate proper just within their own territory. We got girls from all over the North here in the Polar Girls' Prison, really called the Polar Girls' Youth Facility, but we know what it really is: jail. Most girls are placed here because they don't want them in the other smaller communities, they don't have any jails there. Some of the girls come from other areas like we got Inuvialuit lands at Banks Island and Victoria Island, then Gwich'in over Aklavik and Fort McPherson too. Sometimes we get some of the girls from Yellowknife here too. Then there's the Yellowknife prison, it's a youth facility. But they say you get to know worse girls there, like they've been in and out of jail a lot, and they do more needle drugs there and they don't act like us. Like Deanne and how she's been hooking there in Yellowknife and says she's only into having girlfriends not boyfriends, only doing johns for money. Not something I know much about here in Jackfish Bay. Sure we get all the drugs and shit, but if someone is hooking maybe they doing it out of their home I guess, not on the street.

Now Deanne's got her mouth open and she's all talking about getting more phone time to call her friends. She gets it going most days in Group because the rest of us too quiet, except Megan. She's in from Paulautuk and she's got HIV. We're not supposed to know how she got it and then of course we all do, because it's jail and that's how it works. We don't go whispering it to each other, not secret-like. But we're doing chores, dishes or something, and Megan, she just tells us. Us that's on dishes. She just goes, "You won't get it from having your hands in the water with me." We know that anyways, we got them public health nurses coming from Yellowknife and telling us that, but she's just telling us to let us know, that she's going to tell us, that's she's letting us in. That's what Linda and Deb want, to let everyone in and then we get better somehow.

That older worker's here today in Group too, we're lucky that it's not just the Bitch. The older one's got her hair cut real short, it's grey and spiky and she's nodding at Deanne like she cares, she's good at that. I know she does care, but Deanne's trying sometimes, anyone can see that, even me, though she's older than me. She just wants some good attention to her, been without parents and in one foster home after another so long.

"And maybe we can get some more Arctic char for dinner? I haven't had char for so long," Deanne says.

"Where do you think you are, the Mackenzie Hotel?" the Bitch says.

Megan's shifting. "Be fun if we could go to the hotel one night, could we? Like maybe do work training there, maybe in the kitchen like Sherry teaching us some too," Megan says, and she's getting all into it you can't help get kind of excited about it too maybe.

Grey spiky-haired worker says, "Let's get off the food topic, on to other things."

"I just think there should be more phone privileges too. Like every night," Deanne says. She's looking over at me, trying to make me say something about it too and I just nod my head because I know she's thinking about me and Tyler, how I get waiting to phone him. How he's never fucking there at that number and wonder when he's ever gonna pick up the phone and call me.

"Okay, Deanne, we'll look into it, but let's get on to more serious things," the Bitch says. "How was your visit with Sam?"

Deanne's got her own fancy lawyer from Yellowknife, not legal aid from Inuvik like most of us. Because her court case is part of something about prostitution and RCMP and rings. I swallow hard because I'm jealous. Deanne looks so grown up, and she talks about it like it's something. Something not bad she's done, but like street justice. Wonder how she lives with the knowing. Me, don't even know when my court case is set, haven't got a date yet. Might be I get sentenced to forever and then that's forever without Faith too, or Tyler. Only dates have been with the doctors, they figuring out what to do with Faith, testing her. Maybe taking her away and I can't think about that now, don't want them to make me think about that now. Deanne goes on about Sam this and Sam that and her voice never loses that proud thing she's got going on. She can talk about her crime in Group like she done some service to humans.

Deanne winds down and the Bitch asks me: "When's Dr. Petterson coming in again, Trista?"

"Huh?"

"When's the doctor coming in to take Faith for the tests at the Inuvik Hospital, did she say when she had her checkup?"

"Maybe Thursday."

Jail and sentencing and tests and baby and doctors and Group. Makes me happy my mom isn't alive to see me in here, this fuck-up, got enough feeling bad for Auntie and Nanuk. I say something more, but it feels like just all the stuff I've been saying about Faith and how she's eating and how I'm eating. Hollow words that don't fill in for the pain I got in my gut and the period blood that started with Faith that night and hasn't stopped and pushing away the worms inside that want to swarm out of my mouth and scream, What did you do, Trista? Look what you done and what's gonna happen? But the Bitch is checking in with Aimee and talking some with Megan and it's off me for today and I don't want to think about it any more. Everybody piles up the chairs and we leave the Group room, spend some time before lunch in the living room and the workers let me have the rolly crib to myself. I'm holding my baby, warm, she's sleeping. Doesn't feel real, this prison, Faith.

two

"Tyler? Pick up, okay? So I gave you the number last time on voicemail, just call and the workers can put you through. But you can't call until seven at night, after dinner. That's the only time they'll put the call through. Between seven and eight. Ty? Please call."

School day. It's only in here I can hold on to the words in them books they give us. The teacher from down south, Miss Sarah, she's okay, but a little scared of us, I think. Maybe not. She doesn't talk much like the teachers at the high school, and that's good, because lots of those teachers from down south, they're nice, I guess, but they do blather fucking lots at the mouth, they got so much to say. Most days it's quiet in that class, there's only four of us in the jail right now, and the workers say maybe one more girl's going to join us in a few weeks. Miss Sarah, she's big on the reading, like she says we have to read, to understand character and stories. She doesn't always know why we're in here, the workers keep our crimes confidential because some of us still have court and sentencing, but she makes us write journals and most of us talk about it in there. Except Megan. Megan just motors on about her crime in class. Miss Sarah's always encouraging her to talk about it in Group instead. Megan's got no shame and it's not her fault she done her crime. Maybe Miss Sarah thinks I am softer because I got Faith. But sometimes I am out of touch, like Linda says. Detached.

Miss Sarah starts reading aloud again, from *To Kill a Mockingbird*, and I'm thinking that maybe me and Tyler and Jimmy, maybe our story's a little like Tom's, maybe a little like Boo's. But then I look around this jail, I remember that night, and I know I'm full of shit. Some of the girls here, they're all "I didn't do nothing wrong." Aimee, who set the house on fire with her dad sleeping inside because she was sick of him coming home drunk raping her, or Megan, who tried to rat poison her mom's food to get her welfare cheques coming to her like orphan's pay or something, like the welfare worker wouldn't notice. Deanne and her battle with the johns of Yellowknife. Most of them were doing some coke, or smoking heroin or drinking. We talk about it, just not in whispers or anything, but soft. We have to talk about it all in Group, they try to make us. But the girls are different then. We get more hidden in Group. Not showing our bad we feel inside. You can't just give everything up. Where it's gonna end up, what we all say?

Them workers in here, most they know us, they're in the community and been living here for a long time, or like Linda, who's from Inuvik. We got people working here from down south, and once they start living here a long time, they get it. Or you get some women they get older and had their kids and all, then the Gwich'in or Inuvialuit office give them some money they can get down to the university and then come back up and be workers to us, we got them too, they know their shit, been through it like us. Like the teachers at the elementary school from down south, some are not Inuit or native or nothing but some even marry. Here, Jackfish Bay, Inuvialuit, Gwich'in, and also whites doing the oil and gas, and the army used to be here too, with the DEW Line. That's what Daduk told me, he remembers some of the army guys he'd drink with lost their jobs to the computers, left in about '85, then most of them gone fully in 1990, something about Russia not bad any more. Daduk's still pissed with that army, putting shit in the Mackenzie, like their hard metals or something, he's worried maybe it makes the fish sick, makes our water weird, and we have to put more chemicals in to clean it. Daduk remembers when it tasted better, the Mackenzie River, sweet.

Miss Sarah says, "We got two minutes' silence coming up for the eleventh hour."

I think, we been some silent for a while, what we got to be more silent about? After we stand and think about soldiers, Miss Sarah shows us some DVD about the old wars and also wars in Afghanistan they got Canadian soldiers at. Makes me think of Jackfish Bay in summer, looking all dry like that. Except for the garbage the snow uncovers when it melts.

"You girls write more in your journals. Put them up here on my desk, then you can play Scrabble or finish up your workbooks while I check them," Miss Sarah says after the movie. Check them for what? But she's nice. Even I seen Deanne looking at her and smiling a little, not so grumpy in class. Miss Sarah's just started in September, never even been up this far north before. She's got these green eyes that got bits of brown in them and she doesn't wear any makeup, not even lipstick, just some shiny gloss that when she's leaning over your desk you can smell the cinnamon of it, like something Christmas. She laughs like a little kid, we been telling her about the utilidor. She's asking, "What's that covered metal thing for, winding through town like that?" Showing me a picture I drew of it in my journal. Tyler standing on it, whooping. How it takes shit away, and gives us water that's not froze up. "We don't have that back in Lunenburg," she says, then tells us how she go out fishing with her dad, how her house just got some sand foundation then cement, not built up on wood or stilts so it doesn't slide with the permafrost top hardening and melting some come summer. We look up from our workbooks when Miss Sarah starts telling us about her Nova Scotia life. How she goes out sailing and even in a special boat when she puts down metal cages. "Those lobsters, they walk right in there and we haul them up. Plop them in the boiling water," Miss Sarah says.

"Alive?" Megan says and giggles.

"Yup, gross right? We boil them up till they're red and gleaming. Crack them open and dip them in butter. Best you've ever tasted."

I'm looking at that map of Canada, thinking that's a long long way down and away from me and this snow outside, dark outside still and going on almost noon but twilight coming soon and hitting the hard white of it, just so, making it yellow up and gleam through our classroom window.

Sometimes at night the workers come in my room and sit for a while with me and Faith. These walls in here, it's not like they're some kind of jail, it's like they are tan and soft, like the hospital. I feel safe here. No hard edges. The workers on nights will bring me hot milk, remind me to drink lots of water to make the breast milk come more, and talk about feeding their own kids at their breast. They gentle talk and they're almost the same age as my mom would of been. They bring some knitting in and we just sit, listening to Faith trying to suck, her little fist pulling at my necklace.

Watching them knit, I think of Mom trying to make the crafts to get us some more money. How she was good with carving, even how she said I was good at cutting hair when I was little. Used to love getting the scissors and brushing through Auntie's, Nanuk's, Mom's, or even Snow Nanuks' long hair and just trimming off the ends, clean and even. Snow Nanuks said that people used the ulu not just for cutting caribou hide but cutting kids' hair too, for good luck. I was sitting in the living room when Mom gave me the ulu necklace. Moving some little cars around on the floor. She come sit beside me, crosses her long legs, pushes my hair out of my face: "You got to use your clips, Trista, your hair is getting so long now," she says. In my remembering it's kind of slow motion, like I remember I am almost five because it's the night before my birthday. "Such a big girl you're getting to be, cutting the Snow Nanuks' hair," Mom says. Then she traces my lips with her finger and I think she's almost crying and I'm wondering why she almost crying. She opens her other hand and the ulu necklace gleams in it. "I got Daduk to get the mammoth ivory so I could make this for you. See, it's a tiny ulu." And I touch it, the gold part is a little cold, but the mammoth ivory ulu bit is warm, cream-coloured, old-looking. "Long ago, ulu was the best thing a woman could have, use it for skinning caribou, cut up food chunks, or cut hair." She puts it around my neck and the chain is long, not like now where it sits in the hollow of my throat. Then it was long and mornings when Mom would brush my hair she'd tell me, "Hold your ulu close now so I don't pull at it." The hairbrush going down and down again softly but firm through my hair till I almost felt like sleeping again.

Been waiting for Faith so long, can't believe she's here sometimes. Her cheeks, she's got these full cheeks. Linda says that's so good, because Faith is a preemie, and sometimes preemies don't have fat cheeks, maybe they are starving a little. Faith came out seven months, that night. When she's not fussing, I put my mouth to her cheek, she smells like a good sour, like me if I been sleeping long and haven't had a bath in a day, but I can still smell the soap, the fuzzies from my blanket, smell that warm something smell. I know it's my milk and her breath, but I can almost smell Tyler in there with her, like me and him mixed to make her. I got my lips to her ear, just nibble some there, lick it a bit. Me and Daduk ice fishing off the Iceroad downriver, he's jiggling his pole in the icehole to make the fish come up and take notice. Sometimes if you scoop up a chunk of ice, it can taste like Faith's ear. Faith, she gets real quiet when I move my lips up to her. I know she can't hear, that's what the doctors say, and she's some kind of retarded, probably. But I swear she is listening to me hum.

Today got to get her ready for them tests Dr. Petterson going to take her into Inuvik Hospital to do. Her reflexes, and how come her eyes don't track. The way she doesn't hear me until I am real real close to her. How she's so small, and her screams. Doctor says healthy babies don't cry like that. But I don't want her to go. I know they're thinking, Fetal alcohol baby. I know they're thinking, Druggie mother, fucked-up alcoholic teen pregnancy. We got enough of them here in Jackfish Bay. But I wasn't doing it, I wasn't doing it. Much. I swear.

I whisper it to her, our blankets are warm and I pull her out of her crib I got beside my bed. Whisper how Mumma's not all bad, believe me, little girl. Cuddle her into our blankets. When I look at her, when I tear my eyes from the window, from that whiteness that's under the glow of that sun that won't even peek its head out at us, I feel it, her solid. It's like I remember good. Even in the trailer with Tyler I only got it that strong when Tyler wasn't home. My hand on my belly, imagining her face. Looking down at her now and tracing the line from her closed eyes to her pink mouth. She looks like any normal baby. But then I think too much about Tyler, get a bad feeling that starts below my belly, like a shaking goes down there, a trembling like I better make that stop moving or if someone hits me there I'll break up, then it moves to my throat and Faith is wriggling some in my arms. Then comes this joy bubble, this it-might-go-all-right bubble and in my throat there's this fluttering, like I am going to laugh and cry or shout out something, all the same time. Faith doesn't open her eyes and I brush my lips against her cheek, and fuck if she don't smell just like my mom smelled right after her shower. That mixed-up smell of some soap and bleach, because Mom liked to clean the tiles every time she showered. "Just keeping it up, Trista. When you don't got much, you keep clean what you got. Makes it dignity."

I got Faith clean and dressed. Leaning against my room window. I know I'd do anything for Faith. I know I can't keep pushing away what Linda says and what Deb says about getting some goals and thinking about her placement and what we gonna do. Push that feeling of bad inside me about that night, what they gonna say in court, what I gotta face for what I done. Push it all away to look at my baby's pureness. "I do anything for you, you know I will," I whisper against her ear and she opens her eyes and I swear she's looking right at me. Those blue eyes she got from Tyler that are somehow blue and dark, like she's got a flicker of my brown just waiting to come out. "I do anything," and Faith opens and closes her mouth like a tiny fish Daduk just took the hook out of before he push it back into the icehole, too small to eat.

Awake, showers, breakfast, school, or work training, Group, free time, dinner, study, bed. And smoke breaks only because we're lucky because really we're minors and not allowed to smoke, not supposed to be having them. It's like this most days. We wake up, there's this small wake-up bell sound that we can hear in our rooms. The rooms are cells really, but they make us call them rooms. We hear that wake-up bell and get out of the bed and supposed to make our bed. Then we get our stuff for the showers ready. I change Faith because I am allowed most nights to have her in with me and they given me a little crib right beside my bed. Since I had her in here I been waking up early and breastfeeding. At first the workers took her some at night, fatten her up with more formula, but she was only in that incubator in the hospital for a few hours after I had her. So I get her stuff, and get my housecoat on and my bag with the toothbrush and stuff. Then we wait at the door for what seems forever for the big bell, for the door to make that snick sound and then open. It opens slow on an electric swing, you can't push it or the bell goes off like danger sounds, just wait for it to open like if you blink hard enough you can pretend you're the Ice Princess come out of her big bedroom to rule the day on the Iceroad. I think maybe if I don't come out, then they can't take Faith. But I try to push that shit out of my head. I know she's got to get looked at, I know them doctors won't hurt her. Just been like I been waiting for her so long and now she's finally here and I want it to be all normal. But there's no normal waiting for a bell and the door that's locking us in. My arms get tired waiting so I put Faith in the rolly crib they got for me and hang my bag on the side with the diaper bag. Then the bell sounds, door opens, and we all come out of our rooms the same time.

"Hey," Aimee says, her room's next to me and I can hear her singing to herself at night. Just some sad songs like what her Nanuk must've taught her because they sound like the songs on Inuvialuktun Hour on CBC North. Aimee has a sweet voice. Me and Aimee, we don't really look at each other in the morning, still dark out and sleepy in our heads. It's a job on your brain to wake up here because it's crashing in on you while you waiting for a fucking door you can't even open. If we had bars, like the prison shows on TV, if we had the screamers, instead of that all quiet Isolation room they stick us in if we do turn into screamers, or "harm to self or others" like they say, maybe it would seem more real. Sometimes it makes it scarier, the quiet. Megan's got her room the other side of me and Aimee, and she comes over. She's right perky in the morning before they give her them ADHD meds, she nods at me, comes up, pushes Faith's blanket back. "How she doing today?"

"Slept good, some, only up a few times," I says, but she was up five ten times, too tired to remember to count it.

"Hope there's bacon," Megan says. She's always thinking on her belly the minute she gets up and I don't know where she puts it unless she just burns it off jumping about.

"Yeeah. Right. You lucky if there's bacon when the Bitch is here," Deanne says, and we all groan some because we forgot Linda said she had to take this morning off and the Bitch worker is on. She doesn't take any of Sherry's shit, like how Sherry cooks us special stuff. Says, "Just oatmeal for this crew, Sherry." And that's the end of it. Mostly we got Linda or Deb on as our workers, and Tracy comes from the work college training program and helps out some too. But the Bitch sometimes, usually weekends.

We line up at the outside door, by the workers' station to get into the showers. Yeeah and she's up there. "You give Faith to me while you wash, Trista, don't want to go dropping her now," and with that she's taken away my one big fun thing of the morning, soaping up Faith's body and holding her against me, over in the corner shower stall, away from the chattering of the other girls. Just me and my little girl, getting all clean for the day. I wait a bit, don't look the Bitch in the eye, biting my tongue trying not to say nothing. You start something with her and it's never going to finish. You figure that out real soon with her. Megan sees me struggling, says, "Whatever, Trista, just shower quick." And Megan eyes the Bitch like she's gonna murder her. I pick up Faith from the rolly crib and hand her to the Bitch. She doesn't mess with Faithy, I can say that much. She brings her over to the workers' station, gives her to the other worker, and gets in there and coos and teases with Faithy's feet. Faith gets this gurgle that she gets when she's happy, so the Bitch doesn't worry me much on that. Just she's got to control everything about me.

We're undressing in the changeroom right before the showers and Aimee's going real slow with taking her arms out of her sleeves, and then when she's got her pyjama top off I see why. She's got cuts sticking to her top. She sees me looking, says, "Shh," and I look down because I seen it before, sure I have, Keely used to cut some when she was upset. But then Deanne's walking by and she says,

"Shit." Not real loud but loud enough for the Bitch, who's now standing at the door, to come up and say, "What?" Deanne goes into the shower stall and says nothing, but I'm starting to shake. The Bitch is standing over Aimee. She knows. They all know, they know to watch out for Aimee and this, Aimee don't talk about it none in Group, but it's something everyone knows about her, watch her for it. The Bitch gets a softness to her voice that I don't expect from her, takes Aimee's arm, says, "You need some medical care, Aimee." It's not a question and she's leading Aimee out, Aimee looks up as she passes me, kind of says, "Bye," with her eyes, because now I know she's going to have to be in Iso for a while. We get that.

Usually it's for Megan when Linda's got to yell at her just to make herself be heard. "Megan, calm down or you'll need a PRN for it, stop twirling about," when Megan's like she's got some demon inside her and she's too hyper for words, just jumps about. And then Linda bear-hugs her, sometimes takes Deb or Tracy to get in there to hold and drag her down to Iso. We can hear Megan bumping around down there even though it's kind of down the hall from the living room or school room. They got these foamie things on the walls and floors and she just tires herself out screaming. "Harm to self or others," Linda reminds us, when we look at her, scared we're going to be next for Iso. But this is the first time I seen Aimee go in, because I don't think she done it that bad before. She's in there I don't know how long, they're gonna flip her bed, find what she's been cutting herself with. The Bitch being nice to her, calm with her, somehow makes me feel worse. Wish she just upped and smacked her some. That quiet, kind voice coming from the Bitch is like even more control.

Makes me want to scream when I'm under the hot spray of the shower, scream this whole fucking place out and just be on my own in my own tub in the trailer, me and Tyler and Faithy in our own place with no one telling me what all to do or how to do it, no one dragging me off when I'm out of my head. Tyler's got the washcloth, and me and Faith are floating in the warm water and he's washing us down with some mild soap so's it don't make Faith get that rash, and I am humming some good song been going round my head, Faith's hands splashing the top of the bathwater. I press my mouth against the green tiles of the shower stall, I got my hand pressed against the wall, Deanne's next to me, then Megan, we all trying to pretend we're somewhere else. I remember showers with Richard, Mom gone and just me and him in the apartment, before he took off and I went to Auntie and Nanuk's house. Him soaping my back. Or in the big bathtub at the trailer with Tyler, my belly starting to stick out of the water. I press my lips against the tiles of this stupid jail and try not to scream hard enough to get myself to somewhere else. Dream myself fucked up and drunk or high in a bar not thinking anything much.

Funny thing was, before the Aurora Store, I wasn't really that drunk or anything, because I was seven months gone with Faith and keeping mostly clean and straight. It was Tyler who got me like that, Tyler, mostly, who I can hear what he'd say even though I haven't talked to him in a long time. All his fucking do-right bullshit: "We going to have a good family, Trista," fucking loser who ran off not a week before I got in here. But he says soft in my ear when I'm trying to forget where I am. He says, "Tell them, Trista. Tell them about the Aurora Store. It will go right then. It has to."

Long before Tyler come up from down south I was lost in that bullshit dirty scum of snow you see sitting like old shit down Jackfish Bay town to the Mackenzie River in April, two months before the Ice Break Up. We're drinking, and before the whole thing with Keely going and setting me up with Jimmy. I didn't know what to do then, just wanted to go to Barclose at 2 a.m. every night outside the Icebox Bar. Stand with Keely, watch the drunks come out and fight, watch and drink beers with the girls. We're like twelve or thirteen. Mom was long dead from the accident on the Iceroad, and Auntie was gambling every night with the OKO card games and kicking us out of the house, then we'd go over to where Nanuk was playing the TV bingo with the girls and Daduk out at his buddies, drinking, hoping she wouldn't notice. Nanuk didn't care about him as long as we got her the bingo cards, and she'd sit and talk to Maisie Ford and put her dabber real close to her card so she could see them numbers and have that old TV cranked because she's deafer than the Ford's dog.

Was too long ago we went to the Snow Nanuks, me and Keely sitting there listening to them tell us about their young ones now old. Me and Keely got lost from them, don't know why. Starting to drink, smoke up, whatever we could get our hands on. Not all of us went bad. Some of the Snow Nanuks' kids went down south to find work, or just some of them still in town. Like one of Nanuk Marjorie's boys who was doing good working in Edmonton in some office job he got, but then Nanuk Gemma's girls who she never heard from again, went and got lost to the cities, maybe Toronto, maybe Montreal, far far away. Don't know where their husbands went either. Me and Keely just started calling them Snow Nanuks because it was like they just rise out of the snow when we was little and making some snowhouses, rise out of the snow and smiling at us over the pale white of it. Seems like they were the only ones smiling at us for just being us, when we was little. Them and Mom too, before she was gone.

Here in Jackfish Bay, we only have maybe six, seven hundred people, on a good day, when the sun is shining the summer long light hard, and there's some tourists come up the Dempster Highway, ends at nearby Inuvik, they can drive it slow twenty or thirty minutes on our side road the rest of the way or drive a mean Ski-Doo on the trails by the river when the snow's on come September, sometimes even end of August. Otherwise, maybe we got five hundred people. You walk into town and there's the Northmart, used to be called the Northern and it was part of The Bay, but someone else bought it up, gave it a weird name like they got those commercials for on the TV, like that Wal-Mart store down south. Those kids on those commercials, jumping up and down in their new clothes. We just got the same shitty jeans that everyone wears, then you put on a stupid T-shirt that says something, like we think we're from Hawaii or something, with all the surfer shit. You can get Ski-Doo jackets at the Northmart, though, and they're kind of cool, Tyler had one. Makes you feel like when you're riding, you got something to go to, or some camera following you, doing those northern shows we seen on the TV. It's weird, seeing the news, when you got the CBC North showing something here, and you can look out onto the Mackenzie River from your bedroom, but there it is on the TV, talking about some stupid-ass kid going through the ice on his Ski-Doo, because the ice is too thin and he's been drinking.

Jackfish Bay, yeeah, it's a white name. But it's stuck, all the other Mackenzie Delta communities going back to the old names, Holman to Ulukhaktok, Arctic Red River to Tsiigehtchic. Wish we had a cool Inuvialuktun or Gwich'in name to go back to. But Daduk says the name sticks because of the jackfish, that's just what it is, what we are, a small little bay off the Mackenzie River East Channel where you can fucking catch some good jackfish. Oh yeeah, some people got their taste for whitefish or even char, says the jackfish too boney. But we love it any day. Speckled light brown with darker brown underneath, Daduk says you gotta strip it of its skin, can't eat the skin like trout. Their mouths so funny when they first come up, maybe Daduk got them trolling running crank bait and waiting. Their mouths gape open, long almost like snouts, like a fox's snout even I said once to Daduk but he just laughed at me.

Wind comes down from the Beaufort Sea, your scow's moving back and forth a little, the long summer sun's shining down on you, maybe it's two in the morning and you're far away from the town and Barclose and the mosquitoes have gone to pester someone on the riverbank, because you got the breeze keeping them away, and you're just sitting there with a pole, hoping for something to bite, jackfish or loche or maybe some old prehistoric fish just come free from an iceberg he got trapped up in on the Arctic, made his way upriver into the Delta, just to nibble on your line and surprise the shit out of you, feed your family for decades.

Yeeah, Daduk says, just simple Jackfish Bay suits us fine. People think, when they come from down south and they're first working here, you know, like we got some taxi drivers they from all the way Pakistan or somewhere you got to look up in the big atlas at the library, people think we're on some reserve maybe. Like we learned about in school some natives from down south are. But we got maybe two hundred whites, two hundred Inuvialuit, like I am quarter that, like from the Inuit people. My mom and Nanuk both got it up with the white rig-pigs when they were young, and Nanuk hooked up with Daduk later—he's full Inuvialuit from Shingle Point way. Used to call us Eskimos. Kids call each other 'skos as a joke sometimes, whether we're full, half, quarter, or who the fuck knows how much 'sko blood. Then you got maybe a hundred Gwich'ins, they're like First Nations, they came over that land bridge and just kept on going, all the way to South America, some, like Miss Sarah shown us when we looked at them pictures from the mountains they got down there, and the penguins they got in their cold places way down south. My nanuk and daduk, they come from people who walked over that land bridge, got into the Delta, and just said, Yeeah, here's where we're gonna stay. You got ptarmigan, willow and rock, hares and caribou, muskoxen, moose, grizzly, beaver, lots of animals to hunt and trap, makes some clothes and food, then all the fish, and then the muskrat, shit, he's good and tasty when things are running low or they're sleeping the winter. And the ravens and the gyrfalcon, can't touch those to hunt them because they're precious, keep the north together. Then later those whites come up, some doing the army, some finding the oil and gas they're building pipelines out of, to run their cars down south. Daduk says maybe it'll fuck up our caribou runs, the animals can smell them pipelines, will make them go more south and they're deader than shit, no good grasses to feed on, no place to have their young. But Auntie, she wants the pipelines, says they bring in the money and the men, give the town more money now we actually got special rights paperwork for northern hires and treatied proper. Auntie's got her shit together now. Had a few years after Mom died, drinking, me going back and forth from Auntie's to Nanuk's after Richard left. But when I was around nine she got it together. Seems like then me and Keely picked it up, the drinking, drugging. Hurting ourselves.

Back then some two years back, when I was thirteen and fucked up, where else could I go but hang out at the Icebox Bar with my girls and talk some shit and get Keely to go in and get some off-sales High Test beers, because her uncle worked the counter and would look the other way. As if they didn't know, those men been knowing us since we was little, hiding under the coffee table at their piss-up parties. You get to work soon in Jackfish Bay, just because they can pay you less, we all had jobs since we were twelve, and they pay you good at the Northmart, like nine, ten bucks an hour. We always had money, the town's not poor. Maybe that's part of the problem.

We're missing getting ready for the day with Aimee. Even though she's quiet, she's missed. Out of the shower, Megan says, "Hey, my sister brought in some makeup they didn't take, you wanna use some?" We're looking at ourselves in those fake mirrors they got up, sometimes the steam from the showers make us look like something out of the circus, not real glass in them. We might smash it up and cut up. I look in it, Deanne's putting on some blush and I'm wishing

Aimee could be out and doing this too. Feels like we're getting ready to party and Megan's smiling. "Just need us some beers, huh?" I take her mascara, slowly pull out the brush and it feels strange, been so long since I put it on. It's black mascara, and I put it close to my lashes, I got long ones, Faith does too, must be we got that from Mom. I remember her long lashes brushing against her cheek, especially after she put the mascara on. Megan's laughing, she's got the red lipstick on. "Fucking hookered up or what?" she says and wipes it off. It leaves a nice red to her lips. Most of us dress in black or grey hoodies, just jeans. Grey socks we go kicking around in our mocs in here. Plain. Dark. I put that mascara on and a bit of the steam clings to my lashes, it makes me grin, feel some grown-up.

"Okay, girls, let's get going," calls the Bitch. We hurry put the makeup back in Megan's bag, drop off our stuff, and then it's breakfast, and Sherry's on and she's got some colour for us on a boring day already coming up to me and Faith's rolly crib, chucking Faithy under the chin, "She latching on better, Trista?" It gets me warm in my hoodie, feeling what she does for my baby. Like we're not in jail meeting, just like she's down at the Sunrise Café and I come walking in with my kid and she's going to come over and give us up a coffee and talk about the day.

"Yeeah, she's doing better. I think she is anyways. She hums some instead of crying so much. But Dr. Petterson's coming in, take her away for checking."

"It'll be good news, you'll see." Sherry says and she doesn't look right into my face because she can somehow feel that I'm starting to bawl. She goes behind the kitchen counter, gives me a towel. "Clean her up some, honey, she been spitting up." But she puts the towel on my cheeks and I hold it up against my eyes, losing it, my breath funny and starting to hiccup. "Come and sit down with her, have some milk," Sherry says. I sit down and hold up Faith against my cheek, I feel so shaky. Sherry puts a glass in front of me, but my tummy's doing those flips again and I feel like I am going to throw up.

Then the Bitch come in. But she's got the soft voice all over again. Why can't she just be mean all the time. She says, "Dr. Petterson's here, Trista." I put Faith back in her rolly crib. Tuck up the blanket around her. Look outside and it's dark, and I know it's cold, when is it not ever fucking cold out there. "Let me get the other blanket," I says, and as I get up I can see Dr. Petterson, just come from seeing Aimee I guess because I see her coming out of Iso. I get Faithy's warmer blanket, tuck it up around her, Dr. Petterson is saying, "Hey, little girl," and her eyes are warm looking into Faith's. Then she looks at me and she gets this hard look. Not at all like when me and Tyler come in to see her for that first ultrasound, not at all when she believed in me that I was a good kid, but just too young to be having babies. Right in that kitchen room she says to me, "The anti-depressants starting to work, Trista?" I mumble something at her, embarrassed the other girls got to see my shit, but they're used to it, sometimes there's just not time for private time with the doctor. They don't look at me, I can feel them sitting at the table and they're looking away. All our shit just hanging out there for everyone to see.

"Trista?" Dr. Petterson says. "We'll be back in a day, maybe two, the tests won't be long. I've left a breast pump for you, the workers can freeze the bottles."

"You bringing her back for sure?" I says, because maybe this is all just some joke on me to take her and put her in foster care.

"Yes. She's still too little to be away from you for too long. They've said you can have her for two months. We've talked about this already, Trista. Nothing's going to change until we find a good placement."

And as I lean in to give Faith one last kiss, Dr. Petterson pats my back and I know she's meaning, I'll take care of your girl, I won't hurt her, Trista, and I want to believe her, but it's hard to let my Faithy go.

The school hours pass in a blur and before lunch I am on the bathroom chores. I wear gloves, they make us anyway because Megan got the HIV from putting needles in her arms. But we been told we still have to do chores, and we won't be getting anything if we wear gloves and masks, clean properly. Megan is real careful about it and only uses the one stall, cleans it herself. I'm moving the toilet brush around the toilet bowl, thinking too much, maybe it's those anti-depressants finally kicking in some. Because I can think, not feel too sad, but also tears been running down my face. But it's like I don't really feel anything, like I'm me and someone else. Missing my girl. This is the first time she been away from me since I had her and my gut hurts, my breasts ache, and I want to talk to Tyler.

I been thinking how Mom let me think I was such a grown-up girl, helping her sweep the floor in the bathroom, and putting on the large yellow gloves and using the Comet cleaner to scrub the bathtub. "Lookit you, what a big girl, Trista, that's Mom's big girl." I wonder, was she happy before she died? Was she really going up to visit him, or was she seeing someone else? If she had known she was going to die, would she have written down my daddy's name? If she had lived, would she have told me about him, sometime? These are things, I know, I been too worried about, like them things you can't worry about. Because you can never get them things back.

Fucking men at the Icebox Bar, they're not all our dads. Easy to dream my dad whole and responsible up on them rigs. Maybe head of the rig or something, and in charge of all those guys out there on the Beaufort Sea, iced up. Some of the kids got good dads who don't drink much. If they do, they drink at home and then they go to bed early, don't mess with them, and they go off to work in town. There's good jobs, like in the government, or working for the community.

Tracy, who comes to training here and also takes us to job training at the Elder Hospital, her brother is working to be a recreation leader. He goes to Arctic College in the winter and comes back in the spring. He tries real hard, going to the rec centre and even making some classes for us, like two years ago he made all us take tae kwon do, that was fucking funny, watching all us kids doing these leg kicks. You can still go up to the rec centre and there I am in the picture with Keely, giving a pretend kick at her for the picture. Or Lee, Nanuk Marjorie's other boy, who used to babysit me and Keely at the Snow Nanuks sometimes when we was little and Snow Nanuks out carving or quilting circle. He's working the van-driving job, training on driving so's he can be a good paramedic. Was driving ambulance that night I got hauled in even, he works so many shifts. We got lots of money here, for the programs and everything, even I knew that since I was a little kid. Or how Nanuk tries to make us go to the youth group at the Ptarmigan Hall, the Inuvialuit people from her office try to put up. Trying to get us kids into making stuff, doing caribou tufting or making jewellery, bead work for some moc slippers or mukluks and all that.

Me and Keely, we are both quarter-blood, don't talk about that much here. Her mom's some Inuvialuit, and then she doesn't know her dad either, and her mom used to drink some but getting it together, like my auntie. But some moms got their shit together way early, lots and lots have their shit together since way back before they were even moms, and even some of the adults trying to make Jackfish Bay a dry community like they done in Tsiigehtchic. We got some of the kids from there, they sometimes come to Inuvik high school, and skidoo up to hang with us, do some auto mechanic program they're into and they got their shit together. Like I was trying to do with Faith.

"Trista," Aimee whispers to me as we wipe down the bathroom counters.

"Yeeah."

"You going to Greenhouse today?"

"Maybe."

"How you gonna get out of it?" Aimee says. They let her out of Iso, she only got two hours because they found some broken plastic pen she been cutting with, doctor put her on some new meds. Don't know why she don't get some days like Megan when she goes in, but figure maybe it's because Aimee's so quiet and inside herself, not out of control like Megan. Maybe better for Aimee, be out more with us and talking. She hates going to the Greenhouse for work training, says it gives her the creeps, all those vines and plants. I secretly love it, don't tell her that though. The way my hands can squish in the dirt, watering something and knowing it's soon gonna start to grow up. It's dark days so there's not much to do, we're just weeding out the old stuff, planting the bulbs and things that need to set and wait for some months, cleaning up around the place. Light doesn't start to come on until February, and even then it's only about twenty minutes, but you get those twenty minutes adding on and on and on to each other, every day. Some days sun sets at four, and you're feeling sleepy, looking out and not even dinner yet. But then it goes on four-thirty, then five, then before you know it, it's April and it's ten-thirty before it's dusk even and then the light lingers. You get some hope feeling then.

"Not much to do there," I says, and Aimee nods. We bring the cleaning supplies to the workers' station for them to lock up, wash our hands, and go for lunch. Sherry dishes out a big portion for her because she's some skinny that Aimee. Having her baby early, her baby dying, or doing her crime after maybe did it, but I think she was skinny before her baby died too. Even though it was her dad got her pregnant, she cared, wanted her baby and do good by it. But she couldn't have him come after her more when it died. Only time she speaks up, whispers it to me in the living room after Group, she gets on about how she didn't smoke around the baby or party, or let anyone smoke or party around the baby ... Don't matter though what the mom been smoking or what because some girls in the community lose their babies to SIDS. Some doctors even saying it's because they born too soon, like how Faithy is a preemie and we got to watch her breathing, her lung function. Aimee, she's thinking maybe it's God or something take the baby away, like she can't have it because it wasn't made good in the first place. That's why the cutting, maybe. Lots of people would be cutting too, I guess, have that happen. Keely's mom's best friend was depressed like that, near hung herself, they found her tying the noose to the shower and everything, had to go down to Yellowknife to go to the psych ward there for a month, now she's on the anti-depressants too, back working at the Northmart and looking all zombied out if kids come through the checkout. But Aimee don't act zombie-like. She been saying to me, when she's holding Faith, how she's relieved sometimes and I know what she means.

When you're pregnant and you want to be big, you want to be that dream mother you got in your head, and then the thing comes out and you don't know what the fuck to do most days but watch it cry and scream and nothing is changing that. Like how I feel sometimes with Faith. Never like the dream you had of the baby, the family. When it's late and Faith's crying and I am trying to pat her back and I am trying to make the pats soothing and even-spaced, but it comes in my head I just want to pat harder and harder, this thing that won't shut up. Easy to feel that now she's gone to hospital, like she could just be a blip in my life that never happened. Except this bleeding, like a period I had ever since I had her, won't let up. Doctor says sometimes the bleeding goes on for six weeks after birth. The blood reminds me of Faith and the bad that I done the day she came out, and I just gotta put it out of my head. But then can't. Then the light soaring in my belly feeling when she's sleeping and quiet, when I touch her, or my lips brush against her eyelashes and we're just us, quiet, and I want nothing else but my Faithy.

We're waiting for the van to take us to the Greenhouse, just getting shoes on and me, when I'm bending down to put my boots on can feel this whoosh in my belly like I'm going to puke up my lunch, like someone slamming inside my head and screaming Faith is gone, she's gone. Megan nudges me, says, "You think the Bitch will let us have a smoke before we go?" And I am glad I can think of something else, something almost normal. Standing outside us three, me, Megan, and Aimee on Greenhouse work rotation, we can see inside at Deanne starting up her reading because she's ahead of us in school and mostly goes for work training at the Elder Hospital. We got two weeks of Greenhouse every other day, then two weeks of Elder Hospital, they trying to get us used to some work training options. The Bitch doesn't even look out at us, just once she poked her head out to look at Aimee and raise her eyebrows as if saying, Don't hurt yourself, okay? But Aimee knows better than to fuck up her smoke breaks burning herself though. No one wants to be detoxing from nicotine here, only thing we can have that seems normal. Like we're just outside school on break, not waiting for some van to take us out of the jail for a few hours.

Guess no one's all bad inside, that Bitch. Maybe she's got a family she's loving and caring about, maybe she's had some babies she's given kisses to, fed them. The girls too, hard to imagine they done all those terrible things. Like Megan's real nice to us all. Always got something to share. Makeup or smokes or cookies Sherry lets her steal for us. It's weird to think how we had so many people trying to help us be good. How Snow Nanuks gave us good but we didn't take it all.

"I'm gonna plant some daffodil bulbs today," Megan says, she gets that excited. Me and Aimee smoke quietly, me thinking on how much Aimee must be missing her dead kid if I am shook up missing Faithy this much. What good I got to give her, how I used to be. I'm thinking on how much time I used to waste, all that shit going on, school and programs, the government or the band council or whatever trying to make us kids go good, and still we're outside Barclose at the Icebox 2 a.m., waiting for the drunks to come out and fight, see if we can pick up some cash when they drop their wallets. And don't give me no shit about fetal alcohol syndrome, I know all about that what with my own mom drinking with me in her belly, and the public health nurses come in to the high school and tested us all the way back to Great Nanuk, questioned us and shit, and then they had to stop, because the fuck of it is that seemed like lots of kids in Jackfish Bay got the fetal alcohol syndrome, well, not them full whites or Gwich'in or Inuvialuit getting off the bottle, not most anyway. Their statistics fucked up. What do they know about us? What does anyone know about anyone, unless you going to be living here?

Don't think all of the girls who are half- or quarter-blood doing all the fucked-up things, it's not all us Inuvialuit or Gwich'in that are drinking or drugging our lives up either, the north gets the whites here too. Shit we must've looked bad swigging away outside what with the cold blowing out icy with our liquor breath, April and nothing warming up much outside. Keely's smoking and we're passing the butt around because smokes had just gone up again, and we're whistling at the green and white streaks of the shifting northern lights so they don't come down and chop our heads off. Those old geezers in the Icebox Bar, and they're speaking low-like to us, "You girls want making some money?"

"No." Dirty fucker, I know your wife, work with her at the Northmart.

"C'mon, Trista," He's patting my back and I want to strangle him with my scarf. "Let's do her."

"No." You old man, you oil pig, you drunk stinking fucker. They know I can't say no for long though.

They know us, like they known us we going over to their houses since we was little. Me and Keely, we been through a lot that way. Not all the dads or the uncles get to you, you learn quick which ones are which. After a while though, you don't much care. Me and Keely, I remember us drinking from the beer glasses at the parties Auntie go to sometimes, before she got off the booze, started her AA meetings. Keely, even though she was littler than me then, seemed even a whole year younger sometimes, with her heart-shaped face, the way her eyes go up and smiley even when she's not laughing, she was the brave one, going off to the toilet with the older men. Me left sitting out in one of the kid's bedrooms, I don't know whose it was, all the houses look the same, even ours.

But me and Keely felt safe at Snow Nanuks. And my house too. We got our kitchen, this is in Auntie's house now, I moved there when I was seven and Mom died, there's the brown counter, that's some kind of plastic crap on it, and it peels at the edges and buckles from water. The carpet is thin and a dark brown, the colour of shit, and it's frayed in the hallways where Keely's brothers wrestle on it when they're over.

I got my own room, because I don't have brothers or sisters, but Keely sleeps in my bed with me when she's over. I twirl my fingers around her long hair, she's the only one I know who's got some real wave to her hair, even curls when she has it loose and not up in her ponytail like she usually has in the daytime. The bed is bigger than a twin, not like Nanuk's, it's bigger. And the quilt is on it, the one where Nanuk made the little squares of kids dancing, like she has some Gwich'in lady friends she plays the bingo with and they do a lot of those wall hangings with kids playing and some fish scenes and caribou. Nanuk sewed it up good, you can even wash it a million times like we done, and still the dancing felt kids don't come off. I don't have much else in my room, the bookshelf that Auntie made when she was at the high school, she liked working with wood when she was a kid, some books we got at the festival when we were in elementary school. My closet, and I got some jeans there, we used to wear the jumper dresses when I was little, my favourite with the sunflowers on them, all yellow, like they were smiling. Keely's got to share her room with two baby brothers, but they have bunk beds off to the sides, and she gets her own bed. When it's done, when I try and think, What the fuck went wrong? all's I can do is think of our good times and what my mom, auntie, nanuk, daduk, Snow Nanuks give us. With all that stored up against the bad times, Richard, the boys in Tuk, Tyler and where he gone, me and Jimmy—why isn't it enough to make it right?

The van comes to take us to the Greenhouse and we all climb up. Lee's driving it. He says, "Hey, Trista," and he smiles a little at me, hard to see because he's got his scarf almost up to his mouth. But if I didn't know him, I wouldn't seen the sad in his eyes. Thinking me and him the same time about the Aurora Store, how can he not?

I want to think about him when we was little, him jiggling me on one knee and Keely on the other, we're about six and he's maybe thirteen, he was that big even back then. Grinning at us while we watching Sesame Street and each time singing, "L, L, L for Lee, can't you see, that's just me," and every time he says "me," he lets us go so we come tumbling giggling down his legs, right ourselves up off the floor, and clamber on back up his big lap screaming, "More, Lee, more, Lee."

"You girls get yourself buckled in," Lee says, then turns the van onto the side road and heads over to the Greenhouse.

Not all the men were that bad, okay there's Stephen and back then he's maybe not much older than me now, maybe some years older and just barely eighteen and too chicken to do much to make those other older guys stop their fucking around. But I can see him, he's up on the shredded side of the couch from where me and Keely are playing cards, I can see his socks, the right one he's got a hole in, and he's laughing at their jokes, they got low voices. But when he's looking at me, he gets a smile corner of his lips and his eyes sad and I know he's looking at me like a brother. You get that too. The brothers, you just know they not going to do nothing to you, like Lee who babysat us good, it's something you feel inside. Snow Nanuks say it's like the angatkut shaman from long ago, even before they remember it. Sometimes the angatkut good for things, like when you're running a fever and got the cough and the boiled pine needles tea isn't working. He can be healer. But then sometimes you look to angatkut for help and he got so much power, he knows he can use it over you now, he got you. And you better watch out because he can take from you too. Snow Nanuks tell us about our last great Inuvialuit shaman. How he was gentle and powerful, could turn himself into a falcon, even Nanuk Marjorie said she seen it when she was a little girl. A good man, a good shaman who helped his people.

But some of these men, they're not like our shaman. The party, that time that I remember the old men from, they were younger then. This man, he's Freddy's daduk, and he's talking at me, and his breath stinks. I can see me and Keely at that party, we're playing cards under the table, Crazy Eights, and Keely is sneaking their beer glasses under the table, and we drank a couple and already laughing. We were about maybe seven or eight then. The party is all around us, there's music on loud, and someone's got the door open and it's hot from the woodstove, but I can feel the cold from the door, hear Freddy's daduk yell, "You can close the door, don't got wood for hours."

Keely's got hiccups, and she puts down her cards, I look up and she's crawling out from under the table because Freddy's daduk's got a five in his hand, just letting it drop in Keely's hand. I can see the blue of that five-dollar bill. "Be back," Keely says. I don't say nothing, I know what she's going to do. We been doing it for so long, doesn't seem real. Only time them men pay attention to us, and fuck it, it doesn't feel that bad. But you got to get the money for it. My auntie's Paul, the guy she goes out with now, and he's in the AA too, he never did nothing like that, though. Back then, we thought all them men were just after under our jumpers. But later, I got it, that it wasn't all of them.

And then when we're older, that time seems like long ago when we thirteen, me and Keely, the dirty old pigs from Barclose go away but not before Keely's muttering some crazies under her parky hood, and the wild in her black eyes drives them off some, swaying down Tullinqit Road, away from us. Keely about done with them and their fingers, pushing at her to touch them just a bit longer. Maybe they go home to some other little girls. Maybe we're too old for them at thirteen, we wasn't feeling too little. It's funny that, now I'm living in the jail, how I feel so old, and only fifteen, Linda says. "You're only fifteen. You got a world ahead of you." What I got though is a court case ahead of me, placement for Faith, maybe never see her again.

The Greenhouse's not far away, only about twenty minutes by van or truck into Inuvik when our side road and weather good. The snow's swirling and Lee's driving slow and careful. We pass the bars and the bank, the Northmart. Nobody goes to the Greenhouse in November except us for some training, nothing gonna grow there now, just getting things fixed up under the dirt, maybe digging up some old bulbs and putting plastic over the dirt or mulch to warm it some. It's cold in there without the sun to warm it up. I think it's just something for us to do to pretend like they giving us some responsibility, more fun, Deanne said when last March she got to plant real seeds and stuff. We just have to sweep and clean, turn the soil that's under the plastic. Even though I'm away from Faithy, it's kind of nice to be out and pretending to do something like a real job. Lee says it used to be the old arena, and a part of me remembers it, maybe being little and going to a hockey game there before they built the new one in Inuvik, maybe I can even see me and Keely sitting there with Lee, eating fries covered in goopy gravy and screaming whenever our boys got a goal. We pass the liquor store and there's men outside there even now, it's only just past noon.

We pull up to the Greenhouse and Lee starts to grin because Megan starts whooping, you can't put it past her to make you feel better about the day. Twilight's on the snow, we get about two hour of it from noon to about 2 p.m. when there's just enough light to see the fields of snow out back the Greenhouse, a little sliver of sun winking, saying, Pretty soon I'm gonna sleep for the whole month December and you're gonna just wish me back. Megan's already got a smoke in her mouth before Lee can say anything. He doesn't tell her to put it away, just walks up quiet and big, lumbering in that way he has, even lights it for her. He knows we don't got much that makes us feel like we're free. Lee lights up too, says, "Aimee, Trista, you want one of my tailor-mades?" Aimee nods shyly, and I hold back, till he's taking one out and giving it to me. "Here's a light, Trista." Every time he says my name I think about that night, the store, Jimmy grabbing for the smokes. They were Player's Light, not Export A, what Lee offers me. Megan stamps her feet outside the Greenhouse door, rubs her snowboots against the porcupine with the straw quills they got there, the snow coming off in chunks. Pulling in the smoke with the cold is like sucking ice cream or slurpees, hits the back of your throat harsh and tight. Not only Megan gets perked from the smokes, makes me feel like they can bother with their doctors' anti-depressants and pills and PRNs, just give me some nicotine outside in forty below.

"Okay, let's get in," Lee says as we stuff our cigarette butts under our boots and pick them up. He unlocks the Greenhouse door and we put our butts in the old water can inside the door, sign in so they know we not done any violence to others' flower or vegetables beds.

What gets me is the smell, right away, even though it's still winter, it's that smell of earth and somehow of spring. It's a damp, clammy smell, like Nanuk's been cooking her stew all day and them vegetables just simmering there, under the earth. There's about a hundred separate beds, raised so we don't have to bend over. I go over to the one we got for the facility, there's even a little sign some other girls made says "Polar Girls." They don't have the facility part because everyone knows anyways that it means the prison girls. Megan and Aimee pulling on gloves while I am peeling away the plastic, but I don't put on the gloves. Lee grabs a foldout chair and it squeaks as he sits on it, pulls out a magazine about Ski-Doo racing.

"You girls want I put on the music from my iPod? On the speakers?" Lee says.

"You can?" Megan says, grinning.

"Sure, just stay put, uh?" We look up at him as he says it, meet his eyes so he knows we don't pull a runner. Not like we can anyways, go too far, what with the back road going far far into a load of nothing. Just dead is what you find out there after half a day, less maybe. Not even any bear, caribou, muskoxen out there now, that stretch before Shingle Point or the Lakes, or even Tuk. Maybe. Maybe I could get down to the Iceroad, stumble down the road and hitch a ride. But them cars going past, them rigs, they wondering why some northern girl all alone on the Iceroad. Know enough not to mess with danger like that, RCMP after them on the road. What bad they done stays at home, quiet, in their houses and locked up tight.

It doesn't matter much anyways, I got all that I got back at the jail, Faithy coming home soon and I'm not going to fuck that up. And when I call Tyler he'll be there and answer the phone and we won't be fighting about anything, he'll just say, "Hey, babes, just gonna be down here another month and then I'm coming up."

I'll say, "So you gonna be ready for when they let Faith out?"

And he'll say, "Oh for sure I'm gonna be ready. She don't have to go to any foster home. Got money from my mom and it's enough to set the shop up, and Faithy can fall asleep to the hum of the tattoo gun, I'm gonna be doing so many jobs."

I put my hands in the dirt, making little holes for Megan to put her bulbs in. We cover the bulbs with dirt, splash a tiny bit of water to dampen it up some, go onto the next hole. The dried marigolds are on the edges, still orangey and yellow, they crumble at my touch. I sprinkle some of the marigolds onto the earth, Aimee's humming along with the music Lee's put on, it's the first line of "Personal Jesus," Marilyn Manson singing it, me and my Faithy's song. It's some remix song, so the first line of it comes up again and again and Aimee smiles at me, like she knows what I'm thinking. We're just some normal kids, doing some work.

When we get back from the Greenhouse, we go for the snack Sherry's left out for us in the kitchen, wash our faces, and then half an hour later is afternoon Group. Linda's back in Group, we find out we don't got the Bitch coming around for maybe two weeks now, she has to go down to Yellowknife doing some kind of class for workers. Hope they train her to be nicer, but I don't think it's going to happen. Having Linda and Deb around it's like having big and little. Linda's big and round cuz she's had maybe three kids and it looks like she's always pregnant, that belly fat. She's grinning a lot too. I know sometimes fat people don't like their fat, but Linda's just about always smiling and grinning at us, like she likes herself just fine and we're the best kids she's ever had the chance to meet. She's not even into Jesus or anything, like down at the church we sometimes go to if Linda's feeling we need to get out. Linda says she doesn't believe much in a church kind of god, only the kind of god that you can find anywhere, church or home or even between your toes when you're cutting your toenails and the joy of trimming them so they don't hurt and rub against your snowboots. Yeeah she's a strange one, that Linda. Deb is so skinny even though she's got two kids, we never seen skinny like that except maybe Aimee. But Aimee's got the eating disorder thing where she can't eat when she's upset. Deb comes and eats lunch with us and I swear she puts away more than any of us. She's always moving too, leaning forward in her chair in Group, crossing her legs. But not in that restless hyper way like Megan, more like she just got to move, like a dancer or an arctic hare, with purpose. Deb's muscles in her arms are something beautiful, defined like. But Linda's got these big ass arms that make you feel like the shitty world's gonna go away and never come back when she hugs you.

"So let's talk about after-care goals," says Linda.

"What I got when I get out but nothing," Deanne says.

"You got your job training experience at the hospital, how's that coming?" Linda says.

"Some old farts, cleaning up their shit, oh yeah, that's something to look forward to, what the fuck you know about it, Linda? Better to get hooked back up in Yellowknife with my girls and earn some good fucking money. Or good money fucking, you know?" says Deanne. I got my head down. She's so fucking brave sometimes it brings some red to my cheeks. She can talk it in Group. Big Yellowknife city girl. Makes you want to giggle, come bursting out of you like a nerve bubble or something. But Linda just keeps at her.

"You're good with those old farts, kiddo, I read the reports," Linda says.

"Bullshit. Just don't want bad reports from you all. Got to get me back down to YK and out of this fucking small-town bullshit."

"Isn't Yellowknife filled with bullshit too, Deanne?" Linda says, and it's all I can do to look at Deanne, she's blushing.

"So. Least I know what's up there."

"What's the plan when you transfer? You going to avoid those girls at the YK facility?" Linda says, and she's leaning forward in her chair.

"Why the fuck should I? They got good experience, those girls, they know what's going down in town and can fill me in," Deanne says, but she's fidgeting.

"You don't believe in it," Linda says quietly. Deanne looks up at her sharply, like the quiet in Linda's voice makes it more serious.

"Believe in what? Oh, how I'm gonna be all ready and set to live there, what, my work experience gonna do shit for me? You know that's not gonna do shit for me once I get there."

"Are you scared to go back, Deanne?" Linda says.

"I'm not scared of anything," Deanne says. "Fuck off, Linda, don't do that stupid Group-talk shit with me."

"Deanne. It's okay if you are," Linda says.

"I'm not," Deanne says, but her eyes are down and she's sucking her cheeks in and I don't want to look at her.

"Deanne," Linda whispers.

"Shut up, Linda, shut the fuck up," Deanne whispers back. It's like her words are mean, but then she's crying and Deb's handing her the tissue and I got this quivery feeling in my belly like I know it's good for Deanne to cry but it feels out of control. And then Deanne gets up, frustrated-like moves quick to the door. "Let me out, Linda, shit," And she's kicking at the door all getting up angry. "Let me the fuck out!" She screams and Linda just leaves her to kick at the door, looks around at all of us, we're squirming under her gaze like bugs. There's just the sound of Deanne's kicking, and my heart pounding, no one says anything. Deanne slides down against the door and just sits against it. Linda goes over and sits beside her, not touching or hugging her or nothing, just hands her more tissue.

Then Deb takes the attention off them, says, "Megan, looks like you, Aimee, and Trista are going for the first time to the Elder Hospital this week, shadowing Tracy?"

"Yeeah, we all going this week," Megan says.

I panic then. They going to start me on more job training so soon? I can see Aimee's looking over at Linda too, but we don't say nothing. Linda's smiling, like she just had the best conversation with someone and they solved it all, not like she just had a fight with Deanne, like we seen. Linda gets up off the floor with a groan, pulls Deanne up with her. "C'mon, kiddo," she says and Deanne sits back in her chair again.

She's got this shine to her eyes, Linda does, when she looks at us. Like she really believes that with, in her eyes, she just loves us and then we can see the force of those eyes and get better. It makes me look down and scratch my ankle I got crossed over my leg. I get so I can't look her straight in the eyes, that gleam makes me squirm. Like Mom looking at me long ago climbing up on the chair to get something off the counter I was too little to get, like she's mad and proud at the same time that I thought of bringing the chair over and doing it, that's what Linda's eyes are like.

"I think you're ready," Linda says, and Deb nods at us too. And I don't want to think of the time away, from Faith, from trying to get a hold of Tyler. Then Megan says, "But then so, what about more phone privileges," like she's reading my mind and trying to get on something safe to talk about the same time. And I don't have to look over at Deanne to know she's relieved it's off her.

I want to say it clear right up front that Tyler had nothing to do with Faith being how she is, or with me and Jimmy and the Aurora Store. He only come up to Jackfish Bay to get away from his bad-ass city friends in YK, wanted to turn sixteen and do something right and get a job, then he's trying to save me, with his talk of God and goals and dreams, I swear. But now he's not calling me, and I left messages and messages for him. Night-time and I don't have Faith with me and not his voice and it's like right before I met him, alone, and always his roommate or someone, saying, "He's out." He's out he's out and where is he and what's he doing when I am moving from this breakfast to this school day to this Group and the hours lost in between not able to sleep at night thinking about him and I know he'll be calling me soon, he's saving money, just for me and little Faith. And later, fucking Deanne and her mouth. "That sounds like fairy princess wannabe bullshit," Deanne says. We're not even in Group when she says it, just sitting around talking in the living room after dinner and I am so happy because she's here my girl is here, and maybe it's going to be okay because they only took her one night and two days, then she can't be that bad, she can't be that bad at all, and I'm trying to breastfeed Faithy but she's fussing and pushing her fists to her mouth instead of taking my nipple and I am just so glad she's back, I'm shaking, aching her to feed. They had her on the bottle too much there and I don't want to think about what they gonna be telling me about her testing. Always waiting waiting waiting till they have their conference fucking talks with the workers and the doctors and whoever until they finally get to us with their expert stupid opinions and decisions that's gonna turn everything around. We're allowed some TV at night, but I can't keep track of what's on. Never anything good, always some crime show they won't let us see, Deanne flips through with the remote and Linda says, "Nope, not that." Finally Deanne chooses Treehouse and we all watch *Barney*. Sometimes Linda puts on some movies that she knows from long ago and we have to see, like there's a lesson in it.

"It's not fairy princess bullshit," I says to Deanne. And I want to yell at her, What do you know anyways, you only fuck boys for money not love them, but I don't because she's gonna get angry at me and I hate it when she's angry. Aimee moves in close to tickle Faithy, says, "Take some food there, little girl."

"Sounds like you want some white knight in shining armour come and make everything go all right. Had me a friend in YK thought that too, talking about it up in the jail there and thinking he's gonna come and take her away. Like Linda's old *Pretty Woman* movie."

I want to jump over the couch and punch her out. She doesn't know. She doesn't know that even meeting up, me and Tyler meant to be together. He knew me, even before he didn't know me, he knew me, got me. We'd be talking about something, like how he knew I liked to cut hair, telling him about the haircuts I did when I was younger, friends of Auntie coming over and Auntie giving me the special shears kit she bought in YK for herself, thinking she could do some haircutting on the side, but it was me she give them to, remembering how good I was at it, even at my old house. Just to cut out those frizzie bits of her perm one day, it was growing out. But it was me that ended up knowing how to gently layer her hair, cut out the frizzies and make the other curls bounce. Then her friends coming in. I gave them haircuts, took forever they said, I was slow then. But they liked it, give me five dollars.

"We have things we gonna do, plans," I says to Deanne. She just snorts like she doesn't believe me.

Aimee's rubbing Faithy's cheek softly, she loves touching Faith, gets all dreamy, says it helps her almost sleep at night, thinking about Faith. "I believe you, Trista," says Aimee. But Aimee's good people and won't say shit bad about me and Faithy, hard to think she's even done that violence that she done, way she is with Faithy. It's Deanne I want to know how it goes, Deanne should know how it goes. What does she know what love I got?

Me and Tyler meeting up? It started like this last year. Keely called and was all "What are you doing tonight?" and I was just enjoying my smoke by the pot-bellied stove that Daduk had got going in our trailer again.

"Nothing, what you're up to?" I says.

"Maybe walking uptown?"

"Why?"

"Just for looking. Did you hear Tony come in? He brought some guy with him," Keely says.

"Tony out from YK Youth Corrections already?" I says.

"Been two months, he still has to do community service," Keely says.

"That went fast, like yesterday he standing up in court, you bawling."

"Yeeah. You coming uptown then?" Keely says.

So we go walking. The dark's already coming on fast, November, and maybe only a couple of afternoon hours of sun left. The twilight of the day already gone down over the Mackenzie River. That Iceroad settling in some good, small trucks motoring along it. Not strong enough for the rigs, but can see the sensor truck with the bright red lights all over it driving slow-like in the dark, feeling out for cracks, ice patches, making holes to let the water come up, and smoothing it down over the road. It's not that the ice will break and you're going to crash into the river, it's the cracks. The way at dead of night under those mean-ass northern lights that run ghosties in the sky, the ice can up and crack wide enough to sink some coffin cars. Then you're standing there out on that ice, screaming up, nowhere to go as you're wondering when the next car going to crash on top of you. That's what they say can happen. More like you just go off that road and never find the road again, snow's not that high in some places, go off and wander lost for miles and miles into dark nothing and freeze when the gas runs dry. I hate that Iceroad. Lost one too many an uncle on that thing, then Mom. Not good for nothing except going downriver to Tuk to watch some hockey. And well, after what with all that happened with Jimmy's asshole friends, why I want to drive for a stinky three hours on that Iceroad to do that even? Not even a bar they got there, just the rink, and then the Tuk Inn where caribou burgers will set you back more than eighteen bucks, boys who fuck you drunk in the snow and leave you frostbit.

What I see first about Tyler? He had his parky half off, the dumbass, trying to look all Eskimo like he can't feel the cold or something, stupid white boy's not even a 'sko. Then he had these cool teardrop tattoos on both sides of his eyes, and some other black tattoos on his hands. He was smoking some weed, which then we knew he'd just come out of stir, because we don't see much townies smoking weed uptown, the RCMP ready to just haul our cans into Holding for any little funny smoking you doing.

"Hey," I said. "Got a smoke, real one?"

"Hey. Here." And he passed me a Player's, a real expensive smoke from down south, and that was it, we were together. Wasn't much later he started working at Arctic Gas, then Daduk said we could have the trailer he got parked out back for cheap rent, even he cleaned it up for us and got the stove working again like he knew even we were in love and wanted to be together. Maybe that's all too simple sounding, what with all that happened after. But I swear, that bit? It sealed us. Tyler come up that night, I was fourteen going on forever, and he was mine, as was Faith, later. If even for only a short time.

Faith starts up crying and I'm jiggling her. "We are set up good, living together in our own place and everything. He's just down south to save more money," I says to Deanne.

"Right. That's why you calling and talking to him every night? He know you waiting on a court date? He gonna come up and support you? Say he's gonna look after your problem baby?"

"He's just worried about money," I says over Faith's cries, turning to screams now. I try to put her in her rolly crib and move it back and forth. Aimee takes the rolly crib from me and walks her around the living room.

"So worried he don't even know what his own daughter looks like," Deanne says.

"I don't got pictures of her," I says.

"Be easy to get Deb to take some."

"He's gonna answer, he's just busy," I says.

"Yeah, okay, whatever you say," Deanne says, and then she drops it. A part of me is happy, but a part of me feels the cold of that night, sees the form on the floor, her clothes, her sweater buttons shifting, Jimmy screaming at me and in my head alls I can think about is Tyler, not this baby, not this baby here and now and the fear fills my throat, makes me want to puke with the bad of it.

I take Faith from Aimee, but then Deb's there, says, "Let me take her, hon," and she takes her over to the workers' station and I swear she's gonna give her formula and I hate it when they do that because then Faithy doesn't feed right from me.

I go back in the living room and Deanne moves over on the couch so I can sit next to her, but instead I sit on the little couch next to Aimee and she whispers to me, "He's gonna be there next time you phone."

I know she's just being nice, but I don't want to listen to nice. I want Deanne to believe me.

three

Wednesday and we're waiting for Lee and the van, still got our socks on and sliding on the carpet. "Oooh," says Megan because I got her a good one. Faithy is in her rolly crib and Linda is rolling her back and forth with her big toe while she's writing something in the logbook at the workers' station. "Fuck," I whisper, because Megan got me back on a good one and it had good colour too. If you rub your socks about, you can electric shock. Get some good sparks here too, but in me and Tyler's trailer it was the best, real real blue ones. Especially the oil guys have to be careful. Tyler says he went up with Arctic Gas one day, they needed some more manpower at the camp and the men had to wear these special gloves, like a desert up here, what you wouldn't know it with all the snow, but it's super dry. "Fuck you, ow!" Deanne says real loud as I get her one and Linda looks up. "Mouth, Deanne," but Linda doesn't do nothing as Deanne's got me in a chokehold rubbing my head so hard and then she tweaks my tit. She can get nasty like that, almost want to kiss her one day and the next she's pinching or kicking at me. Don't want to kiss her much then.

The workers tell us over and over again that we have to do other things besides the school, because they want us to look toward what we maybe have to do for work when we get older. They have to do northern hires at the hospital, and some of us don't even have to finish all of high school to get some good jobs. That's the thing with the pipeline going in, you get some jobs even you're young maybe, Tyler was only pumping gas but then maybe he gets older he can do some work training courses too, don't know why he wants to fuck it up looking for work down south in Yellowknife, they got more work coming up here and Inuvik too maybe. The Inuvialuit Regional Corp and then the Gwich'in band, making sure they got us some money when they treatied the oil stuff but it took a fuck of a long time to even do that. Mom didn't have much from them. She took up with Richard and I think he was full Inuvialuit, then he got some money coming in. But it's not too bad to rent in Jackfish Bay, we didn't have much money coming from what Mom did, think she was up the Northmart, can't remember much. Auntie works some at the Northmart and then Keely's mom got Auntie also coming in and trying for that counselling job up the treatment centre they got for adults. Good to have some people who been there to be your workers, only if they got it together and Auntie's now got more than five years sober in. You wouldn't think it to talk to Nanuk, she's still hard on Auntie.

We're in the van and Deanne's singing this old song, "Don't Worry, Be Happy," but she's not singing much, just doing that whoo whoo under her breath. Makes me cheer up some because it's hard to leave Faith with the workers and come out of the facility especially since I just got her back. Tracy's smiling too and I think she's looking grown up with her hair cut short like that pixie cut she has and her dark glasses, even though I know her from school and she's only about three years older than me. Hard to believe she's already in Arctic College and doing job training with us at the facility, seems I remember her dancing at the Ptarmigan Hall just yesterday, wearing her long blue dress all fancy and getting beaver shear mittens from Nanuk Marjorie for graduating grade ten. Also I am nervous because this is my first time going to the Elder Hospital instead of the Greenhouse. Aimee looks kind of nervous too, so I'm not the only one. We see kids coming up the road, it's not time for school just yet, before 9 a.m., and they're walking with their heads down against the wind. Most of them have parkys or Columbia ski jackets on, but they're wearing no snowboots, just runners and shit I'm thinking they must be cold, remembering my toes in my shoes, walking to school with Keely.

We pull up in front of the Inuvik Regional Hospital and Tracy leads us round the corner to the Elder Hospital, and I'm thinking it looks a lot like the facility: kind of grey painted walls, and that look, like those buildings could go on forever in the snow. Up here you get some view of the town too, the lights glistening in the snow, makes Inuvik look a lot bigger, not shit small like Jackfish Bay. They don't cuff us, where we going to go? Up the back hill and then into nothing, we know that and they do too. Just as I get out of the van after Aimee, I almost fall forward, Deanne behind me, grabbing at my parky to hold me up. She slips her hand up my wrist inside and tickles some there, moves in close to my neck. It's sudden, this closeness, and I shiver a bit, imagine we could go back to my room and Faith in her crib and I can hear her humming and really have Deanne's hands on my arms, my belly, her mouth on mine. But I got to put it out of my head, them thoughts about Deanne, at day, at night. Sometimes I am so mad at her, then other times I only can look at her mouth and imagine. Lee sees us to the door and then says, "Bye, girls." Deanne pulls me toward the door, hand rubbing my back. And why I have to go with these girls when I got my Faithy to tend to, and now them workers get to have her all morning while we here. Megan's behind us and I can see her orange hair sticking out from under her hood. She's grinning and I think she's some crazy because she says she's gonna love coming and washing the old people.

It's hard to imagine they let us do this. What we done to some people to get into the jail and now they letting us put on gloves and the singlets and fill the tubs. But I'm not gonna think about that because I got to focus on just this, just this day right now. The nurses and other workers are there too, to watch us. Linda says this work is good for the soul, to see the nanuks when they old and lived a long life, and care for them. I get the sponges like the other girls, and I wipe down a nanuk, but I don't really see her. I see my hands mixing with Deanne's. I see us up in our own trailer and we got Faith and I push that memory smell of Tyler and the soap suds, he's doing the dishes and I'm just feeling safe. This nanuk's belly and her stretch marks from the babies she's had and Aimee is washing her wrinkles, mixing the soap suds with her belly, rubbing and this nanuk's sighing in the warm water. That warm water that smells of babies clean and something of God.

When me and Tyler just started going out, I'm not into that "get with your spirits and elders" then. Had the Snow Nanuks, but seemed like they been long gone I been to see them. But then Tyler talks about it, and he's not even fucking native or nothing, all about getting clean with God, or he calls it the Goddess Upstairs, Gus, like Tyler thinks it's all about women and how they can give birth and the Earth is Gaia, some spiritual being. His mom is a hippie, he says, thinks there's room on this Earth for everyone. I don't know Tyler's mom, she's down in Yellowknife and I never met her, but I think about her, maybe think I want her to be my mom. Maybe I even think it's the Goddess Upstairs. Tyler is real good about other people getting their spirit god whatever way they want. And he's been always talking about setting up with his tattoo shop. He's got goals. I never been around with no one who got goals. It was easy to think that once I was big with Faith, me and Tyler were going to make it different. Like not how Tony and Keely always fighting. When I knew? I always had my period every twenty-seven days, since I been getting it regular since I was twelve. Day twenty-eight, twenty-nine, thirty all go by. My tits hurting like they been pinched then rubbed raw. Me and Tyler been partying back a few weeks and I just knew we messed it up. But he was real good. Come up behind me in the bathroom the next morning after I told him, me with red eyes up all night without him but he came back. "Gonna be okay, Trista," he says in my ear. Put his arms around my shoulders and pulled me against him. "How it gonna be okay, Ty?"

He pulls me against him and hugs me tighter, looks at me in the mirror. My toothpaste in the corners of my mouth and he's kissing my neck. "Whatever, Trista, we'll take care of our business together." And I believed him.

"Trista, you come on over here and help me out in this tub," Tracy says.

I dry my hands and turn to help out at the next bathtub. Tracy's washing the nanuk's face, but when she moves the washcloth aside I say, "Nanuk Marjorie," and Nanuk looks up at me, blinking: "Who is it, honey? Come in closer, don't have my glasses." And I move my face in and Nanuk's face crinkles up, "How's my girl?" I move back from her because her wrinkled face soap smell makes me want to kiss her, but I don't think she knows it's me, how could she say that if she knows it's me?

But I don't want to think about that. I wash Nanuk Marjorie and think about Tyler's soft lips, that little bit of fuzz he'd get on his upper lip, hardly had to shave, that white boy. Some like my Faithy's hair, how it's growing in all rough in some patches and then soft up around her ears. Nanuk Marjorie's hair is like that, swirling in the water as the pillow holds her up. Tracy's washing her arms, sudsing with the blue puffy thing. Aimee's behind me at the other tub humming that song Deanne was singing in the van, and I see a little bit of sweat coming on her forehead, it's hot in here, the water's so warm from the bathtub.

I can see myself maybe in the future doing this. Not with the smock I wear at the Inuvik Hospital, the smock that was a hand-me-down. Not with that one on. I can see me with my own nurses' clothes, bright-coloured smocks with bears on them, and blue daisies, or red bells for Christmas, dancing caribou for New Year's. And my own nametag, I can see it, in that gold like the nurses got at the hospital. Trista LPN. The way I can look in the mirror at the changerooms at the hospital, pin my hair up and away from my face, scrubbed, clean, and ready to go to work. And maybe I can take my haircutting tools in and cut their long old hair for the nanuks. Give them new haircuts that make the hair go out of their face when they sleep, sleep good, and wake up with the wrinkles round their eyes and smiling.

Nanuk Marjorie is smiling and she's got her eyes closed, but she says, "You some good girls." I feel good, washing her cheeks, rubbing some raspberry-smelling shampoo into her hair, and Tracy's got the washcloth over her eyes so the soap don't get in. I want to feel good how I want to feel good again.

Saturday and visiting time and me and Keely go and sit in the small room off the Group room. Keely's come in with her head ducked down a little because she knows I'm always looking past her, see if Auntie or Nanuk come this time. Auntie calls. Says she wants to come in, but she got her shift at work during visiting hours. Maybe one day she can get a shift off, but it's hard this near to Christmas coming up. She says Nanuk's still mad at me, won't come alone, can't go look at me in here with what I done and I don't want to think about how her face gets when she's angry, her upper lip get that twitch to it, her hard eyes big in her reading glasses staring me down like she's never gonna see me good in her eyes again. Auntie says don't worry about it, Nanuk's gonna feel better for Christmas, maybe the holidays soften her, maybe the pictures Deb took of Faithy and sent to them gonna warm her heart. But I don't know, take a long time to forgive something like what I done. I know that hate she got inside for me, been pushing it down in me too, but it comes bubbling up flashing like some mean hangover headache you can't think about or it gets worse.

The visiting room's got carpet and it's warm, but they won't let me bring Faith to see Keely. She brung some pictures of her brothers.

"We got them Crazy Carpets, they been going on that hill out the utilidor," Keely says.

"You made that hill for them? They got the utilidor fixed?"

"Finally. Our lights would go weird on and off, shit was frozen and backed up too, couldn't flush for a few days. They come up fixed it last week. Yeeah, me and Mom, we packed the snow up, was hard, it's the old snow so it's all crispy and hard to move, got the shovel from Lee," Keely says.

"This one of Robbie is funny," I says.

"Yeeah, he kicks Adam's ass on the Crazy Carpets, Adam gets his fists up all angry."

"Lee come too?" There's a picture of him and he's got Adam by the scruff of his parky, Adam just about going to slide down the hill and Lee's climbing up behind him. Lee didn't do well at high school. But he's doing something instead of drinking about town, like getting his paramedic driving hours in. He come in sometimes and talk to us, when we were in the high school. Maybe come in Socials class or something, talking quiet like about choices and things we can do than drinking or drugging, maybe work more or study more, like the teachers think he's some poster boy for going to college. He's no suck or anything, he never come at us like we got to do this shit and you know in his dark eyes he just setting there wanting to help not judging us or nothing. We think maybe he'll be like Tracy and study to go to the boy's jail down YK and help them out, where Jimmy ended up.

"Lee tell you he come up here, drive us to work training?" I ask Keely.

"Yeeah. Says Faithy's looking real cute now," Keely says and she's picking at her jeans again. I know she wants to see Faith, but them workers won't let Faithy come in with me for visiting. But Lee's allowed.

I know he saw me the night I went in. Was his auntie, that woman at the Aurora Store that night. When me and Jimmy been there. Doing that. She gives us candy when we're little, me and Keely and all them other kids we run around with after school and heading to Snow Nanuks, she's like a Snow Nanuk. Lee, he come in here to pick us up and look at Faith when the workers holding her, he push aside the blanket and I wonder what he's thinking, does he want to talk to me about it all. His eyes are intense when I look up at him and I think he's gonna say something, I get these squirms in my belly wondering what he's gonna say. But he just looks at me strangely. And I don't know if that look means he's sad or he wants to punch me out, punch Faithy out, take it all back to when we was younger and I was little and maybe he could have made me good.

"You're lucky you don't got school all day," Keely says.

I think about washing the Snow Nanuks, think about telling Keely I seen Nanuk Marjorie up there on work training. That is lucky. But then think how Keely can just go and make her own bed, up and go to school. Have a smoke whenever. Like when it's 3 a.m. and trying to nurse Faith and I'm so tired and she's screaming and I don't want to nurse. Just sit quiet and have a smoke back cozy in the trailer months before. Watch Tyler sleep. "Almost Christmas break soon, Keely. Then you don't gotta get up early. You gonna take more hours at Northmart?"

"Yeeah," she nods, getting excited. "Save up for gas, shit, my Ski-Doo so old I think the tank's leaking slow fuel. Get it fixed up." She's smiling at me and then suddenly I got this pain in my chest like someone reached in and stole my next breath away. Jealous feeling. Keely looks up about to say something and I know she seen it. "But work sucks too," she says. "Hey, think they let us out for a smoke break?"

We're outside smoking. Linda's by the door, she don't smoke, but she's watching us. She's good people, because she sorta stands there and watches but not watches. Lets us know she's not really listening.

"Tony heard some more about Tyler. When he's down at YK," Keely says.

"How come you didn't tell me before?" I say.

"Busy."

She gets this grin on her face and I want to smack her. Like she's saying to me that I am fucked up in this hole and now she and Tony are the one's who all mature and setting up house and knowing how they can get on. But then she look up at me all concerned. "We been cleaning. Trying to go clean the Snow Nanuks' house, get some spare money." And I feel bad. Because she is trying. She is trying to be real and get it together and I am a shit, a stupid mean shit.

"What Tony say?"

"Just Tyler not there. Not at the coffee shop any more working," Keely says. Her head is down and she's concentrating on smoking real hard.

"Yeeah. Figured as much. Probably fucking using again, sleeping in all day and sucking off his mom."

"But, Trista. He's just going down south more to earn better money."

"What better money? He can earn better money here, even if he had to work the Northmart or something. You know what all them say, who been down south. There's no jobs there. What, now you're sticking up for him?" I says.

"Nah, just. It's what I heard."

We smoke for a bit, seems like sometimes them smokes gone so fast, and then sometimes they go on forever. Keely comes in to the visitor room again. Linda steps inside and leaves us be. I look at Keely, she's got her Columbia jacket draped across her knees and she's got her jeans, muddy down at the bottom and kind of white where the snow dried and the salt makes white. She's got all this black eyeliner round her eyes and I can tell she's tired because she probably put that shit on yesterday and just rubbed under it with a washcloth this morning. Brushed her long hair. Looked in the mirror and just figured, This'll work today too, took the washcloth and didn't wash right into her eyes but just under the lid and wiped. Brushed her teeth, put on her clothes, and came over. It's early still. Early for the old Keely. This new one, who been cleaning the Snow Nanuks' house with her boyfriend, this one I don't know too well. Who gets up early and comes visits her best friend in jail at 10 a.m., who is this one?

I think about what all she says. How she's trying. I think about saying to her, like in the movies, Why don't we talk any more, Keely? And she says to me, What's there to say? And she opens her eyes all moody and meaningful. Like there is too much to say.

I start to giggle.

"What?" Keely asks.

I shake my head, cover my mouth. I hate the crooked teeth I got.

"What?" Keely says again. And she's got a little thing that come into her eyes, like she wants so hard to laugh too, like we been meaning to have a good belly laugh for too long. She's missing it. Not the belly laughing we got into when we was also into the vodka or whisky. But the belly laughing we did when we was kids and at the Snow Nanuks' house and eating popcorn, almost choking on it, throwing it at each other and the other kids at sleepovers. Keely's looking over like she been thinking I'm going crazy. I know they got her and Auntie, even Nanuk some, on the phone, telling them to look out. For what I don't know, maybe me going completely crazy.

"What you been doing?" Keely ask in this false kind of voice.

"Nothing much. Just setting around some. We got schoolwork."

"Yeeah, what book you doing?"

"Something about some gangs down Texas. Boys," I says.

"That one about that Ponyboy? We done that last year," Keely says.

"Yeeah. Doing it again. Don't remember much reading it last year."

"You the one who gave me all the answers," Keely says.

"Yeeah."

"So it the same as at the high school, school here?"

"Some. The girls are okay. First I thought they … you know, some coming from Paulautuk or Kug, maybe be—"

"Screwy."

"Yeeah. But they're fine. Just quiet."

"They letting you out, come down for the fireworks on Sunrise?" Keely asks.

"Don't know. Maybe. Some of the girls been talking about it. Maybe first time I don't see them."

"Yeeah."

"You and Tony?"

"Maybe. But you not going. Maybe I thinking on staying home too. Hard to see the Snow Nanuks come out for Sunrise and you not there."

I don't say anything to that. Probably should. Probably should be blabbing my head off to that, bawling or something, like Linda think we all should be doing in Group. Spilling it all. Getting our guts out messy on the floor.

Some things don't want to get out. Thinking on the Snow Nanuks, what saved me and Keely from not sleeping and our moms and boyfriends drinking and partying all night some weekends. Fucking Snow Nanuks. Where are they now? Sitting at their house, looking after some more little ones. Are they thinking on me? I got all this self-pity going on it's like coming up in my throat and setting there like the sour candies me and Keely used to love to eat after school. At the Aurora Store we could get all the good stuff like we seen on the TV commercials, Hardy Sours and Powersour Balls and Lik'em Sours, me and Keely eat them all. Mavis say, "You girls gonna turn into some sour wives maybe." And she's got a smile in her voice. We take them bags of sours back to the Snow Nanuks, set up with the kids and watch cartoons, or Mr. Rogers, maybe even we play with all the pillows they got in the kids' room. Wasn't ever any of the Snow Nanuks' kids actually living there, them all grown. But they kept that room up there so we'd come down. If someone got his face kicked in from his older brother coming in drunk, or a girl and her stepdad at her again. Me, I stayed there too. Running there maybe in April or May, when the lights are on almost all night. Just sick of Mom and Richard all cuddly together.

"You remember my mom telling us Fox and Ptarmigan story, Keely?" I ask her.

"Yeeah. Kinda. Used to be I fell asleep so fast. Something about him not eating her baby."

"Yeeah."

Linda pops her head in. "You girls ready? Keely should be going now."

"One more smoke, Linda?" Keely says.

"Yeeah. Hurry it," Linda says.

We go outside and I wonder why Keely's wanting to smoke. Usually she comes but is happy just to get the time.

"So, Tony."

"Yeeah," I says.

"Tony says he heard from Tyler. When he was down there. Seems like he was in his own apartment."

"Seems like or was."

"Was." Keely's got her head down and I know she can't stay that way long, the smoke's going up her nose and gonna make her sneeze.

"He's down there setting up. Going to school even. Taking some auto mechanic course after school."

"Hmm."

"Tony says he sounds good."

"Yeeah. Would be good that. Setting up. Maybe having his mom set him up. He down there in Yellowknife."

"I'm just saying," Keely says.

"Hmm."

Keely stubs the smoke butt on the ground, picks it up, and drops it into the can. I feel too numb to even think of Tyler, what, where he is.

"You see about getting a pass for the fireworks, ah?" Keely says.

I smile at her some, what am I gonna say to that? She know and me too that I don't know what's coming up the next day even, what do I know about next month or more. What them workers going to say is any good for us. Maybe we get out. Maybe they think it's not a good idea. Keely grabs for me sudden-like and hugs me hard. She's rubbing my back, but my arms just go by my side and can't move. She pushes my hair out of my face.

"Stay gold, Ponyboy and all that," she says and grins at me. But she's got the sad back in her eyes. The things you see. The things you notice when you got your best friend visiting you in jail. It's hard to say much to her. I know sometimes she's just up and feeling uncomfortable. This somehow sister of mine.

It's afternoon Group. My leg is all jumpy, like seeing those pictures Keely brung in makes me want to get out there and be little again, slide down on the Crazy Carpets and climb back up the hill again and again, have Nanuk call me and Keely in for some Eskimo pies and hot chocolate before she's got the bingo on the TV, sit up with her at the big table and do some crafts that Auntie bought from the V&S store, make some Christmas decorations or wreaths for the Elder Hospital. Nanuks's got some flour on her nose and I wet my finger and lick it off. I look outside and it's dark, only 4 p.m. but so dark and I feel it wash over me.

"Feels good to have them babies," Aimee says. "Because we can and then that makes us warm."

"Feels good to have them maybe," Deb says. "What about taking care of them, when they finally come?"

"If you're set up okay, it works," I says. "Have a place and your boyfriend has a job, it's gonna be fine."

"You can't trust those men to do shit for you. Got to look after yourself, not have babies until you're older," Deanne says.

"Easy for you to say, boy killer," says Megan but grins at her.

"Yeah well, not into redheads either, babycakes," says Deanne. I don't look at her because I hate it when she plays older like she's got her shit together, when she looks at Deb and Deb doesn't grin at her much, not like the Bitch. When she's doing that in Group and siding with them, the Bitch sometimes just laps Deanne's parrot-talking counsellor shit up and I think Deanne doesn't really believe it but does it anyways. The Bitch gives her some more phone privileges so she can call her girlfriend on the outside, waiting down in YK for her or so she says, and so Deanne believes. Sometimes I don't know what makes me more mad, her girlfriend or the way she does that sometimes. Deb doesn't fall much for it.

"Yes, you should wait. Some of you have your moms or aunties come through for you, help take care of the babies. I have seen some girls even get to grad, or close to it. Get into a work program."

"You done that too," I says to Deb. She told us about her kids and how she's a single mom, how her littlest one, Danny, always sick with something, the cough you get up here because it's so dry, the bronchitis that you cough with and it doesn't go away till Ice Break Up.

"Yes, I did it, am doing it. But I wasn't so young when I first started. I'd finished my school, even half of my college program before I had my first."

"Hmm."

Deb looks about, she knows what we all thinking, I bet, she knows we're thinking, What do you know, been down living in YK and not up here, yeeah Yellowknife is north, but not so far away from them people and the way they live down south, and more people there and the big city, so what do you know, Deb?

"What I want to look at, what I want you to think about, girls, is why"—we all look up, even Aimee—"why do you think you are doing it? Not using the condoms the public nurses make available to you. At school. At the clinic. What happens, that conscious decision to make that baby? Or those of you who didn't get pregnant, who used protection. What did you learn? You need to come to terms with that. To look after your babies. To look after yourselves." She goes on talking about some stuff then.

I am listening but not really. Like I can look into the brown carpet and see Faithy. See her walking down to the Snow Nanuks, me at work and her going with her best friend, just like me and Keely long ago. The Snow Nanuks setting in the living room, doing their knitting or caribou tufting and Faith comes in, they put their stuff aside, "Chee, girl, you grown big, c'mere." And Faithy runs up to Nanuk Marjorie and she's got those big arms around her, like the sinews of the caribou themselves, just strong and holding her up.

"Where you been, my girl, where you been my Faithy? Haven't seen you in long long time, like dark days you been gone." And Faithy snuggles in deep and she talks, she sings, she sings an old song to Snow Nanuk, one song been gone a long time, the things she seen, but the bad all cried out and Snow Nanuk hums against her in time with Faithy's singing.

Babies and babies. Me being unsafe with Jimmy before Tyler came along, we was just lucky. When we little, the men at the parties giving us money. Richard. How me and Richard lay together after Mom was gone. His hands under the quilt and me only seven. Being with Tyler and kissing him and knowing when he's inside me that we could get into trouble and me not caring because by then I'm long gone from Snow Nanuks' house. Not that they didn't want us no more. Their door always open and we known where to go. But then, then me and Keely, older and wandering uptown after school. If we even went to school that day. Crashed out at my house, Auntie working and Nanuk not knowing we so stoned, just thinking we're in my room up and quiet at night. We were always quiet stoners, me and Keely. Only when we got hold of a bottle from the men down Barclose maybe we have to walk a long time before coming home, maybe hide behind Ptarmigan Hall, where it's still warm from inside and drink the big bottle of forty Jack Daniels there, cold fucking cold still though we been huddled against that back door, listening to the old-time dances from inside. We're feeling like we're grown up. Like we known something about relationships, or how to live. Babies. What I done to her and what I'm doing to her and when Faith grown, she gonna turn out like me?

"Trista?" Deb says. I'm lost in my head and it takes a second to really see her. She's smiling at me, a question in her voice.

"Yeeah," I says.

"You want to tell us something. About babies?'

"Me and Tyler. We made it right. Didn't want no abortion. We got our trailer and Daduk help us set it up, gave us some money. Was doing good. Still doing good," I says.

"How's that, still doing good?" Deanne says. "You ain't seen him, he's not come up here to visit or what."

"Shut up," I says.

"It's true, Trista. We never seen him visiting days," Megan says and her foot's jerking away she's jiggling it so much. I don't want to look round at them, all their faces on me I know it, and Deb's not even saying anything to break up that bubble we got in the room, the pressure.

"Just fuck off," I says. "What you all know, he's calling me back soon."

"Yeeah, we heard that one before," Megan says.

"What do you know about it? You ever lived on your own with your boyfriend?" I say.

"Have you been able to get in touch with him, Trista?" Deb says. She knows I haven't, why the fuck she keep asking?

"No. He doesn't answer the machine."

"White boy could give a shit about you," Deanne says. I jump across the room at her.

"Just shut the fuck up!" I say and she moves, quick. I fall just short of smashing her face in. I go to get up but I'm so mad I fall forward again and the empty chair beside Deanne dumps over and I kick it. Deb comes up behind me and bear-hugs me and she makes me go down on the floor. I am so fucking mad I can pound her face in, but she's got my arms pinned, then grabs at a pillow and shoves it into my hands and I punch and punch at it, feeling it's stupid, but it's also Tyler's face all the same. Then I start fucking crying and Deb's rocking me, and I know my ears are burning because all them girls are looking at me, now I am the freak who's freaking out in the Group room. But I don't care, it's like my head is flaming up and I just scream out his name, "You fucking cocksucker, Tyler, you fucking asshole you shit you shit!" and my throat closes up with tears and I bend over Deb's skinny arms and they loosen, she's rubbing at my arms. I swipe at my dripping nose and I just can't stop shaking, but Deb says, "Breathe through your nose, Trista, deep breaths." And I do it a few times and after a bit say, "Okay. Let me go," and she does. She rights the chair and I can't look at them girls. Deb gives me the tissue box and I hold it, almost breaking the cardboard.

It's quiet for awhile, then Deanne says, "Well, I got something to say about smoke breaks: how come they so short these days?" and Deb says, "Go on," to Deanne and even though I want to still punch out Deanne I love her right then for taking it off me.

Before I met Tyler I went to this party next to Keely's house, and me and Keely were drinking beers. Keely really wanted me to talk to this guy that she thought kind of looked like me, Jimmy. "C'mere, Trista," she said and pushed me toward the kitchen.

"What you're up to?" he said.

"Nothing, just talking, how 'bout you?"

"Nothing. So I hear Keely figure you and me had moms who were cousins," Jimmy said.

"Yeeah. I heard her talking up something like that."

"So your mom's Gloria? She got relatives from Tuk?"

"Yeeah," I said.

"Her mom's sister, that's Nanuk Ethel. My mom used to live with them when she was little. I come from Tuk just now."

"Maybe I heard something 'bout you. You working up the Beaufort?" I said.

"No. Just staying with my uncle, in Tuk. He's saying maybe he'll get me some job on the rigs out there."

We didn't talk much more, but he wanted me to talk just him and me in the bedroom, and then before you know it he's doing it to me, without even kissing me and I'm thinking, This guy is my cousin, maybe, and what the fuck because it don't matter anyways. I'm drunk and it's not like my uncles haven't been in me, calling me slut skank whore, at least Jimmy is nice about it, and comes quickly, and gets the hell out of the house after, skulks around all week, though. That time in Tuk happened after, when he was drunk there after losing the hockey game against Tuk. He's out on the street around Tuk, his buddies take me down outside, each one of them, the fuckers. He said he was sorry that he didn't see me or help me, way past sorry. But he wasn't there then. That shit makes it numb. Laid me right ready to believe Tyler and his talk. Thinking how this guy's not from our town, he's from down south where they do things different and he's gonna be better just because he's not from here. But didn't take long to find out he was full of shit too.

I didn't see much of Jimmy for a while in between. Heard his uncle did get him on the rigs out in the Beaufort, but then I heard someone say that he'd called me a slut for what happened in Tuk, said Jimmy just said I probably fucked anything that moved and was after his rig money, which he came into Jackfish Bay to drink up at the Icebox Bar anyway, so as if I could stand at Barclose, when all the drunks come out of the Icebox, and get money from him. That one time, it was that only one time that he'd come down from the rigs, and was jacked up on some coke that them guys got for him, and also was drinking at the Icebox Bar. That one night before we went to the Aurora Store to get smokes. I hadn't seen him in such a long time. And look what he went and did. Look what we did.

Tyler says that God is all about responsibility, and owning. Owning the past, the present, and the future. Tyler says, if you're straddling all these things, like if you're spreading your legs to get across the creek, then you got one leg in yesterday, one leg in tomorrow and you're pissing all over today. I'm trying not to piss on today, Lord, I'm trying.

Eating breakfast and we try to string it out. "You girls just love me too much, that's what," says Sherry. She's joking some, but she's right too. We like to sit there in the morning with her cooking and the lights are bright. Sherry's behind the counter and she's mixing up some stuff, maybe something for dinner.

"Where you go to school?" Megan asks her, because what with going to the work training at the Greenhouse and then the Hospital, the workers get us asking everybody.

"Went to a cooking school in YK," Sherry says.

"Easy?" Megan says.

"Not too. Had my little boy with me, up at the daycare they had at the college. Was hard to do the homework, him being all around and up on his feet walking new, then my roommate had her little girl too. But she was six and sat up at the kitchen table watching the TV."

"You ever feel like quitting it?" Aimee asks.

"Almost every morning. But my roommate, she was in the office assistant program, she was good at computer keyboarding, organizing stuff, she kept me going. She was sick of being on welfare, the food bank. Having to ask them for clothing allowance for another shitty winter coat for her kid, arguing with the worker whether you spent your transpo money right or being stupid up at the bar when you know you not seen the inside of the bar in two years, stuck down in your apartment with your kid."

"What was it like? Getting the graduation paper, walking?" Megan asks and she's got this look on her face like she can see it. I got my head down, jiggling Faith trying to get her to take my nipple, but I'm listening.

"Everything what they say. Hard not to cry. My roommate was there with my boy, Seanie, it was during the day so her girl was in school so she brought him with. He was too little to know what was what. But I knew he was there, watching his mom get those papers, all what that means. Getting a job, having something you can do except fill out stupid welfare forms. Was always good at cooking, even my mom said so, when I was younger," Sherry says.

Megan's grinning at her and she's got a piece of egg stuck to the corner of her mouth. Her tongue flicks out and gets it, and she's chewing. When I am breastfeeding Faithy, it's like I want to kiss everyone, that feeling you get in your breasts and it goes right in to the centre of you, feels a little like you got to pee and you're having sex. I want to kiss Megan, the way she's looking at Sherry. Deanne grabs her breakfast tray and rubs up against my arm, smiling, funny how she can know me like that. I wish I can breastfeed Faith more, but most days she's more taking to the formula they been giving to her to fatten her up.

"So, what you making for dinner?" Deanne says.

"How about quiche?" says Sherry.

"What?"

"Quiche. Just fancy for ham and eggs in a pie." Sherry's mixing and wiping her hands, pulls at Deanne's cheek. Not many who can get away with that. Deanne lets maybe Linda in, not even Deb so much. Deanne pulls away, but she's got that look in her walk that says she's feeling loose, not uptight.

There's no sunlight coming in the windows, but I want to stay under the fluorescent lights forever in the kitchen, even though Faithy is fussing. She keeps putting her fists in her mouth, and going ah ah ah. It's like she's singing a little song, or trying to tell me something. Deb said the doctors coming in again soon. More of what they can't tell me shit anyways. Looking at her again, like they come in every two weeks. Been a month now. All they don't tell me.

The shit they do and I don't want to hear it, it's fucking shit, just block it out. How she's so squiggly at night, trying to sleep, and I worry about getting food into her. Maybe they don't find a placement for her in foster care and then she can just stay with me here, always. Imagine maybe they don't got to take her away and I don't got to go to court after Christmas. Don't have to face the crime and talk about it and think about it, push the evil feeling away. Don't have to listen to doctors gonna tell me something bad, more bad news and I can just stay here in this kitchen with Sherry and the girls and never have to go out again and face anything. Can't imagine that Faith's never been with me, but only been a month since that night me and Jimmy fucked up.

This baby. In old times, Snow Nanuks be walking out on the land and the young ones like me have their babies under their parkys, on their backs or if really little snuggled up close in front. Then my Faith can pull at my breast just when she needs to, even if I'm walking with the group and trying to find a good caribou cache so we can have some meat. Imagining we're out in old times on the land, trapping small game, mostly hares and muskrats, some beaver if we come up on a den. When I look back to the town, I expect to see the houses with the lights twinkling, maybe see the cars along the Iceroad. But I don't. I see only the icehouses and the whirling wind. I can hear Faithy inside my parky, her ah ah-ing. I go to the icehouse and Snow Nanuk's inside, "C'mere, girl." I go to her and she pushes my parky back and takes me in her arms. I lie against her and feel the shearling against my cheek, she helps me bring Faith out, and Faith latches on to my breast and I fall back, feel I am swimming in Snow Nanuk, me and Faithy swimming, this warm.

We have morning Group today. Miss Sarah is sick so we're in for morning. I'm not allowed to wait outside for a while to breastfeed

Faithy, even though my boobs are aching for her to try to feed more. They ache but they're drying up and she can't get much out of them anyway. Megan's freaking out because Linda is grilling her about her crime, trying to make her talk about when she bought the rat poison, if she knew in her head what she was gonna do with it. So Megan's trying to change the subject, talking about being taken off privileges for smoking in her cell. "It was just late, and I was shaking," she says.

"Where'd you get the smokes? The lighter?" Linda says.

"I'm not fucking telling you that. What you're gonna do? Come and search my cell, and take it all away, and I just got them pictures from my nanuk."

"Calm down."

"I'm not fucking calming down, okay I'm calm, fuck, you just come in and fucking take it all, don't you? Can't call my friends or my nanuk, and you talking about claiming our culture and all this shit, then you cut off my phone privileges and I can't talk no fucking nothing with no one, culture shit or not!"

I feel all sleepy. Times like this? In Group with these girls, I feel so old, even though they're all like fifteen or so like me, okay, maybe Megan is only thirteen, but she's bigger than me. I think of Faith older, running outside, with her little feet in her snowboots, pumping strong in the snow. Driving on the Ski-Doo up the back hill. Riding our Crazy Carpets down the hills by the utilidors. Kissing Tyler down by the river at Winter Jamboree, before we fought and he went to Yellowknife. Before Jimmy come from Tuk, and things got so fucked up. Just one day, one night, even some hours. And just like that it was all fucked up.

Make a family, make a home, Snow Nanuks say to us long ago, we all huddled around them playing string games. With Faith inside me, was trying so hard with Tyler to make a family, put out my head those fights we had. I don't want to think about the fights. Deb says, "Trista, think about the times it wasn't good with Tyler. There are reasons he is not here in Jackfish Bay. What are the reasons he left?" What he says, sometimes he could say it so good, sometimes he had me believing so hard. Get a shop, get some tattooing going, get some money in. Gonna save my money, gonna save so we got something, Trista. Maybe my mom give us some money, we get our own place, not have to pay rent. We get Faith to daycare, and you doing good getting your grade twelve, maybe we get out of here, go down south and make a shop. Good money in tattoos, every one and his dog wanting one now.

Then he's all right for a week, all right for two. But then him smoking weed, him up nights drinking and then screaming at me, saying, "It's all shit and why are you knocked up? Why didn't you get rid of her? Why am I not just taking off and heading down south without you and this shit?"

"We got Faith coming, Tyler. We need to save money for her," I says.

"That's what I'm trying to do, can't you see that? Working all these shifts for you, and what you only got one shift Northmart, and still you're taking classes at school. Why should I be the only one working so hard?" Tyler says. He flings his joint at the pot-bellied stove, then jumps up and gets a piece of foil out of his drawer, throwing our socks and underwear onto the floor.

"Where'd you get that?" I say

"Some guys," he says, going through the fork and knives drawer, looking for a spoon to cook up.

"You said you didn't do that shit no more, Tyler. You promised," I says.

"Yeah well, you're stressing me out. This is my home, maybe I just gonna fuck off to YK, get my own place. Do my own shit on my own time," he says. I go into the bathroom and lock the door, can hear his lighter snicking on and off, on and off. Yeeah, why don't you. Tyler. Why don't you fuck off.

Megan's arguing more with Linda, but I don't hear what she's saying, it's like I got Tyler screaming in my head and then I'm shaking and Linda's saying, "What's going on with you, Trista?" And I say to them, "Stop fucking fighting about it, you're always fighting." Deanne's looking at me weird and Megan says, "Just leave it alone, Linda," and Linda focuses on Megan again and they start up and I curl my fingers around the chair's arm and push it down, push it away and their voices get softer and Group's done again and it's like I am losing time.

"Jailbird."

"You ugly."

"What you thinking on, ah. You thinking on some *drugggsss*?"

"You ugly, go cut."

"You feelin' like what, you're gonna die."

"Wait … hold on … don't do nothin' … let me get you a sharper knife."

Maybe it's Deanne who starts it, but soon's as you get into the facility, you gonna be doing it soon too. Hawking. Most times it starts with someone new, they coming into the classroom. At least when they get to being able to be in the classroom, and they making that girl go to school again, we know she's out there to be hawked. Didn't take me long neither to whisper under my voice soon as Aimee came in, "You gonna die. You feeling it?" Then Deanne whispering to her, "You feeling some sad and sorry for yourself … I can go get the gun," not even looking her in the eye. When it was Aimee she near cried, put her fingers up to her corners of her eyes and pushed hard. Yeeah, it was fucking shit to see that. Then she looked at Deanne and said, "You want I go get my daduk's rifle for ya?" And her lips went up some, and Deanne and Megan, they just howled laughing until Miss Sarah told them to be quiet.

Sometimes it starts in the living room, like now it's break time after lunch and we don't got any work training today, just homework time in the afternoon.

"You ugly," Deanne says to Megan, who's putting on some lipgloss. It could be Vaseline she got smeared around her lips because it's so dry in here but it don't matter. "You ugly."

"Yeeah, you wish I'm so ugly," Megan says.

"Oh, yeeah?"

"I could ugly your daddy with my ugly mouth, bad, I could ugly him till he comes and have to give me that ten bucks he promised to you for last night," Megan says. She doesn't miss much that Megan, don't even look at Deanne.

"Ah," Deanne says and then starts in on Aimee. "You so ugly when you finally get around to cutting up that face a yours instead of those arms, coroner going to come around and say, 'She too ugly to put into the ground.' Then you just gonna ghost your ugly round town screaming and yelling for the coked-up kids to see your ugly dead face."

Aimee doesn't say nothing to that, but Megan gets up and kicks Deanne and they go down on the ground wrestling. If Linda or maybe even Deb's on the desk, they don't do nothing. At first, sitting watching Deanne getting it up with someone, or even Megan, I wonder about that. The girls are fighting, how come they don't go to Iso after that? If I have Faith in my arms I just move away some, they don't get me into it if they're wrestling. It's fun to watch, but feels some lonely too. Like they are more friends when they are doing it. Then Linda come about, "Okay, girls, get up, stop getting all the carpet on your backs," and that's it. They're breathing. They're smiling.

If someone sees you're thinking too hard, maybe depressed-looking: "You want I go get my daduk's gun?" You can't help and then smile some on that.

"Yeeah, and tell your daduk I got a present for him," Deanne says.

"Ohhhhh, not your lipstick on his dick again? Damn, I had to wipe that off last time," Megan says.

"Yeeah, maybe left me some AIDS spit on there too for you," says Deanne.

"Oh yeeah, thank fucking Christ because I just finished with the pills and thought I didn't have it any more. Good because now I know for sures your brother's got it," Megan says.

"He had it before that when your trannie mother fucked his behind."

"Yeeah? Thought she was down with rear entry. Had enough from your daddy when he was down from the rigs. He got tastes for it up there with all his fag buddies in the Beaufort, yeeah."

The trick is you can smile a little, but you can't laugh right out before you're down on the floor. The best times are when Deanne knows Faith is over the workers' station and she knows I don't got to attend to her. I'm just setting reading some book because that Miss Sarah's got us reading so much I don't think I can ever keep up. Something about this weird place called Narnia and this kid likes Turkish Delight that he thinks is "grand." But it sounds like muktuk to me and I can't get muktuk down no matter how Daduk tries to tell me it's any good.

"Jailbird. Think you some reading, jailbird?" Deanne says.

"Yeeah. Gonna kill me some YK whore," I says.

"You can't find me, jailbird. I'm living in the big city of Yellowknife, not up here with some small-time jailbird."

"Oh yeeah. Can smell ya way upriver the Peace and the Mackenzie. Coming for ya right now."

"Smell what? Your last boyfriend."

"Same smell as your last trick."

"Oh yeeah? Must be the same smell of blood because I killed my last trick."

"Jailbird."

"You."

"Yup. Gonna killa you," I says and I got her down the floor, hands in her hair and I'm tugging, hard but not that hard because I like Deanne, like a sister-brother-friend-something kind of like her. Sometimes not, sometimes something else. She's pushing at me and trying not to laugh as I rub my face hard against her cheek.

"What you trying to do, nuzzle me to death, jailbird?" I push her against the chair and she loses her breath. I go up to her, hands off, worried I pushed too hard and she grins. "Had you, ah? You don't know your own strength," and she shoves me into the couch. Aimee gets up and just manages to get her books out of the way. Megan goes and turns the music up and starts singing, "Killa, killa, killa in our midst" from that rap song we're always playing from California. I imagine me and Deanne some gang girls and it's hot and there's lots of buildings around us. She pushes me into the water park and we're getting all wet.

Deanne says, "Oh, you got some fight to you yet. You want something from the store, little girl?"

"Only razor blades to cut up your whore face, YK skank," I says.

"You wish you had some of this face," Deanne says.

"Yeeah, so I can cut it up and make whoreburgers for your family barbecue."

"Hm. Loves me some whoreburgers on a hot day. Go down by the Mackenzie and get it fired up, little girl."

Then Deb's in here: "C'mon, you girls, stop your scrapping and do your homework."

Deanne makes a show of putting it on some more, shoving me. "What we got homework for? No one in here going to any school outside ever again," says Deanne.

"Don't be so hopeful, girl," Deb says. "You might get yourself a job in the Shopper's in YK." And Deb smiles at Deanne while she moves some of Deanne's hair back. Deanne lets her because Deb gets it. Deb is funny with us, like she knows. They sometimes tell us some of their shit. Like about their kids or something.

"Yeeah, you'll be lucky I get a job there, you got to come in for your vagina cream," Deanne says to her. Megan bursts out laughing and even Aimee's got to smiling.

"Oh I would only place my vagina cream orders with you, love," Deb says right back to her and Deanne huffs off to her room but you know she loves it.

Before dinner we're all in the living room again and Deanne's milling about because she's got that restless to her again. I know I feel it too sometimes, but not as much as her because she's from the city and takes it different. The dark days don't go on so long down there, they're different. Faith is in the rolly crib and she's finally sleeping, not crying that high-pitched squeal she gets like she's being electrocuted or something. Linda calls me over.

"Trista, Dr. Petterson's here. Go into Iso. She wants to talk to you."

"Can I bring Faith?" I say.

"Sure, just go in now, she's heading home soon," Linda says. I wheel Faithy into Iso and Dr. Petterson's sitting on a chair she must've brung in because there's no chairs in Iso usually. She points to the other chair and I sit in it, and she goes to close the door.

"We're going to try some new medication for you, Trista," Dr. Petterson says.

"Why."

"Trista, the workers say you've been having a hard time in Group. Detached. Not coming to terms with things."

"What things?"

"Are you tired? The reports show that you seem to be sleepy. Is Faith keeping you up nights?"

"They don't let me sleep in. They get us up to do all their chores," I says.

"You have to follow the program, Trista. The chores, school, it all provides structure. I'm going to continue Faith on the formula. I think you are almost done with breastfeeding. Your breast milk seems to be drying up fast. And this medication might not be good for her long-term."

"So you coming to take that away too." I look at her, those brown eyes and long long lashes she has, make me remember how she was with me and Tyler when we come in for my checkups. When she liked me. When she thought me and Tyler going to be okay and raise our girl up right. When we told her, "We're going to name the baby Faith," and her face lit up and she said, "That's a perfect name, full of hope."

"Honey. I know you are sad. I know this is hard. But you have to start facing things some time. Your case is coming up soon, and you need to be healthy."

"Healthy so they can kill me?" I says.

"There's no killing in Canada, Trista, you know that. Now you've got until after Christmas. I think you're slated for January. There's a foster family in Inuvik, the mom has some experience with special needs kids. We'll have to see if they can take her. Or Faith might need to go down to Yellowknife. There's a special care unit there."

She's got those sad eyes looking at me. She was so nice when I went in with Tyler, all putting that ultrasound goop on me, treating me like some real pregnant girl, not feeling sorry eyes on me like some drunk-ass loser types in town. Back then she got all hopeful in her voice, and happy when we first went in and I tell her I don't take no drugs, don't do no drinking, and not even smoking, not that much anyways. Now she's thinking, Evil child, liar, bad mother. And I am. Why am I so stupid? What did I do to that lady? What did Jimmy do?

We was cold. I just wanted Jimmy next to me, in a warm bed, Tyler gone, and me drunk, my head spinning, why did Keely call him up, why was I with Jimmy again? Where was Tyler and why isn't he coming back? Keely crashed out on our couch, my cheek against my hair and the stink of it.

Me and Jimmy, we're snorting coke and drinking and I am giggling and thinking nothing about fucking it all up, feeling Faith finally move in me, so messed up that one night I felt her move inside me, as if to say, No, Mumma, don't do it, Mumma, falling asleep with my hands on my belly feeling my little girl. Jimmy shaking me awake and then we went to get the smokes, and we're walking to the store and I can't stop laughing, Jimmy whispering "shush" in my ear, and I start calling him Tyler, and he's saying, "Tyler's fucked off on you," and I'm saying no, and he's pulling me up the stairs to the store, goes behind the counter, and I hear the clerk, I hear Mavis say, "What you kids want back here?"

"Trista? Trista, you have to eat more too," Dr. Petterson says. "Otherwise these pills will give you a stomach ache."

"Yeeah. Yeeah. Okay."

"Linda tells me Faith is still crying at night." Then that doctor goes on about it being Faith's detoxing still, but I don't want to fucking talk about that. How's it been a month and she can still detox? When I look at her sleeping in here she almost looks like a real baby, all healthy, and I can imagine just being in some friend's living room, not here.

"Trista?" Dr. Petterson says.

"Hmm."

"Did you hear me? She's delayed, honey. We don't know how much yet, but we know she's got some hearing loss. And the crying is indicative of fetal alcohol syndrome. There's going to be an FAS specialist coming up from Yellowknife in a week, and we'll take her in again to Inuvik Hospital to see him."

"Can I go now?"

Dr. Petterson nods. I pull up Faith's blanket around her and Dr. Petterson comes up from her chair, slides her fingers under Faithy's chin and strokes her there. "She's so peaceful when she's sleeping," she says and I nod, wanting to get out of here but also wanting Dr. Petterson to just wrap us both up and take us home with her and away from here and this.

"You got a smoke?" Deanne says.

"Yeeah."

"Come out and smoke with me."

Tracy's on and she stands outside with us, she smokes too but stands apart so we can talk. "So you getting out when?" Deanne says.

"Don't know. Got the court case after Christmas."

"Yeeah, got mine in a month, up for review. Maybe get transferred down before Christmas, out of this boring piss." Deanne touches my hand and I can feel the warmth of the smoke. "Maybe you get down south too."

"Maybe," I says.

"You're good with your baby. Never know what happen."

She's smiling at me, the way her upper lip's got that swollen bit in the middle like Faith's after she's done feeding and I get this thing happening in my belly. Makes me think of Tyler, the good times. Makes me think of Deanne, holding me in bed and holding Faith and we're all just in a big bed with Snow Nanuk's comforter around us. The one with the kids jumping on the caribou skin, doing some high-jump blanket tosses. I close my eyes and I can feel Deanne's breath on my cheek. She kisses me and I get this rush come up inside. I open my eyes fast and Tracy's on her cellphone and not looking at us, probably on with her boyfriend, and I turn to Deanne and kiss her on the lips. She's grinning under my lips, I can feel it. I pull back from her, my face feels like a campfire flash and she giggles, brushes my hot cheek.

Snow Nanuks said the angatkut shaman was a really private person, not talking much to people when they on the land, but there if you needed him. Snow Nanuks said maybe our angatkut was from the Mackenzie River, flying high. Other families got their healer who speaks with mountains, animals, the Arctic Ocean. But Nanuk Marjorie says, "We got ours flying like a gyrfalcon above the river, sometimes ice hard solid, sometimes pulled blue by the current. We always have the river, Trista. Even it's hard or unmoving, or flowing fast. It's Freeze Up or Break Up you got to watch though, you kids. You watch for that power coming up from under the ice. There's no gyrfalcon shaman coming for you, can save you when the river gets that way."

When the families roam, they usually go in small groups, hunt the caribou and, when there was none, come up upon small caches set aside, the stones pointing the way to food. Any family could come up to a cache and, if they were hungry, take from it. But in the same way, they gave back and they filled the caches too with caribou or game when they caught lots. Some thought the angatkut had animal powers. Change into animals and went through amulets, some bone necklace, or mammoth ivory bracelet. Maybe even in the power of the mammoth ivory ulu pendant I got from Mom. I touch it, it's warm against my throat. That angatkut, he's just like any witch or shaman from long ago. Makes you learn to look out for yourself. Makes you learn to be careful who you give your heart to, to protect yourself.

"Must be fun here in summer, for Ice Break Up," Deanne says.

Looking at Deanne, feeling good thinking about the river, the good times. "It's been a long time since I been actually swimming in the river," I says.

"We got the swimming pool in YK, swim there some, or Great Slave, but not that it's really swimming, more like dipping or getting throwed in by friends," Deanne says, and she's facing the Iceroad, trying to see if she can see some cars moving along it.

"Yeeah, the Mackenzie's fucking cold in July too," I says.

"C'mon, let's go in," Deanne says and she slides her fingers against my cheek her fingers cold and smelling of tobacco.

"Tyler? I got the court date now, gonna be in January. And they say Faith might go with this real nice family in Inuvik, maybe not have to go down to YK. Ty? If she goes down to YK, you go visit her? You go visit her if I'm still up here? She's got your blue eyes. And your fingers too, like she maybe play some good guitar. Fuck. Why won't you pick up?"

"Trista? You there, girl?"

"Hi, Nanuk," I says and I am holding the phone so tight not even believing it's her voice.

"What they feeding you up there?" she says and I want to say not good food like at your house, Nanuk, not your hot chocolate or your caribou stew or your dried whitefish or even just your mashed potatoes and corn out of the can.

"Nothing much, just regular stuff. Heard Maisie won the big bingo."

"Yeeah, like nothing you ever seen what she ordered outta the Sears catalogue for her house," Nanuk says and she starts laughing and coughing, and I can see her on the grey couch with the blue and yellow blanket she crocheted last year, her eyes crinkled up and the tears coming out, pushing up her glasses so she can wipe at her eyes and it makes me start to cry, my belly starts to shake and I press my fist into it.

"You there, Trista?" Nanuk says.

"Yeeah."

"Miss you. Seen them pictures of your girl."

"Yeeah."

"You get better soon, maybe come home," Nanuk says and I think it's like she's talking like I am in the hospital not jail and maybe her voice isn't angry but now it's like she's not thinking about the lady, the lady on the floor and the blood. "You give Faithy kisses for me," Nanuk says, and we say some more stuff but my head feels foggy hearing her voice, hearing her feel so close. I want to run out of this place and into the snow I don't care, I don't care, pack up my baby warm and run back to her voice safe.

It's another Saturday and Keely's come in to visit again. We only get an hour and it takes Keely a while even to say much.

"You hear from Tyler yet?" Keely asks. Deb tells us we got ten minutes left of visiting and I can't believe it's gone so fast and I don't get to see her again till next week maybe. Keely's someone I've not seen for less than a day my whole life, and here she is going to be gone soon again for a whole week and I don't know how I feel about that, what all been thinking about, how come she call Jimmy up that night. That night going round and round my head and why she never liked Tyler.

"He hasn't called, been trying to call down to YK," I says.

"Maybe he's saving his money."

"Yeeah. He's full of shit setting up shop. He don't have any money to set up shop for nothing."

"He stood by you and Faith, Trista," Keely says.

"Yeeah. For how long? For shit. You forget the fights?"

"He did tell Tony to say hey, when you first come in."

"Yeeah. What's hey gonna do me? Why you suddenly liking him now?"

"Not his fault you in here," Keely says.

Then I want to punch her, it comes like a rush. I want to scream at her, Yeeah, whose fault is it then? Who calls up Jimmy and gets me messed up with him again, who's got booze and fucking coke at her house and then we're fucking things up again, who's going and partying with her best friend when her best friend is seven months' pregnant and too fucking gone from her boyfriend leaving to know what's up? I flash this at Keely, don't say it. She knows and starts getting her stuff ready to go. Then as quick as it comes, it leaves out of me. I can't stay mad at her. Wasn't her that put the coke in my nose, drank that way that night, went to the Aurora Store with Jimmy and fucked things up. And she knows about the times me and Tyler weren't perfect, slept over enough on our couch them times he gone off after we been fighting.

Keely's sitting there like she always does and it hasn't been always, only been maybe she's come visiting three times. But it feels like forever we been in this room facing each other in these chairs like they got down in the Inuvik dentist and doctors clinics, same chairs as the RCMP and hospital, orange plastic, with a hole just at the bottom at the back, slippery.

"Don't go yet," I says.

"You okay?" Keely says, half-looking at me in that slidey way she has. We been in each other's beds since we were both little bits, pretending makeup lives when we're gonna be grown-ups, talking about who we'd marry, what we gonna do to make money, what curtains we gonna have in our own houses. Both just little bits, talking till we're both yawning and drowsy. We been together standing in front of my bathroom mirror, or hers, even at the Snow Nanuks' house when we was little, practising makeup. Me brushing out her curly hair. Seems then was the only time Keely could really look at me. When she was saying, "I got this eyeliner globbed on here too much, ah?" me giggling because we're pissed on Daduk's Scotch he stashes under the bedroom window in the snow, thinking Nanuk don't know, thinks we don't know, me and Keely been pouring in water and Coke to it since we was eight.

"Yeeah," I says, the anger seeping out of me.

"I gotta go," Keely says.

Keely leaves and I'm looking out the window at her walking down the road, the lights on the street swallow her up, pools of light on the snow. She's not going far, she lives maybe ten minutes walk from the jail. But it seems forever far to me.

Making love with Tyler is different from them other guys. The first few times we done it we wasn't drunk at all, and he hadn't even smoked up none. This one time we'd put more wood into the pot-bellied stove, and he went out and chopped up some more, so we didn't have to chop in the morning, and then he played some Nine Inch Nails for me, and told me what guitar licks to listen for, and why some band guys sing about death a lot, but it all doesn't make kids want to kill themselves, well not him anyway, only just the once and that was his dad that was getting on him, not listening to Nine Inch Nails. I tell him about Jimmy, and the assholes in Tuk, and I don't cry or nothing, and Tyler gets a new needle for his tattoo gun, and he puts a teardrop on my right inner thigh, and he kisses me right there, and on my face and cheeks and when the tears do come down my face, hot and hard, he kisses those too, and he makes love to me so slowly it feels good and hurts the tattoo spot at the same time, but it just means it is right, and I know that tattoo night was the night we made Faith.

Faith's sleeping finally. It's late Saturday afternoon. I see Deb through the classroom window, talking at Aimee before Group. But I don't hear them. I stroke Faith's face, it's so soft. She's got new skin, some white bumps that I want to pick. But otherwise her skin is so smooth. I kiss her and take the bottle out of her mouth, she's half-asleep and doesn't notice. I leave her with Tracy at the workers' station, go to Group. Before the Iceroad is cleared, before you see the blue and the cracks, it's like Faith's face. White and smooth with the new snow. You don't know if you can even walk on it yet. Then a month later and they get the trucks coming over it smoothing it down and it's forty inches thick with ice. November and it's set in and you know the Fruitman's going to come up from Vancouver soon to bring something fresh from his rig. Then it's like you lie on that Iceroad, you put your feet and hands up, take a picture and it looks like you are skydiving on top of the world. The cracks looking like the Earth beaming down on you like something from that space station they got up there Miss Sarah been teaching us about in school. Whole world in that ice. Mom and that night she goes and leaves Richard and me, the last time I seen her. Except in my dreams when I see her and she's rising out of the car and the car isn't smashed up from the ice cracks, her body is not white and frozen. That smile she's got when she's looking at me and it's bedtime and she's humming that fish song, "You gonna be a big fish soon, gonna rise up out of the river, and catch us with your love, Sleep now little fish, sleep some good, and then you'll be big to rise up and catch us with your love." She's singing and I can see her, rising up out of the ice. She's got her crafts bag and she's showing me: "Here's the doll I made for you, Trista, isn't it good? She got your hair, and a parky with beaver shear mitts, some wolf around the trim. And look, a tiny ulu necklace, just like yours. Out of the mammoth ivory, so old and he's only telling me where he found it, and one day I will show you. Out out far past the banks of this river, this ice, he dug deeper and deeper because they came to him and told him, Snow Nanuks pointed the way. Here, little girl, hold her tight to you, and you and she will always have the ulu to protect you, your amulet, your own angatkut. They can't drag you under the ice, you won't come under the ice, I'll tell them never to take you."

Richard tells me what Mom looked like. When he gone down to the morgue to identify her body. He tells me and I hear Linda's voice in Group saying, "You weren't old enough to hear that." But he tells me. We're on the couch and he's holding me, not touching me, but I want him to, I want to see that grin he gets when I am holding him and he gets hot and there's the look on his face like I am making him the happiest man in the world. But he's holding me and I am not touching him. The crocheted blanket is not on us. He's drinking Jack Daniels and it's the third time I gone and got him ice. "She was grey and frozen. Her arms crumpled and legs pulled toward her belly. Didn't even look like a real person, Trista." And then he's holding me and I am pushing his hair away from his face and I don't feel nothing inside.

"That's because you were only seven. You were too young to take away an adult's pain," Linda says.

But, I think, I am old enough. I am old enough to kiss him and want to make that dip in his lips go away and he kisses me back because he loves me and I don't want to think that I am glad, happy even that Mom is gone and we can be like this on the couch forever without her walking in on us and Richard pulling away from me and I got him all now and he's mine.

Tyler and I knew to name her Faith, because we went to see Dr. Petterson and had all the ultrasound, and knew it was a girl. It was so weird to have Tyler touching my belly all goopy with the jelly they put on you. Keely was seriously being beat by her boyfriend, and I was down helping her out some nights, as if I was doing so much better, me and Tyler. But early on we were, we were trying so hard to be perfect. Not doing drugs, eating right, not fighting so much. "You should be sleeping," I said to Keely, her head was against the couch and her nanuk was listening to the Inuvialuktun Hour on the CBC.

"I'm just tired. You know, of Tony, and his bullshit. Always stealing, then coming home, fighting with me, and slamming me up the wall, and now look. Five Ski-Doos, Trista, he even stole three from in front of the RCMP," she said.

"Least he wasn't coked up when they found him," I said.

"Yeeah, well, couple of more hours and he would of been."

Faith was in me right then, though I couldn't feel her yet, her little fish body swimming inside of my six months' womb, Keely's boyfriend, Tony, in jail, Keely's nanuk singing her old songs with the CBC, and I can tell she just wants the Jamboree to come so she can get out and watch the jigging, dream of the jigging girl she used to be. I had Faith inside me, worried for Keely and thinking me and Tyler going to do so good. And get our shit together and be happy perfect families.

Linda says, "Who are you getting perfect from?" I look up at her and think she's gonna have some angry around her mouth. But she's smiling some.

With Faith in my belly, I get Tyler to get some lotion from the Quarter Store, the good kind they get from down south Edmonton, not that shit from the Northmart that gives me a rash. Nights, when Tyler is home from his job fuelling up cars at the Arctic Gas, and we got the pot-bellied stove all wooded up, Tyler pushes me gently onto the couch and turns on some old Ministry, lifts my hoodie slow-like, rubs the lotion in his hands, and smoothes the warmness on my belly, round and round, until I am right relaxing, almost sleeping. "She's gonna be an artist, I can feel it," he said that night.

"Don't know about that. Maybe. Daduk was a right good carver before heading down to the Icebox every night to drink up his cheque. Nanuk can make some good slippers if Auntie gets her some beaver pelts and caribou skins. And Mom knew her crafts."

"Or a swimmer. I can feel her twisting in there, spiralling, jack-knifing, just like the jackfish in the bay."

"Too damn cold to swim up here, most times, Tyler, them fish sleeping." But I am grinning at him, hard not to dream inside his dream. Moving my hands around my belly.

He's got his ear to my belly. "Can almost hear her, just like a Sik-sik, whispering and calling out from her little squirrel hole." He moves his lips against my belly and I squirm under the tickles.

"Or a dogsledder. I can hear her yell, strong-like, to the dogs and they perk their ears up and listen to her, because she is some northern woman and she wants to be heard."

"You're full of shit," I said. But I stroke his head, he had his hair shaved off mostly. My white boy. The redneck kids from around Inuvik, they tease him some when they come to gas up at the station, but Tyler, he don't care.

"She can still be that strong woman, Trista," Linda says. I look up at her. Look at the girls watching me. Aimee smiles shyly at me and says, "It's beautiful, Trista. She is your beautiful Faith you dreamed up." I can see the hope in Aimee's eyes, shining kind of fierce like an arctic hare out on the land, knowing where he's going. I want to suck in that hope and have it inside me, put down the trembling I got in my belly.

"Trista, you have an incoming phone call, come over here to the workers' station and take it," Linda says. I get all excited, bring Faith over to her, and take the phone. "Hello?"

"Hey, it's me."

"Keely?" I say.

"Sorry. I know you expecting someone else. But I just. I just wanted to … Listen, when I see you I just want to talk to you. But then you're in there, and I just …"

"It's okay," I says.

"Trista."

"Yeeah." I can hear she's breathing funny.

"What?" I say. My skin feels wet inside my hoodie suddenly, like I been running hard in slush.

"I only called Jimmy to make you feel better. That night," she says.

"I know," I says.

"No. You don't. Listen. I fucking had it, all that shit talk about Tyler. Me and Tyler this and me and Tyler and Faithy gonna do that." Keely's voice is hard and coming out in a rush.

"It's okay," I says. I want to hang up, tell her to fuck off, and go hide under the covers with my baby girl.

"No. Trista, I fucking did it. You would of stayed home. Just stayed with me if Jimmy hadn't come over. Never gone out with him." Keely's full on crying now, can almost see the tears on her cheeks, see her swiping at them.

"What's it matter now, Keely?"

"Matters to me," she says.

"Why?"

"Matters to me you know. We all fucked up. We were all so fucked up that night." She takes a deep breath. "Doesn't get to be just you, Trista. Shouldering the blame on just you." She hangs up and I'm standing there with the phone in my hand. I put it down. I'm shaking.

I'm standing at the phones and I know Linda's looking at me like with them warning eyes. She doesn't say it, but I hear her in my head saying, "Okay, Trista, use your breathing," but I don't look at her and anyways Tyler's got to be home this time, he's got to be. So

I dial the number and it rings and rings and I think, Maybe they don't got the answering machine on, and then I am picking at the peeling hard plastic on the speaking part of the phone and before I think I'm never gonna hear his voice again, Tyler's saying, "Hello?"

"Hey. Hey, Tyler, it's me. Listen, don't hang up."

And before I even got that out he's hung up fuck fuck fuck, and then I smash the phone against the wall and rip that fucking little piece of hard plastic and rip it, and the phone half comes off and then I punch the fucking thing into the wall and my fist and over and over again and then Linda's behind me and she's trying to grab around me and she's hollering something but I don't hear her. I smash my hands into the wall and it don't hurt, it don't even hurt, and then Linda and Deb's got my arms and pulling them back and hauling me off to Iso, and Deb lets go and Linda's fat ass is half-sitting on me, why won't she fucking let me up, but then she moves and makes me lay on the mattress, she's trying to hold up my arm and there's blood coming off my hand and I am screaming my voice is screaming but I don't hear anything. Linda comes around and puts my arms in front of my chest and makes me hug myself and then hugs me from behind, Deb comes in with a needle and hauls down my pants and ass sticks me with it. It don't make me sleepy or nothing right away, just I can feel Linda's arms loose as my fight goes out. She props me in the corner against a pillow.

"Fuck him, Linda, why won't he talk to me?"

"Shh—shh," she says, and she says some more stuff but I can't hear again, then Deb comes in and puts some brown stuff on my hands and wraps them in bandages. Then I feel sleepy. "I can't go to sleep yet, where's my baby, Linda, where's my Faith?"

four

I wake up with my face against the pillow, Linda's sitting against the wall, ready to give shit. "What were you thinking? You have a baby to take care of. You were getting somewhere, Trista, talking about your mom, your feelings about Richard. What you're doing to yourself, this false hope with Tyler. These are steps backward."

What I'm thinking? I'm thinking I've had enough of this fucking crap and it's all I can do to keep from being real good for like a month, so I can go for a smoke with Tracy and then climb over the gates, get Keely to drive by in her Ski-Doo and steal me off the road so I can go down the back road and smoke up or drink a two-four or fucking snort some coke, and just fuck it all.

I can't hear her, but I imagine Faith there, wherever they got her. Maybe at the workers' station and she's all crying, I'm crying now because after days of being dry now my fucking milk is coming out and wetting my stupid fucking shirt. And then Linda's not here any more and I wonder if I fell asleep again and Linda's talking at me through the intercom in the Iso, and I know she can see me crying, because she's got that mini camera on me, and I can't help it, I just scream, "Let me call Tyler again, I got more long-distance privilege, come on, you fuckers!" And I got the snot running down my nose and it don't do no good, all my screaming and fuck I know if I don't get it together I'm going to be in here more than a few hours, maybe days, maybe more than Megan ever got, them bringing

Faith in to me only for two-hour blocks, then back in her crib, her eyes all wet-like, and that mouth of hers gaping like she does when she sees me, she needs me, fuck why am I such a fuckjob? Oh great, here comes Linda with more fucking meds, now they're going to fuck up my milk more too and Linda makes me put the pills under my tongue and I do but throw the juice cup against the wall and Linda just leaves me and I start to feel sleepy, jesus what the fuck they giving me and I lean against the wall and look out into the dark, press my fingers against the window, trace the wires they got in the safety glass, my hands starting to ache.

Mom used to make up stories, help me and Keely sleep. Mostly when it was colder out and the dark days were on. Weekdays before she died we were sleeping over Snow Nanuks, then I sleep over at Keely's too, especially when her mom started getting it together and not drinking any more. But this time we were at my house and Richard's not home, off to the rigs and working some again. Me and Keely snuggled up in the blankets on the floor, Mom stretched out beside Keely, Keely snuggled in the middle, she's smaller than me.

"I'm going to tell you a story. Your nanuk made it up and it might come from the elders or it might just come from her head. About Fox and Ptarmigan, they were always having talks and fighting on the ice. Had to. Was about survival, not much to eat when you were a little animal. Fox was like the cold North wind, always roaming. And Ptarmigan was looking over her nests in the spring, but flying about too." I can smell Keely's hair, still wet from our bath, that apple smell from the shampoo. I put my arm around her and snuggle her in. I always liked to be on the outside holding her in to my inside. "So Fox is saying to Ptarmigan, Why shouldn't I eat you? And Ptarmigan is saying, You got nothing with my baby, my baby is too little for you. All's you get is some bones and stuff, not even enough for you to go on roaming for a day, so why bother. Fox says, Only thing I got out here is you and your baby. Soon the snow's going to come more and there will be nothing to eat. Ptarmigan says to him, But if you wait. You let us go on now and you wait. Then my baby will be big and fat, like me. Been out on the land for a while and got some meat to him. Why don't you visit us then?"

Keely giggles at this part, she likes the idea of Fox, him being so smart, but still kind of scratching at his head at Ptarmigan's thinking, more like Ptarmigan's fast tongue. "And all the while," Mom says, "all the while she's talking, Ptarmigan is flapping. Flapping her wings for that little bit of distraction she knows will set Fox to moving on. There's nothing Fox hates more that getting some snow up his snout and Ptarmigan is flapping, gently at first, but enough to make a wind come about and get it up Fox's snout to irritate him some. Makes him think of moving on. But what do I eat? says Fox. And Ptarmigan says, Yes you got to worry about that. But just this once you can let us be in this field, just pass us by and take your hunger farther afield. And so he did. That Fox moved on. Now Ptarmigan folds up her baby in her wings and pushes him just so, moves him along to get nearer the nest. She knows that it's not everything, it's just one day and further along there will be days when Fox isn't going to be so kind, when he's also going to be more hungry. Won't listen to any logic then or let her flapping wings irritate his snout longer than snapping onto her baby's neck and running her baby away from her forever. But she's got this one day. And that's enough."

Mom leans over and kisses me, Keely's far gone in sleep. "You have good sleeps, Trista love, you have good sleeps tonight for your one good day tomorrow," she says, pulls up my blankets, and I snuggle my face into Keely's hair and close my eyes.

My nipples are cracking. My hands keep rubbing them. It's real dark out. They got some big windows in Iso. Thick so's you can't smash them. I put my hands on the window, the streaks my fingers make, the thick soreness. The press of my nose. The light from the jail outside is on the snow. I don't know what time it is, feels like forever. The snow is a road. No Ski-Doo marks on the road. It's dead outside. Maybe some stars? I know the Big Dipper. That's it. No northern lights out. My nipples ache. Where's Faith? When they gonna bring her in?

Those stupid calm drugs they give you. They're not like heroin, not like pills we get on the outside, not like a long drunk. Like some fucked foggy wrapped-up and warm inside feeling. I dream about having Faith with me. She being close to me. Soft milkmouth smell, top of head, watch her soft spot. Faithy smells of her and me and us in between somewhere. The night worker says, "You're just in for the night, Trista, give the meds a chance." Please let Faith in with her crib, just for a few hours, a few hours please. But she shakes her head no and then she says, "Eat your muffin" and "There's the bed over there" and I crawl over to it.

I'm holding on to the extra blanket and pretending it's my Faithy. I think about how before I'm lying on the couch in the trailer, Tyler out working at Arctic Gas, and the woodstove is warmed up with enough wood. I can feel her, in my belly. I dream about this little girl, swimming in my womb. Thinking about how some of the town nurses come to the school and talk to us pregnant girls, they don't want us going around, they say, encouraging the other girls with our bellies. Like we got some glow around us, some of God around us. It don't matter what them nurses says, how many times they come in with their awful films and pictures about herpes and genital warts and little FAS babies all fucked up. On the couch in the trailer I dream up my girl, and she has dark hair like me and curls like Tyler, but I never seen his curls, he's always shaving his head, stupid boy, don't know why, it's cold. I push him out of my head and think about her swimming inside me again, back when I was trying to get it all right. I can see her just moving against my hand. Those mornings I was six, seven months gone, it seemed so easy to get up for school, walking down the halls with my belly under my Nine Inch Nails hoodie, not too big because I am tall, almost as tall as Tyler and he's at least five ten. And there's some girls sitting on the hall floor, Jenny, Frannie, them girls, they're a year or two younger than me, and I say, "Hey," and they nod at me, but their eyes are looking at my belly. I know I'm not supposed to, but I get happy about this piece of mine in my belly, a little hand is pushing at my walls. But I know it's just me thinking I am some kind of lucky because I know they thinking about me and Tyler and Faith together.

There aren't too many kids at our school, we got most of the northern kids going to the big high school in Inuvik. But we got about fifty high school kids, then about sixty little ones in the elementary section. There are big double doors, for fire or something, they got to be closed, but we hear the little ones, and me and Keely go and pick up her little brothers when we're done. I know when I moved up to grade seven and the high school section I felt big. When I think of their eyes, Frannie and Jenny, their jealous, kind of wanting eyes on me, I think of Faith. Even then I thought of her, scared for her because me and Tyler fighting more than we making love, but pushed the feelings away. Me the perfect mother. Me and our family the perfect example for the girls.

Our public health nurse wouldn't let me talk much about me keeping Faith, even when I was in the class and we was all talking about it, when we talked. Some girls talking plans for giving the baby to their mom or auntie so's they can finish up more school. Them nurses didn't believe much in the birthmom really keeping the kid, not for long anyways. I sat at the back, looking out the window. You can see the Mackenzie River from the windows and it was hard not to look, the nurse was saying, "You can come pick up condoms at the Public Health any time you want, girls. And you should, if the guys forget. Then you have them. In your purse, your pockets. Ready." She didn't, she couldn't understand, how could she fucking understand. We, me, Jenny, Frannie, we all wanted to get pregnant. It was too much having to stand around at Barclose at the Icebox Bar and see our aunties or daduks, even nanuks, though most were in playing the bingo, drinking it up. We're picking up the little kids from school and taking them home and making them Pizza Pops or what. It was like we was the moms already, and why couldn't we have our own little ones? Why couldn't we try to make it different from the running around we saw.

Yeeah, okay it wasn't all. It sounds like bullshit on a stick. That's what Linda would say. Yeeah, I listen to her, what she says in Group. She don't think so, but I do. "You close up too much on us, Trista. You need to talk some more, work through this." Work through what? Shit like I am using and not caring and who is with me in my trailer, who is with me at the store and angry and evil. Shit like I'm walking down those school halls and the light's on outside so much and we're just starting school and I am glad I am showing, I am glad that those girls know what's in my belly, and they're jealous and I am glad they are. Fucking Frannie, and then Jenny, Anna, and her little sister even. Getting pregnant to hold something, have something that's theirs. I don't need to say much. Those girls in Group, they got their eyes all hooded down too. Minutes I am just counting and counting down till I can go out for the smoke break. I can close my eyes and imagine the smoke sucking in, getting the cold in there too, and the stars are out, it's dark days and I feel inside my own little womb, being little all over again.

It's morning but Linda's not come in to tell me their decision for my Iso. Them workers tell us the rules again and again. Like we don't know them, like we even thinking about them when we get upset. "Outbursts, self-harm, harm to others, one to two days." Was from them I learn all them big jail words. Isolation, Medical Constraints, Adjudication, Restorative Justice. Don't know what shit they gonna make me talk about once I get Restorative Justice in Group for the phone being broken. Aimee had to go all into it the day she was in Iso for cutting, telling us in Group what her self-care plan was.

In Iso they let me out to smoke only every four hours and the other girls not allowed to come out when I do, only Deb or Tracy's on to watch me. When I'm outside, I got my parky on, and I can almost see that river, I can almost see that Iceroad because we're up high on the bluff and I'm looking down. It's dark, but I can see some cars, their headlights weaving in and out of the road like Nanuk's silver needle on her roses embroidery. In the dark days you'd be in the shelters, the Snow Nanuks told us, long ago. You play some string games the elders make out of the sinew of the caribou, this is an iglut, this is a caribou, this is a sled. You got the dogs sniffing outside, they're burrowing in the snow to keep warm, it's a small sled, maybe only two, three dogs. The elders, maybe the daduks tell some silly stories, or some of the stories about trying to find some shelter before the snow blind you up and freeze you to the ground. You also play the ayaqag game with the seal bone and sticks. Sometimes in playing, the elders tell the stories that meant to teach you something, Snow Nanuks tell us. Tell us about the caribou, how to be quiet with them, got to respect them and talk to them while taking the ulu and shedding off their skin. Yes, they're dead, says Snow Nanuk, but while you're cutting you have to talk to their spirit, in low voices so's not to scare them away, and say thank you, thank you, dear caribou for this and this and this. This hide you been giving me to make my kiddies warm, your bone to make my tools and games to keep the spirits fresh and up when we have the long dark days in the iglut, the flesh you give us to keep our bellies warm and our kiddies healthy and running with the red in their cheeks the healthy blush to keep them through winter.

I'm smoking and Tracy says, "C'mon, Trista, let's go in," and I look at that Iceroad, can almost imagine them on the river in the summer and it is thawed and blue and flowing. The women in their umiaq and the men in their qayaq, they're floating up slow and turning, winking at me, making me feel the long summer sun on my face and get this dark dark winter out of my head. We take off our shoes and Tracy closes the Iso door behind me again.

The baby isn't here, my Faithy isn't here. I just want to smell her. When it gets like this and I can smell Mom on her. I can smell me and Mom and like I am bending down like Mom bent down to kiss me, top of the head and it's Faithy's head, and oh Mom why did you go that night, why did you go down that long Iceroad, smash it up there, smash into that cracked ice and never come back?

Linda says, "Baby, you got to let it go. You aren't to blame."

Who is your baby? Who is my baby? I can hear Mom, she's rocking me to sleep and it's one of those nights that she brings me to bed and Richard isn't there, Richard's gone off drinking with his friends and me and Keely don't have to go down to Snow Nanuks, and Mommy says, Baby, go to sleep now.

"I pushed her away."

"No you didn't, kiddo," Linda says. "You were only little. She went up to sell crafts. It was the night before Jamboree."

It was the night before Tuk Jamboree and everyone was excited because Mom had enough stuff to sell and we might make some money and then we could all get a bigger place and Richard was going to move in for reals. "I'm just going up for a few nights, honey, will be back soon, Richard's here and Auntie's coming tomorrow to cook for you." Her face in the lamplight, my bedside lamp and she's so excited, I remember her eyelashes against her cheeks, dark and fringed and she's got this glint in her eyes like she can't wait to open presents. "Then you me and Richard we going to be a family and you can have a bigger room. Maybe even some bunkbeds like Keely's brother's got, when she sleeps over you have more room." But I'm not thinking about that, even then I'm not thinking about that I'm thinking about Richard and me, having more room so's he can love me some more and Mom being away. I don't want her to go away but I do, so me and Richard can be alone more.

And then the RCMP come up to the house, it's late. Richard's sleeping on the couch. And they say she's dead. And I can't think about it any more.

The workers say I can come out of Iso tomorrow. For Restorative I have to do anger workshop after Group with Linda one on one.

Linda, thinking I'm standing there at the phone slamming it over and over, because she says I am "dissociating" or living in my head.

"Trista, what was going on before you got to the phone? Let's start there," Linda says. She and me on my bed and she's got her back against the wall, not really looking at me, her foot's out and she's pushing at the crib to rock it. Faith's in there ahh-ing, not asleep but almost. I look up at her, I got so much to say and I want to say it all, I want it to come spilling out of me all these thoughts and shit in my head. I think in here, in here it's quiet and it's just us three and maybe I can tell her, here. But how am I supposed to talk about Richard, those boys in Tuk, Jimmy or even Tyler in Group, with the other girls. All that time in school thinking I was gonna be better, we was gonna be a family and a good one, just me and Tyler and Faithy no one else.

Linda says, "You need to learn to stop displacing your anger. I know you know it's not a good coping skill to escalate and punch walls. Can you think about some ways we talked about before, to calm yourself? To start before it gets too bad and then gets out of control?"

She thinks I don't fucking know that it's not good coping skills? She thinks I got something better to do, when it's all coming down and all I can think about is punching the walls, and digging my fists, seeing my hands crack, the blood, making them feelings go away?

Linda says, "That's what you got to learn, Trista, how are you going to do it differently?"

"Yeeah, different," I says. Even outside, not just in here. Maybe it's cutting like Aimee does privately, or Deanne fucking everything that moves, or Megan putting needles in her arms. Does it have to be some deep psycho thing? Because it's not. I just need that release sometimes. And hearing Tyler's voice. That close to me. But that far away, airplane far, not roads far, not even the Iceroad or the Dempster goes down to Yellowknife. That faraway space sound at the end of the phone line. The cut-off sound. I just don't want to think about his shit any more, or anything, this all, Faith, the case, being in jail. It all seems so unreal, and I'm not feeling anything.

And then I do it. I say to Linda, "When we lived together, seems like those long months before anything got bad, Tyler said, 'You gotta talk to the Goddess Upstairs, she'll help if you give it over.' So I try. I ask Gus, 'Why did I go with Jimmy that night? Why did I go to the Aurora Store and do what I did when I should of been home waiting for Tyler to come up from Yellowknife?' Wait quiet-like for Faith to be born and take good care of her and get the trailer ready for her with quilts and warm blankets. Why didn't I wait, Linda?"

"It sometimes happens too fast for waiting, kiddo," Linda says.

It goes around and around my head, as later after Linda goes I sit on my bed and pull Faith's crib over, her sleeping and me stroking her soft head. She lost all her birth hair, and now she's as bald as a jackpine stripped of bark in April. She rolls her head back and forth while she's sleeping, and I think, "Gus, should I save her? Should she even be here, waiting on some foster family, maybe no one ever take her." I think sometimes I should take her away, give her to Gus. Nights, when it is dark outside, the sun gone for the winter, the hallways in jail dim, lights out, just me and Faith, out on the land. I think of giving her back to God.

They've taken her in again, Faith, and all her formula and they took her to the hospital this time to see the special doctor. It's Dr. Petterson who come and take her. Says she's got some other doctors coming from Yellowknife and they have to assess her for that foster care maybe she have to go to after my court case. Just wrapped her up good. I don't fuss over her going this time. What good it gonna do she's so used to everyone holding her and not even crying for me and my belly feels hollow inside. It's like she's in my arms and we're just quiet inside the room, and then she's not here. The girls and me in Group and some are talking. Deanne's gonna get to go down to YK soon. I'm off in my head, can't stop thinking about Faith. What if the doctor says, "No, she's too severe. We need to send her down to YK right away." What if they don't let her come back?

"Anyways, it's a good halfway house, my lawyer said, the women go to some courses at Arctic College. Or you can even get a job in town," Deanne says.

It's too quick and I don't want to think about her going, why she get to leave, why she get to go away so soon?

"Have you been thinking about the courses? Maybe talk to Tracy, she can help you look up on the website what's offered for spring," Deb says.

"Yeah, Tracy said that she'd help me. Gonna be hard though, to not want to hook up."

"That's always going to be a struggle, Deanne. Because of the money. Many women have trouble exiting the sex trade," Linda says.

"Straight job never pays," Deanne says.

"True, not money-wise. But self-preservation and safety-wise, it's a better gig, honey. And less trouble managing your recovery," Deb says.

"Fuck sex. I'm going to be like an old maid and never do it with no one again," says Megan.

"What if you find someone in the future?" Linda says.

"Then I'm telling him right off about the HIV, and he will probably go fuck off scared," Megan says. "Anyways, I'm done with sex."

"It's okay to want a life. It's okay to want to be with someone, when that someone cares for you. You don't know what'll happen in the future. And then you can be honest. There's ways around the HIV," says Deb.

"Oh, a fucking condom? That's not going to make them come running," says Megan. She all clams up then and Linda sighs knowing she's not going to get anything more out of her. We kind of all look at the carpet. I look at the carpet a lot in Group. But the workers don't push it. They know it's a big hot topic, HIV. We know some girls who got it up north, that or other STDs. Girls who are done with life because of it and on the AZT cocktail, taking lots of pills but still boozing it up because what else have they got? I'm lucky to get away with not having it, I know that much, and I'm thinking the rest of the girls are thinking this too, or thinking about their girlfriends or brothers or whoever they know got it, or whatever other STD we're fighting. I know I been checked for the genital warts since I got them when I was twelve, fuckers around here they give you everything. Lucky I don't got the herpes, like Keely got, have to be careful and eat good and she takes some medicine when they come up, hurt awful to piss some days, she says. I know one time she was in the bathroom so long with her period and all because she has to dry it up, the sores hurt so bad when they come.

Linda sees me private again. She doesn't push me in Group, I think she is going to, about the phone slamming again. But in one on one she doesn't talk about it either.

"You're thinking about what you want to do? Like your trade schooling, have you looked at the books?" Linda says.

"Some," I don't tell her when. When did I get time to sit there and get all hopeful about my future? When I get time to dream and wonder what I'm going to do with me and my baby and where we going to live and what we going to do, and how we gonna do it, if we ever are? Linda looks at me. I don't look up but can feel her eyes on me. "I've been busy. Faith. Her fussing."

"She's not been fussing that much," Linda says. And I know she's meaning that I been in Iso and Faith's been away and she's too nice to say it. "I've been thinking about how you were talking at lunch yesterday. Saying how you used to cut your friends' hair. I see you with the girls. You do up all the girls' hair good, like you did last week. You're good with hair, Trista." I don't say anything to Linda because I'll get this hitchy in my voice. If someone says nice things you can't say shit to them, maybe they'll go away. Just let it sit in your head like you gonna polish it, like a stone you got down from the river, rubbing it in your pocket and keep it special some. "Maybe we should get a Career Training worker in, like Tracy or Lee but one who went to hairdressing school. I know Verna up at the shop went to a place in YK, maybe she can come up and talk to you about it, during Career Training time." Linda's got that hope thing going in her voice, that way she gets when she's trying to talk all casual, but you know she's been thinking about you, maybe been writing about you in that logbook they keep at the workers' station. "You might be interested in that?"

"Maybe."

"They got a good program down YK."

"Yeeah."

But still all I can think about is talking to Tyler. How can he make all this shit in my head go right like he always done before. Like that bubble we was living in when Faith was in her own bubble in my belly. We made so much real and kept lots of the shit out. Even though it's starting to bust up and float away. That bubble's breaking and gone greasy like oil on the Iceroad, brown to muddy in some spots slick, but other spots glowing with its own special light-ups of colour against the truck's headlights.

We're back in the Greenhouse for work training, I got my hands in the dirt and planting some bulbs. Lee says to us: "When you here in the summer, say come in about May, June, you got to work quickly. Get in as many bulbs that you would've got in maybe February down south. Light's so intense through the arena roof." I look up at the wide domed roof and it's all just dark even though it's only about four o'clock and I wonder if I'm going to be here even in May, got the court case in January.

"You never know which bulb's going to sprout and rise up, which one won't make it," Lee says. Deanne's over by Megan, Aimee's home with a cold. Megan and Deanne are talking, but I don't feel jealous because Deanne's looking at me sometimes, she's looking up and she's grinning and I get that flip-floppy to my stomach. Like when I am kissing Faithy in my room and it's night and I think of all the songs I'd sing to Deanne, if she were mine, I'd hum it in her ear, then lick her earlobe a bit and she'd get that grin and I think we all in her family, our own place and out of jail.

My Faithy is coming back today and I can't wait to see her, Linda said this morning she's coming back some time before dinner, so maybe right when we get back from work training. I mix the dirt with some fertilizer, it stinks some, but not that shit smell, more like a good growing smell, I move my hands over the dirt in the boxes and make sure the bulbs are down enough like Lee says. He comes over and checks my depth with a Popsicle stick, "Yeeah, that's good, Trista," and I get a little feeling in my belly like I done something right. I can think about how maybe I will be a great gardener. Have to go down to YK or even Whitehorse or something, where people actually got some gardens. Even then they got a slow growing season too. I can bring them new flower shoots to put in, and help them arrange their flowerbeds. "No, here is where the hyacinths should go, and you want to get some perennials in there for colour." Like I could make something beautiful for them, they get up in the morning and look at and sigh, thinking on some beauty they got right there in their own yards.

I imagine Faith with me, toddling along nice sturdy legs. Going to people's houses with young plant shoots and bright flowers. I can see my little girl, how I want her to be, whole and healthy. This girl, this little girl. I can see it for her, Faith. Her babyself trying to get out. She tries so hard to move her hand up and down my cheek and says, "This is your cheek and this is your cheek and this is your cheek, and I am kissing you now, Mumma, please don't make me more wet with your crying. I am kissing you now, and you must listen listen listen to this love."

"Hey, daydreamer, ready to go?" Deanne says, bumping my hip. I pat down the dirt and sprinkle it with some more of the water and vitamin mix Lee taught us to make. Megan's washing up at the taps and flicking water all over and Lee lifts up a plant and says, "Hi ya Cynth, get it?"

Megan says, "You're cracked, bro," and we dry up our hands and pile into the van.

When I was little, it was like we were so with the town. Not the bad parts of town, but the good stuff, the smells and the nature. Me and Keely, out until Mom calls us in, we're real little and I wonder, Do I remember that far back or is it just being in this place, being off the shit I got into that night with Jimmy, being not pregnant any more, makes me remember, think about this stuff? Linda says it happens like that, this slow unwinding, she says, like some spring leaves unfurling. She talks like them poetry books Miss Sarah makes us read sometimes. Like the snow talked to us too, when we were little and outside, me and Keely. Before Mom went up the Iceroad, before they moved her cold, stiff body long ago. When playing outside was still fun and Mom was inside with Richard but Richard wasn't really my boyfriend yet, he was still Mom's and I didn't care about that. I cared about the Snow Nanuks.

Keely and I went to the back houses, you just go along that one utilidor outside my house and climb up it where there's the wood plank, run along it, then jump down into the snow pile, there's the Snow Nanuks' house. Some were sisters, I think, some just old ladies without their husbands any more all set up together in a house, drinking the Red Rose tea with Carnation milk that they give us too, tastes so good when your hands are near froze getting there. We can see the Snow Nanuks, like our own nanuks, but these nanuks are older and tell us stories, like they coming down from Shingle Point or something, coming after the caribou or maybe chasing some arctic hares or foxes. The tails are good for making things with, or the wolverine, that wolf too, he's good for doing the trim on their parkys. They are big women, they move slow and steady and their Mother Hubbard parkys are blue with little tiny daisies or red, with berries. Tiny tiny, they are far away but it's like when I remember I can see them up close, they're coming to gather round me and Keely. Some Nanuks are inside the snow, like they're telling us about how they were out on the land and getting their icehouses ready, the men already made them. And Keely, she's little, on the carpet and at the Snow Nanuks' feet while they're talking story, Keely's pretending to be the big daduk, "Just gonna cut this here, then here," she says and she's making some square icehouses big cubes, but they're not cubes because she can't get her little hands around them, she's so little.

I remember the Snow Nanuks on those spring fireweed hills, up past the lakes, we could see them, like it was all snow down where we were playing in their yard, but then I say to Keely, "Lookit up there. That's where spring gonna come."

Keely looks at me and her eyes go all big. "That's where the Snow Nanuks take the babies not born yet." I know she is not saying the truth, she's just playing, we both seen the babies come home from the hospital and our Mommies' or our aunties' bellies a little flatter, not much, but a little. And then Auntie's saying to us, "See what the Snow Nanuks brought you," But we know it came from their bellies then. The ice is so crusty and dry and we are breathing heavy and my hands are cold though I got my good snow mitts on, the shearling ones Nanuk made last winter, they still fit. But we don't want to go in. Keely whispers, "Can you see the flowers, Trista?" And I remember looking up that hill, up that back road, like it goes on and on forever snow like it does most days. But I can see them sudden summer flowers, the purple and red of them, mid-June when the Iceroad breaks up and the snow thaws. The sun's out forever and we get those sudden bursts of fireweed and brush berries, all up the back hill. They was there for me to touch, and knowing I can go into the Snow Nanuks' house when I get cold when I can't feel them no more.

I got my head in the door of the jail and I am stamping the snow off my boots and Linda is already walking toward me with Faith and I am just grinning. Linda jiggles her in front of me while I get my parky off and slippers on and then hands her over. Faith's cheeks are chapped. "Teething maybe," Linda says. "Come, I got her bottle ready." I sit on the living room couch with her and Deanne strokes her under the cheek. "Didn't mess you too much up there, hey kid?" She smiles into Faith's face. Faith's eyes move back and forth and I move her to snuggle in more to me.

I pull on Faith's hands, moving them up to her face. "This is your cheek, this is your chin." She gets all quiet, pops the bottle nipple out of her mouth, stops her ah ah ah voice she does when she is not crying. That ah ah voice she gets when she is happy, I think. She can't really see me, but her eyes move to my hand, like she can feel-see me. "This is your forehead, this is your ear," I says. Then she starts ah-ah-ing again. I try to put her to my breast, but she won't take it. I think they been giving her too much formula when they been taking her up to the hospital. I can feel the water coming up in my eyes, but I press my fingers into the corners of my eyes, just so glad she's back with me. It's hard to put her back in her rolly crib while we have our dinner, I keep her near me. It's hard to look at her and know Linda's gonna talk to me soon, tell me what those doctors think about my Faith.

Times when it was near Break Up on the Mackenzie, you could bend down and feel the snow singing to you. Like under it was something moving, something thawing, something going to go down the path and through the trails where some people cross-country ski, and down through where Nanuk picks her berries, the short way through town and down to the river, to catch there and get into the pressure, the ice wanting to just bust up with that river-flow underneath. I can hear its thrum and lull like whispers inside water's waves. The feeling is like those minutes right before sleep here. I got my belly full of some cookies Sherry made us for dessert, and even hot milk. Sherry swears by the hot milk for making us sleep. She swears too: "You girls smoking too much before bed, that makes you up and thinking dark thoughts."

"But we got our smoke breaks," Deanne says.

"Doesn't mean you have to take them all the time, and look what with you too sick and hacking." Aimee just nods, sipping her milk.

Sherry fills up the big sinks, says, "Trista, you're up for washing." Faithy's sleeping and Deanne's got her foot on one wheel of the rolly crib, pushing her back and forth. Some days it's more Sherry I can talk to, over a mouth full of potatoes, or carrots, her laughing. She's wiping up the counters and sometimes she's singing some old Emmylou Harris or something like Auntie used to have on when I was little. It's old country stuff, but we know it too. She knows what we're up to, been working here for years and makes me feel like I can get out and do something. It's Sherry starts that talk about hairdressing, when Deanne first started asking about my hair, why it's not long like some of the other girls got.

"You hear any more about work training for hair, Trista? My little sister, not much older than you, she just went down to YK, got into hairdressing class. When Cara's done, maybe she'll do some apprentice thing for you," Sherry says.

"That'd be good," I says, moving the suds around with the sponge.

"That one store they got in Inuvik needs some competition, you know," Sherry says. She goes and grabs Aimee's arm: "Get some gloves on and come get some steam in your face. Actually, Trista, switch with Aimee and dry, she needs the moist for her cough." Aimee peels on the yellow dishwashing gloves and plunges her hands into the water as I pick up a clean dish-drying towel.

"Or maybe Cara can open her own store right here in Jackfish Bay," Sherry says, starts to hum as she wipes down the steel cupboards.

"You can get us all in there then, Trista," Deanne says. "Aimee can sweep up, mouse can't stand too many people, uh, Aimee? I'll set us up right businesswoman, do the books or something. Megan here can answer the phones long as she doesn't hog it all with her fucking yapping."

Megan says, "Screw you."

"You wish, come on over," Deanne says, and Megan moves up but Sherry says hey to them, pours them out the last of the hot milk left in the pan. Aimee finishes up and lets the hot water out and the girls all go off to watch TV before lights out. Sherry says, "Sit, Trista, nice and quiet here now," and I go sit next to her. Sherry tucks Faith's blanket up under her arms. "You might have to spend lots of time with this little girl in her lifetime, Trista, you mark it good. She's too little. Littler than I seen up here in a long long time. But she born for something. You get a good foster family can take her for a while. A family that knows their stuff, special care. Get yourself good and ready to work hard for her. For when you have her on your own." She rubs my cheek quickly and just turns away and if you didn't know her you think she's saying it cold, but she's not. I know what she say is true. I know Linda's gonna tell me more later tonight and I am scared of what she's going to say. I know my little girl gonna need a lot of care in this world.

In my room at night, Sherry's milk starting to work and I feel sleepy and I want to make them go away, the people in here talking at me, having to tell me all this truth shit. I am sleepy and I can push my body like it's outside, not in here with all these girls and problems, remember a better time, but it's like the snow of the winter and fireweed of the spring, all mixed into one season, and I am plodding round in my snowboots, getting lost. The way the white spruce is sometimes scary and seems to jerk in the cool Arctic wind that lifts off the Beaufort and smack your face even in the hot summer sometimes, unexpected. The way the jackpine seems to mock you and call out to you, "Hide and seek, Trista, wanna play? You'll never never win, little girl, you'll never never win." But I pick up my feet and keep running, and I don't stop to sleep in that barren land. "You sleep, you die," Daduk always said. "You go out on the land by youself. Then you sleep, then you die. It take you away 'fore you know it." When I wake up, I feel like I been running in snow all night.

I seen that woman in my head. The woman from the Aurora Store. Nights, she's on the windows when I'm looking through, and I seen some kids skidooing past the jail. I try to look past her face. Sometimes those kids are looking in at us here at the jail, there's lights on and stuff, it's pretty cushy here, not so much like we hear Yellowknife Juvie is, all bars and stuff. I seen some kids, maybe Steffie and Ben, and they're skidooing down the Kuglingitt Road past here and Steffie's holding up her forty-pounder and she's laughing and I can even see her smile so wide and those metal fillings back of her mouth. They're not wishing us bad, no, I know Steffie would want me to come along, she's kind of like my sister anyways, what with her nanuk and mine known each other for a long time back when they went to Tensle Hall residential school and all that shit that went down there.

I seen them pass and I'm thinking about the Vaseline she's smeared under her goggles so she doesn't get no raccoon eyes from the frostbites, and they're burning it up the back roads, and maybe skidooing past some bear they've shaken out of his sleep, looking groggy for berries that won't come till June. That Steffie holding Ben tight around his belly, her parky hood's fur whipping in the wind and she's smelling the wolverine fur round her face, just sucking in the tight cold air, like chewing icicles. Lord, I want to be there with them, just skidooing, drinking, not worrying 'bout nothing. Not seeing that woman's face staring at me from them window panes.

In my room and away from the girls, I think about a lot of things. They don't think I do, them, Linda and Deb. Maybe they think I'm avoiding, like they say to our faces when we're in Group and not talking. Maybe they think I'm in denial, like not seeing that when life was shit with Tyler and he always messing about with weed and coke and junk. But he was thinking lots about his place and getting his business set up down south, like he was always making some plans and that seemed like it was right to me. Lying in my jail bed and the red light from the camera, and it's something to get used to, knowing they can just stare in on you like that whenever. But you do get used to it, feels almost like it isn't any jail, more like they're just checking in like I remember thinking about the Snow Nanuks, how they were always outside there, outside our house and just off the side in their cabin or snow house and looking in on us when we're sleeping. I see Faith with them too, like she can now come in and see them. She's sleeping, she's got a little snore to her breathing, like her tiny nose is stuffed, but it makes me happy I can hear her. I reach over the crib and hold her little foot, and imagine she can see the Snow Nanuks too, maybe they can be giving her something, like they gave to Keely and me.

Auntie says Nanuk is real sick. Auntie's on the phone, telling me all this and I wish she could just come by and see me. Yesterday Nanuk didn't take her insulin and she was playing the $15,000 bingo with some of her sisters come from Tuk to play the big one. Didn't win it, and so her one sister took out a forty of rum and they went at it pretty good. Auntie was working till 9 p.m. at the Northmart and comes home, finds all them old ladies drunker than shit, laughing, but with tears running down their faces. Auntie says to Nanuk: "Mom, stop that pouring, you're going to get sicker than shit" and Nanuk just answers back: "What you know, ah? Got some kid and grandchild in jail, putting me to shame, my own great-grandbaby in jail like that? She shoulda been home with us instead of out that trailer with that Tyler." And then they just get to fighting and screaming at each other. Nanuk's sisters put their parkys on and make out for the Icebox Bar to get some more booze, leave them fighting alone in the house.

"You know I helped you raise Trista good after the crash, not my fault what she done," Auntie said.

"You let her run the street when she wasn't higher than my knee, after scroungin' round town with them kids, drinking so young," Nanuk said. "Raising her? That girl not been raised by nobody but me, you whoring around Tuk and back."

"Then who you saying whose fault it is? I been trying, Mom, I been trying to get straight with that girl, and working get you and her some groceries, pulling in more shifts at the Northmart."

"Need to stay home with them babies," Nanuk said.

"I'm not taking her baby, Mom. She needs special care, you know that."

Auntie tells me all this. What the fuck am I supposed to do about it? Auntie's sometimes like my mom, then not. Yeeah, my mom. She was only thirteen when she had me. My daddy? Who knew, could've been any number of men down from the Icebox Bar, some rig-pig. That don't mean she was a slut though, Nanuk's got that wrong about Auntie and Mom. Mom had a big heart in her, too big is what I think. Auntie sounds cold for not wanting Faith, for not even thinking of taking Faith. But I hear it like she tells me: "Honey, it's not that I can't take her because I don't love her. I love her too much and I worry I can't do right by her, she's sick. I can't think straight then, keep my job, keep me off the bottle wanting to suck me in every turn." It's no mystery why anyone does what they do. It never was.

"Trista?" Auntie says through the phone. "How's the baby?"

"Linda says the YK doctor's going to come in and talk to me. But I know what they're gonna say."

"You don't know," Auntie says.

"She's retarded. She's fucking retarded," I says.

"That don't mean much, honey, words. She's had a rough start and she's a preemie. A lot can change, you seen it yourself here in town, other babies when they've come out early."

"Think Nanuk's gonna be okay?" I says.

"Oh yeeah, she'll do it. You know how it is, Trista. We fight but those are words too. She knows better and it was just the once. Her doctor give her shit and you know how she dotes on him. She's been good for a long time now, it's a slip. Worst thing is getting her off the chocolate," Auntie says.

"She find your hiding place again?"

"Like a little kid, hand in the back drawer, you know the one with the old spoons Daduk had when he was a baby. 'Just looking for an extra spoon, they're all dirty,' she says and I don't bother opening the cutlery drawer show her the ten we got sitting in there clean." Auntie starts to giggle and I can't help it I do too, seeing Nanuk in her slippers, that scarf she put her long grey hair up in at night, the way her mouth without dentures like a small pink puppy's nose.

"Gotta go, sweetie. You hang tight now. I'll try to come in before Christmas, get some time off on Saturday. You know Daduk sends you a hug too, baby, it's just hard for him."

"Okay."

"And this one's for Faith times a million and two," and she kisses into the phone.

There's something in me that can be happy. There's something in me that I think why am I happy when I don't know what to do about Faithy or this bad feeling about what I done inside of me. But hearing Auntie's voice makes me believe it might all just gonna work out.

Deanne comes up behind me, know it's her, can see her body move in the window, says, "Dinner," and she pushes my hair back and kisses behind my ear. She's getting braver doing that when she knows there's no workers coming up, stolen moments. I close my eyes and she's rubbing my neck and I just want to turn around and kiss her for hours, have her take me into her bed and just feel little and have her baby-hold me all night.

The Snow Nanuks push me like I'm a tiny sandpiper that's burrowed and burrowed and has finally found some seeds left after the cold has seeped itself out of the ground, found its wandering way to the large runoffs that rush to Mackenzie River in June. The Snow Nanuks are pushing me forward, I can feel their warm hands against my back. I'm crawling on the snow, and Keely is up ahead. We must be real young but I can remember this, it's bright, like the crunch of the snow on my knees. I got a white and blue snowsuit on, and it is hard to stand, though Nanuk is behind me, "C'mon, Trista, hold on to the rock, stand up."

I want to turn, to look at Nanuk. But her face and hair gets mussed up in the thickness of my hood. I can feel the wolverine fur the Snow Nanuks sewed around the hood of the snowsuit, and I see the rock, it has snow all over it, save one little grey piece sticking out. I crawl toward it, breathing hard, and the snow is squeaking under me, so hard it must be January, been on there for so long. I climb up the rock, put my rabbit fur–mittened hands on it, stand up, and turn, meaning to see Nanuk and the other Snow Nanuks. I can hear their clapping, and as I turn from the rock, I let go. Even Keely is starting to stand, I can see her in her little pink parky seems she had for ages, and she is trying to clap while standing and she falls. Nanuk is laughing. "Look at you, strong girls," she says. I turn away from the window then, go into the kitchen and wonder how do I remember all this, wonder if I want to make it up to have some memory of somebody loving me as much as I'm loving Faith, that hurt you get when you want someone to do good.

"So you girls been thinking about what I said," Linda says at dinner.

"I'm not doing it," Megan says.

"Why not?"

"Stupid. If we saying a grace why don't we just pray and get over with it. Not sing some stupid songs. And I'm feeling sick," Megan says.

"You can't be using the excuse of those pills, Megan. You're going to be taking them for the rest of your life," Linda says.

"I'm not talking the rest of my life, I'm talking now."

"What about you, Deanne?"

"I don't know."

I look down because Linda will get up on me next and I think Deanne's being chickenshit because usually she's into this thing when Linda gets going.

"I'll do it," I says.

"What?" Linda says because she knows I never do nothing.

"Me, I'll go first."

I get up and I look at them all. Then I start singing that one song I know that Richard used to like me singing. The Dolly Parton one called "Jolene." I don't know the right words. But I'm standing there and I close my eyes because right before I go into it Megan's got this look on her stupid face like she's gonna laugh me down. I sing lots of verses and just put some words in for the ones I don't know. I belt it out good and I'm singing and then I open my eyes. No one is laughing at me, but they're grinning. Megan starts to clap right off and Linda's giggling and says, "Whoo-hoo, we got us a singer!" And Deanne's starting up and clapping too so she gets up and gives me a hug. When I'm done I yell, "Grace!" and sit back down, Aimee's pushing at my thigh, giggling.

"What made you sing that one?" Megan asks me.

"Don't know. Just one Mom had kicking around. Richard liked it some too."

"You dance with him when you sing it?"

"Some. Mostly watch them dance. Mom could dance real well when she got going. Liked to jig too. Keely can remember better than me. Always talking about my mom jigging at Jamboree."

"You should learn some then. When we get the elders in here. Get them to teach you up some," Megan says. I know she's thinking about her own people over there Paulautuk. How she'd like to be there instead of here. But we still got our smiles on.

"Jailbird," Deanne says. "Never known you had it in you to belt out like that."

We tuck in and eat and Linda starts talking on some stuff about her current events things, like what's going on about town and that, up the rec centre and Ptarmigan Hall. She starts talking about what more work training we got to keep up with, how we getting out of the facility to get some work skills. But her voice is light and I see her sneak a smile over at me. I feel this flush up my face and I feel good that she's pleased. I rub at the floor with my sealskin slippers. Wonder down at my feet and think maybe I could be as good as Mom at the jigging. Maybe them Snow Nanuks could come up here and it be like when we was little and down their place. They could come in and teach and love us girls up. Maybe they forgive me some. Maybe they know what that was like for me and Jimmy. But I don't think about that, can't think about that and I put it out of my head and look at Linda smiling and telling us about the Christmas Jamboree and maybe we make some more things after the school is out, maybe we can get some more supplies from the Tru Valu and some skins from the nanuks and learn to make some jewellery or more hookrugs. Learn to make some tufting from the nanuks come in and teach us. Maybe we can learn so many things that it's like they used to be there in my head long ago when I didn't drink and hang around Barclose and was feeling special and good about the Snow Nanuks, just me and Keely being little again.

"Trista."

"Yeeah."

"Phone call." Deb puts the phone down and looks at me funny. I put down the embroidery I'm working on. It's kind of late, almost eight o'clock and almost lights out. "Hello?"

"Hey."

"Who is this?" I say, but my heart is pounding. I know who it is I know it's him and why the fuck is he calling now and where the fuck is he and his voice sounds so good and, "Hey ..." I say.

"You doing good?" Tyler says. His voice sounds slurred and I think he's down there in YK shooting up and his mom's given him money but he blown it on junk but it's his voice it's his voice and I start to cry. "Trista. C'mon. Don't," he says. And I can see his hands, his hands he's cut his nails down so much so they easier to wash and the ragged bits where he pulls off skin with his fingers when he's talking and his mouth when he's frowning at me, across the room and I am telling him something small and silly like, Get some paper towels on the way back from work, or his knees, his knees that don't have any hair on them but his calves do, he's got curly light hair on his calves and I can see them glinting in the lamp light. "I thought you wanted to talk to me," he says.

"Yeeah," I says, but not this way not in here with these girls they making their eyes go through my shirt they know it's him and Deb is walking over from the workers' station she knows it's him and I just want to be in our trailer and talking to him on the couch and showing him Faith, see her eyes, Tyler, you got them shape eyes because they don't come from me and they don't come from Mom and they don't come from Daduk or Auntie or Nanuk and I squeeze my eyes shut and Deb's got her hand on my back and see her hands, Tyler, her little little hands and the way her pinkie go in and I don't got that and no one else, but you, fuck you. "Where you been, Tyler?" I says.

"Here and there."

"You promised," you said and you talked and you said and laughed and talked plans and me and you and Faithy and, "You coming back?"

"Trista, listen—" he says.

"No." And I hang up. I don't pound the phone on the wall and I don't punch the walls and I stand there and it's like the numb just crawling up from the carpet deep into my bones.

"C'mon, let's go sit on your bed," says Deb and she sits with me but I don't say anything, feel suddenly tired and say, "Let me sleep."

"Okay. You come out if you need a PRN," she says.

Tyler and his fucking bullshit. "Trista, I just need to go down and get some inks. If I get more colours, I can do more tats, and the thing is, then I won't be pissing around doing them here and there,

I can actually try to set up shop,"Tyler says and he's drinking whisky, I can smell it.

"I don't want you to go, what if Faith comes and you're gone. Remember what Dr. Petterson said?"

"Yeah, but then she might not come and here I've gone and blown this deal and I won't get anything set up because then she's here and we'll be busy with her, me sitting on my ass with shit welfare money coming in giving us nothing."

"There'll be enough food, the cheques will cover it. You don't even know if the deal's for sure," I says.

"Trista, just let me go down south, I'll only be in Yellowknife for a week, I can get the flight on my uncle's North Flight airmiles, he's not going to offer them again once he pisses his money. That's like a five-hundred flight for free."

"I just don't want you to go. I feel crazy with her, Tyler what if she's dead in there, and you're not home."

"Trista. Don't think that way. It's not going to happen that way."

And he rubs my belly, puts his fuzzy head against my side, and speaks to her: "C'mon, Faithy, my girl, chyat, chyat, start running them dogs, get out there in that snow. C'mon and see us love you."

But I push him away from my belly. "You're a fucking liar, Ty."

"Trista, stop getting at me," he says. He gets up from the couch and into our bedroom and I can hear him digging for the bottle he got under the bed, that bottle he thinks I don't know he got under there. "Fucking small trailer for you thinking I don't fucking know," I says, getting up, my back hurting, pains shooting through my lower belly. What if she's coming, I think, too soon too soon, but then the pain goes quick like it come and I think it's those fake labour pains like the nurse said might come.

"I'm not hiding shit," Tyler says and dumps down on the couch swigging at the bottle of Jack.

"Ty. Please. Don't get pissed tonight."

"I don't need this, Trista. Man should be able to have himself a drink after work."

"What work, you not fucking worked in days," I says.

"Shut up," he says quietly. And I know I shouldn't go there. Not when he's getting quiet.

"You know what we said, we promised," I says.

He leans in real close to me and his breath stinks of the whisky. He twists my arm, hard. "Shut. The. Fuck. Up." And he pushes me back into the couch. I'm getting ready, hurry put the pillow in front of my gut, hurry close my eyes. But I can only smell his breath, heaving, going in and out fast. He pushes sudden against the couch, smashes the bottle against the stove, runs to the bedroom. He throws stuff into his green duffel bag, comes out, and puts his hoodie on with his fur-lined coat, his breathing almost regular now, almost like he's only just getting ready to go to work. He makes sure there's enough firewood for the stove, throws some money on the kitchen table for food. And just goes.

"Fuck off then if you're gonna go," I whisper.

It's Keely who calls me up that day, a week into Tyler leaving. He hasn't called and I shouldn't be all worried or lost feeling, but I am. Because it's gonna blow over, he's not going to be mad for long and he's gonna come back I know he is. My back's aching, and I took two baths already, moving the warm wash cloth over my belly, pressing my belly, "Swim, little Faithy, swim for me," But nothing works, nothing moves inside me. It's Keely who tells me Jimmy's in town.

"What you're up to tonight?" Keely says.

"Just watching the TV. What you're doing?" I say.

"Hanging with Jimmy."

"Why you're going to do that? Trash like that?"

"C'mon, Trista, he wants to see you, make up like."

"Why I gonna see that fucker? Didn't he just stand by when those other guys fucked me over, left me for dead in the snow?"

"Trista, was him that brought you to his uncle's house in Tuk that night. Was him that wiped your face, taped your cuts."

"Keely, was you there?"

"No. But he told me."

"He told you shit. Where was he, ah? I was screaming for him, I didn't see him when they was kicking at me."

"Trista. He wants to talk to you. He wants to be friends. Fuck, you gotta give him that at least. What you worried about anyways, you got Tyler now and Faith, some family, he's got shit. Your auntie won't even look at him when he walks in the Northmart. Like he's not owned by no one," Keely says.

"That's his own fault," I says.

"He just wants to sit and have a smoke, or what, give him a minute. He's not even ask what you're up to. I'll come too, and we'll just sit."

Keely did come and she brings Jimmy too. An hour before they come over I was in the bathroom, puking, making deals with God.

Linda's getting me to talk about Tyler calling in Group. Says it will help me, make the figuring out of it all a little easier and clear my head. I sit and listen to her. But I still can't talk much. I got Faith to keep calm for, that YK doctor still not come to tell me much about her tests. But I know Linda and Deb knows, Tracy even, can see it in their eyes. Today Faith had her two months shots. Dr. Petterson come in. She let me hold Faith while she was giving her the shot in the leg. Then I put Faith in her rolly crib. She's got these brown eyes, Dr. Petterson, but one is a little blue too. It's like she's a half, maybe she is, I never asked her. She puts her hand on my forearm and her hand is so warm. I want to just be four again, and crawl right up to her, and tell the whole thing right from the start, just hum my whole story out to her, and have her stroke my hair, tell me it's all right and the men from the living room are gonna go away, Mommy's crash going to go away, Snow Nanuks are having a party with popcorn for the kids, and Nanuk's going to come and we're gonna make cookies for breakfast and lunch and dinner.

"Hey," Deanne says, and I open my eyes and I am back in Group again, like time seems so so long sometimes.

"How did he sound?" Megan says.

"Wasted," I says.

"You hear where he was calling from?" Aimee whispers.

"Just his voice. Like someone I known long time ago."

"What does it bring back?" Deb says.

"How he was with her. In my belly still, I mean. Talking sweet and hope. I want to go back to that face of his on that couch and punch him fucking silly," I says.

"You have her to think about now," Deb says.

"Think what. All's I do is think."

"If you face up, it comes out, like slivers. Gets better," Deb says.

I'm thinking it's not slivers coming out, but rocks and driftwood and fucking ice cold chunks hard and jagged.

It's after school and we all go into the living room. Tracy brings out some muffins that Sherry's made for us in the morning, she's gone now. Gone home to her kid and we won't see her till morning. It's the best times in the afternoon but I still feel shaky thinking about Ty's voice.

"You gonna hook some?" Deanne asks me and I nod. But right now I just pull Faithy out of her rolly crib, hug her to me. Watch Deanne go get her stuff and sit across from me. Her hair is getting longer and her bangs get in her eyes. I want to put Faith to my breast, but she's not into it, she's less and less into it. Sometimes she will, but not pull or anything and I know I am just being some hopeful. I put her back in the rolly crib and go up to the workers' station, get some formula. Pull her up again toward me, try with the bottle. I stroke her head, she's got such fine thin hair, just wispies now.

"If we were out, we could watch some show, you could come up to my apartment," Deanne says.

It's a game we play lots. What if. What if we knew each other and were out, just living.

"Yeeah. You can come up my trailer. We can start a fire in the woodstove, get warm some," I says.

"You can meet some my YK friends, they're good people, got some good shit, always bringing stuff with them to party." Deanne starts whispering because we can't talk drug talk.

"I got nothing at my place, maybe some beers," I says.

"Beers good," Aimee whispers and giggles some.

"Hmm. Make something?" Deanne says.

"Yeeah, only some, maybe brownies," I says.

"Pot brownies. Better than the shit they give us in here," Deanne says.

"Trista," Linda calls to me. I think she's heard what we're talking about but she says, "Go into Iso, Dr. Petterson's there and wants to talk to you."

I go in and she starts to talk at me. About Faith. Test results. Placement results. Firm dates. But it's hard to hear her and I think about the Snow Nanuks.

The Snow Nanuks say, "Trista, come here," and they put an arctic tern chick against my ear, move my lips to try to help me make the same sound. The Snow Nanuks, they are cutting the caribou skin from the body of the animal, the warm flesh smell rises up. They use the old ulus and the skin slides off and onto the snow.

I wrap the skin around me and dance, and here on the snow, my feet move quickly and I look down at my toes in wonder, because I can walk now. But where's Keely? Seems like in this memory I got the Snow Nanuks all to myself and we're out on the land somewhere. It's day and it feels later in the day, which could mean it is night, but April or something. I don't see Mom and wonder if she's gone. But then, no, if I'm just walking, she should still be here. I see my little self totter up to the Snow Nanuks, and they giggle, let me fall at their feet while they sew and talk and laugh, the other tiny beings open their eyes wider at me, they cannot dance. There are babies all around the Snow Nanuks, little babies. I remember them, like the Snow Nanuks were babysitting us all while our moms were out working, like the Snow Nanuks looked after us and made sure we did stuff, not sit in front of the TV too much or eat too much candy the men give us to be quiet in the house. I'm wondering how I could forget about all them babies all around all the time. Maybe that's why when Faith came she was so easy to hold on to, that practice we all got being over at the Snow Nanuks. I can see in their eyes that they cannot wait to dance, them babies, their little feet wriggling. They look so different from my baby, and I watch Dr. Petterson in this place, this white place that we're in.

This doctor says, "Trista. Have you heard me?" She puts her hand on my arm. "The foster family in Inuvik has decided to take her. She'll go there right after Christmas."

I feel tired and sleepy and I just want to go away to a floaty place, out on the land. Taking my baby away, they gonna take my baby away. Again. Like that night I had her. They take her away and incubate her.

"Trista? The doctors say Faith has fetal alcohol syndrome. Faith cannot hear. Faith is brain damaged." And I want to scream at her.

Dr. Petterson leaves and I'm outside myself, outside, it's cold. Why did that Trista do it? That weirdo girl that I see in my mirror?

Why did she go with Jimmy? Why couldn't she just wait for Tyler? He wasn't gonna be gone that long maybe. He didn't leave her, maybe. He wasn't sick of the fighting maybe. He was getting cash for Faith, inks for his tattoo gun. Monday to set up shop. Why did Trista do it? What kind of girl we got here?

No one asks me these questions. No one's coming up to me asking nothing. I can see the lady. With those glassy eyes, those window eyes. She staring at me through the window. Even she don't ask why. She just looking at me. Nothing in her eyes, really, nothing like she's mad, or sad. Just black eyes looking.

I am pulling on my smoke, it's good to smoke and the air is so icy, sun gone and one o'clock but there's the twilight, and feels good to be outside.

There's no one skidooing on the back road, and the wind is quiet. I can see jackpine and scrub holding up the snow, like their branches grew strong white-grey muscles, and they're just showing off to me, showing me their northern strength.

The light is strange in December. We still get some light, but it's a reddy yellow twilight, like the sun saying, I'm not quite ready to come up here, I am tired from all this snow, and I can't lift my head much, so I am going to just raise my eyelids a teeny tiny bit and give you a little sliver of light, a small shiver so you can see the things I got sleeping around you, pine, frozen river, white snow pocketed on the side of the road like clouds taking a little nap.

"Lotsa Christmas lights up already. Seems more and more each year," Tracy says.

"Yeeah."

"Something to look forward to, Trista. You'll see. Day at a time," says Tracy.

We're going to have some kind of Christmas in here. Auntie, when I was little, she done up Christmas real nice, for an auntie who set to drinking soon after dinner was up. But then she quit drinking when I was young, seems a year after Mom died. When I was older, she and Nanuk would make a caribou roast they had sitting in some good sauce juices for some days. Then I come off of working at the Northmart December 24 night, busy night in Jackfish Bay, that Northmart manager's got every kid older than twelve working for him come Christmas overtime, everyone happy and spending cheques on food and candy, me walking home from work and just dawdling some, even though I'm excited about dinner, because the lights are all out, and some fake plastic Santas on people's porches and their plastic smiles making me think everything gonna be okay.

Auntie and Nanuk are allowed to bring me one present in here, but they're not allowed to come and see me or Faithy until December 26, and maybe after that we get to see Sunrise celebration on January 4, maybe, but we don't know nothing yet.

Miss Sarah is getting us to make decorations in class, telling us a Christmas story about an old guy who gets these ghosts coming over and they're telling him how he's fucking up in his life and why no one loves him. I know that might be me soon, and I can't think about it, because it makes me think of Faithy and where she will be and where I will be and where Tyler will be, and will we ever see each other again, or ever be in the same place, seeing? Who is my ghost?

"Then you roll the ring around, and add another loop. This way you can make a string of them," Miss Sarah says. She is showing us how to make crisscross hearts to put things in, like Christmas cards we're not getting from anyone. The lady from the Aurora Store is at the window again and I am trying not to look at her, think that she's not going to have any more caribou roasts for Christmas, or hold her baby's babies no more.

"Then we was doing coke behind the school, last year, right before Christmas," Megan says quietly because she doesn't want Miss Sarah to hear.

"Hyper you and coke, fucking give me a Xanax, that'd be too sick," Deanne says, pulling her red paper over the white.

"Trista," Megan says, ignoring Deanne, "you ever done it? Only a few times? You lucky, because it gets in your head, gets a hold of you. Like when you're doing it you can do anything, just off of one little smoke. I can feel it going down and then my head just about taking off. And making love on it? You ain't never had anything better, Trista, seriously. I miss it so bad."

We're not supposed to be talking about drugs, outside of maybe in Group when a girl's freaking and needs to talk it out to get it out of her system.

"I done coke once or twice, maybe it was crack," I says.

"Yeeah. It's not the same. Crack's got more shit in it."

I can hear Faithy crying at the workers' station and I feel my breasts itch, even though I haven't been trying to feed her for almost a week now. I don't know how I feel about these other girls. Like sometimes I can put that lady out of my head and imagine I have Faith in our trailer all normal life. Tyler is working and I am getting ready to take Faithy over to Auntie's so I can go to school for a couple of hours and get some computer credits. We got a coffee maker and even a microwave and I can heat up Faith's food and drink some coffee to get more awake, because I am a little tired because Tyler and I were up late last night talking about the tattoo shop and how to decorate it, like how he's going to put his drawings and best tattoo designs up, so if someone is stuck and they know they want a tattoo, but just not which one or where, he can show them visual-like and help them with that, like consult them or something. It is a big decision.

The workers come into class, Linda and Deb, and Tracy even, to join Miss Sarah, like they having the team meeting thing. It's kind of like Group, but more they try different things to do counselling with us I guess. They give us colouring books and we sit around the big table. I get this colouring book with Santas on them and little kids dancing around the Santas, so I colour them. While we're colouring, Linda and them come around and sit with us one on one. There's this soft music, like lullabies or like classical hour on the CBC, and everyone is real quiet and them long beam-like lights aren't on, just the lowlights from the stand-up lamps in the corner. It's nice, kind of sleepy. And the blinds are half-down so where the lady usually stares at me from in the class window, well, that is kind of half-covered and I'm not going to look over there anyway, I am choosing crayons, red, then green. So I am just colouring the Santas and Linda come sit by me.

"You ever colour like this when you were little?" she says.

"Yeeah."

"Okay," Linda says. I can't hear Faith crying no more, and I feel a little sleepy, and Linda's voice is soft and sounds nice, she's talking about some Christmas things she done with her kids, some decorations they making at home. I choose another colour, fill in the little girl's coat blue.

"Remember when you were seven, Trista? Can you see yourself, what your hair looks like, your face, see what's on the table."

I can see my hair. I always had such long hair, even up until the Aurora. I cut it in the hospital after, all of it. Wonder the nurse gave me the scissors. I am seven, but little and still don't have no teeth in the front. And the Inuvik dentist had to pull out some of the back ones, because they were rotten from candy. "You have to brush after you eat candy, Trista, you have to take care of your teeth," the dentist says. Mom is in the room with me, and she helps me pick out a ring from the ring tray the dentist bring after. "The blue one is nice," she says. But I pick the pink one.

"... sitting at the kitchen table in your home. Can you see what you are wearing ..."

My tongue is pressing against the holes in the back of my mouth. I don't want to eat candy ever again, I think, but I know I will. I'm not at the Snow Nanuks. I am waiting for Mom to come home. It is dark and Nanuk is at our house, but I don't remember much, because I am only seven and I like to listen when Nanuk talks on the phone to her friends or Nanuk and her sisters are playing cards and drinking tea, and they let me have some tea with Carnation in it, lots of Carnation milk from the tin and I like to lick it from the side of the teacup, that little drip that's caught there and it's sweet. And Nanuk and her sisters are talking about Auntie, who is not doing good.

"She been drinking up that cheque long time now. Shouldn't take long for her to come home then," Nanuk said.

"Hmmm, she'll be back soon, don't worry."

I'm just drinking tea, playing with my string people. My hair is long and black. It hangs thick and heavy, so heavy that sometimes I am sick of it, and it makes my head hurt. It don't tangle much and I remember it feels nice when Mom pulls the brush through it. "Trista, you got hair like the Mackenzie River at Break Up, heavy with thick ice, flowing fast and dark blue almost black and swollen from Tuk, water pushing against the Arctic Sea," she always says, mornings. She pulls the brush through my hair and I close my eyes, feel the brush against my back and the tickly good feeling of it, Mom's breath close to my ear, she's humming a bit, some song I could never figure. But she's not here now and I know she gone somewhere, just can't remember where.

Then time jumps, not long after, and I am sitting alone at the kitchen table, pressing my tongue in the holes in my back gums, playing with my string people, twisting the Daddy string person around my hair. It is late and Mom is not home. I want to call

Nanuk, but I am afraid she will be worried too much. I don't know how late it is, because I fell asleep a little bit. Richard was sleeping on the couch and I come in to see him, he wakes a bit and is sleepy still, and says, "C'mere."

"Where's Mom?"

"Gone on the Iceroad to Tuk."

"When she back?"

"Doan know. C'mere, Trista."

I don't want to go because he stinks of High Tests beer. But my feet are cold, and I do want to go because Richard is a little rough but mostly he loves me. He says he loves me and he is quiet-like and whispers some in my ear.

Linda's saying something about how she and her kids sing some of the songs they got on the TV come Christmas. How there's the words on there and they sing some Christmas carols together and look at the fake Christmas fire. I'm colouring. I'm colouring in the kids' clothes and remembering Mom and Richard. I can feel the tears coming down and I can see them dripping on the paper and the crayons slide. Linda keeps talking and she puts her hand on my back.

Richard calls me his Trista-kins because we are kin and I am his. He lets me cuddle under the quilt and he makes circles on my belly and I feel like I am breathing like I been running. I am wearing my favourite shirt. I don't got too many and I like to wear it lots because it's got some dogsled puppies on it and their eyes are black and crinkled like they smiling at me when I look at my shirt in the mirror. It's got purple on the part around my neck and then some pink and green stripes that go down my arms and then some bows on the pocket and around the part near my hands, but one bow got torn off when me and Keely was playing with the string family and then Keely got mad and pulled the string daddy out of my hand, and the bow went with the string daddy. But Keely said sorry quick because she known it was my favourite shirt that she torn from.

Where's Mom? I am on the couch with Richard and he's smoothing my back under the quilt and his eyes are closed, mine were too, but then I peek at him. He's got hair on his face, I don't like that part. He kisses my ears, says, "Trista-kins, c'mere," and puts my hands down on him and I close my eyes then.

It's still night when I wake up. Richard's sleeping so I don't wake him. I crawl out and go look in Mom's room, but she's still not there. I look in the fridge for some milk but we got none. I get a biscuit from the cupboard. The biscuit is hard and old, and I have to push it to the side of my mouth because my holes where my back teeth used to be are aching. I go get the Bayer from Mom's bedside table and swallow two with some water from the tap, even though I know Mom would be mad if she known I been taking Bayer on my own.

The clock on the stove says two two eight. I know my eyes should be tired but they're not. I'm worried Mom not home, she should be home now, it's too late. I throw the rest of the biscuit out, and sit at the kitchen table. I must've fall asleep again, cause then I wake up and Nanuk is there and Richard is coming out of the bathroom and has clothes on, and the RCMP is in the living room talking low-like to Nanuk.

"Found by a semi going up to the camp, gone off the road, was quick I think ..."

Nanuk's not looking at the RCMP, her eyes are on her hands, and I'm thinking I should go get Nanuk some cream, because she's moving her hands around and around each other like they hurt and I'm thinking if I got her some cream, that would fix the cracks.

"Trista. Tell me what you are seeing," Linda says.

I have finished colouring the little kids. They are dancing around the Santa. Their coats are blue and green and yellow. Santa's suit is red, and I made the bottom part green. He's smiling at the kids and the kids are jumping. I wonder if this Santa underneath is a good man.

I remember the presents and the tree, and how the Snow Nanuks tried to ban the bingo-playing during the holiday season from being on channel 14 for one whole week, so that mothers could spend the IRC cheques on their babies, their children, and not on numbers, not on hours with dabbers in their hands, watching. And I can smell the caribou, see the Snow Nanuks skinning on the plain, see the steam rise on the arctic ice from the skin being separated with ulus from the flesh, the flesh cut and packed into large long containers, the swipe of the hunters at the head, the bleeding and drawing out of the beast, the calm way it falls, and the others, those good caribou friends, who lift their heads and keep going on, not even running from the crack the shot makes. The crack like a sound in the ice, this is what they know, my Snow Nanuks, this is what they've known for decades, and one lone hunter on the ice will not change it, one herd-friend lost will not change the line, the long line of caribou crossing the arctic plain, unaware the whole time. This is how I remember the story of the old old Arctic Snow Nanuks and Christmas, how they left presents for good children outside their doors, the children's hands stiff from cold from opening the door, the hard chocolates, the frozen raspberry drops, the caramels with frost inside the shiny paper.

We pack up the colouring and stuff and the classroom is real quiet like we all had some together sleep. Linda doesn't say much just gives me a squeeze on the arm and I go get Faith from her crib. I'm here in my room with Faith in my arms and she's not moving much and I can taste them all together, raspberry and caramel, like my mouth just made them up while thinking on it. When we going to get out, if we gonna get out? Will Faith get out before me? How's it gonna end?

The doctor from down Yellowknife comes up today to see me and Faith together. Maybe I don't really want to know how bad Faith is. Maybe I don't wanna know. Like I tell Keely on the phone,

I tell Keely what Faith can't do, like she can't raise her head, or she blinks her eyes funny, like she's not focusing or seeing me right. Keely is really nice about it, let's me ramble about Faithy, even though Keely's never even got to see her, only pictures.

The Yellowknife doctor does these tests on Faith with his small light. He flashes things, and Faith is lying there on her blue blanket. I put on her pink jumper, the one Nanuk gave, and then the sweater Nanuk knitted too. It makes me sad Faithy maybe never gonna know her real Nanuk. The Nanuk who makes things for us, and who's cooking dinner and telling us to come down to her house and eat up good, and the Nanuk who makes me tea and rubs my pregnant belly and telling me how Mom got born. Not the Nanuk who plays TV bingo with her friends and kicks us out of her house. But we're not all some TV family. I lean down and whisper some to Faithy, whisper I'm going to take her to the Snow Nanuks soon if I can.

The Yellowknife doctor is pulling at Faithy's arms, swinging them in front of her face, and almost poking her eye out. Saying, "Hi. Hi. Hi," in Faith's ear like she's just gonna up and say hi back to him.

"When you were breastfeeding, did Faith ever look right at you?" The doctor asks.

"No. She just dreaming and looking up or wherever."

The Yellowknife doctor does more tests, then takes Faith to the exam room, and is gone for only a half-hour. When he gets back, Linda comes with me and him and we go to the one-on-one room. I am holding Faith, and she is sleeping now, tired out from all the pulling and poking.

"Like Dr. Petterson told you, we have a foster family in Inuvik that would be suitable for Faith. The foster mom has years of experience with special needs children, especially kids with fetal alcohol syndrome," the doctor says.

"She doesn't have fetal alcohol," I says.

"Faith presents with some classic symptoms. The bridge of her nose is flattened, her eye spacing. Deafness. It's hard to tell cognitively yet. And then her other problems."

"I never been drinking when I was big with her," I says.

"What about the first months? And, Trista, when they took you in, you were drunk," Linda says.

"That was that one night. Just then." Both Linda and the Yellowknife doctor are looking down knowing I am full of shit. The Yellowknife doctor is pretending to write some notes, and I know that silence, that pausing, like they thinking I am out of touch with my crime, like they keep saying that I am dissociating and not facing what's real, and I'd better face it soon and see it soon before it all just passes me and Faith is gone and I am sixteen and in the Yellowknife Women's Facility and living in a dream and taking heroin like some of them women there get smuggled in, and then I'm hanging, I'm hanging from the shower posts.

"I swear it was one night," I says.

"Regardless. Faith has a lot of problems, Trista," he says. "And with your court case in January, it'll be good to have her settled in after Christmas."

"I know that. Don't you think I know that? Dr. Petterson told me, why you keep telling me?"

Facilities. Care. Group. Meditation. Worker. Court case. Lawyer. Defence. Disease. Alcohol. Fetal Alcohol. Fetus. Baby, our baby, what have I done to our Faithy? Facilities, she and me, locked up, white sheets and people paid to look after you, people paid money to look inside themselves and remember a paycheque makes them care. Retard.

And while the Yellowknife doctor checks more over Faithy, I think about how Tyler hasn't even tried to call again. What is he doing? Is he going to movies with his buddies, talking about tats? Is he sitting at that coffee shop, pouring Carnation evaporated milk into his coffee and putting ink in his drawing book? Is he colouring in the swirling designs of a mean-ass dragon tattoo. Does he think about Faith and me? Does he think, Never mind those fuck-ups, Tyler, never you mind and put them out of your head. You ain't their god, you ain't going to ride your truck up Dempster Highway and come and take them away no more. You just got yourself to think on now, never you mind some black-haired 'sko girl, and those black eyes, and her smiling at you while you kissing by the pot-bellied stove on some night when the lights are green ghosties across the sky. Never mind how those lights lift your stomach, your gut, your centre inside your belly, somewhere deep, and you're kissing her and watching the northern lights out the window swirling, feeling nothing's ever gonna go bad again, you got family in Trista and Faith in her belly and this little trailer and all right in the world, you are not bad and you will be a daddy. Are you drawing them northern lights in your book, Tyler? I think, Are you drawing Faith who can't see, who will never hear her daddy's voice?

The doctor hands Faithy back to me, and she's not crying, not now, even though I want to, bad.

"When will I know when Faith goes?" I say.

The Yellowknife doctor looks up at me, and I stare him down. He doesn't have any anger in his eyes and that makes it worse, that makes me want to drop tears, but I keep staring at him, dry-eyed.

"I am hoping December twenty-seventh. Let the family have their Christmas, you have Faith in here with you for the holidays."

What holidays? What's holy about them taking my Faithy away?

Deanne is going to turn sixteen soon, so then she has to transfer down to Yellowknife Juvie again, maybe YK Women's, she doesn't know yet. She's going to her court date and Deb been doing one on one with her to get her ready. Deanne's not been saying much about it to me, but she's seeming different last few days. More lighter, happier. I don't want her to go, she goes and then Faith goes too and shit what I got then.

"So what's going to happen is you read what you've prepared. We might ask you some questions, and the girls might have something to say to you too. But our role here is to listen," Deb says. Deanne's folding and unfolding her paper and looks real nervous, even though she seen some of the girls that were here before and left done the ownership reading in her time. Deanne's the first one we all seen go, though, so it's easy to feel the jitters with her. Linda's brought it up in our one on one. How I gotta work toward writing about what happened, what I done, what I going to do about the future.

"When I first did my crime, I blamed everyone. Specially I blamed that one cop at YK RCMP. I come in one night and told him about the rape. But because he had hauled me in before for working on the street, he didn't believe me. 'How'd you go and get yourself raped when you're taking money for sex, Deanne?' He said and just ignored me. I wanted to go to Rape Relief. I thought about it, and some of the other girls said, 'Go.' But this guy who raped me, he was a trick before too. And I just thought, No one's gonna believe me, fuck him one day and nothing happens, get raped the next. And this guy, his name was Frank, he was big in selling coke and junk in YK. Not one of the main dealers but part of the crew driving it up and selling. So he could get me that way too, I make trouble for him," Deanne takes a deep breath and crosses her arms in front of her.

"You're doing good, sweetie, just keep reading the paper," Deb says.

"Then. Then I just holed up until the bruises he give me fade.

Girls come and give me some food, got me the morning-after pill and make me go get HIV tested because he raped me bareback. And I just watched a lot of TV. After about two weeks I went back to work again because the rent wasn't paying itself and I figured, What the fuck? I am okay to do this again." Deanne starts shaking and puts the paper down and tells us the rest without reading. "Then I seen him with his buddies, coming out of the YK Inn. I pull my kitchen knife out of my purse, go up to him. Frank didn't even recognize me. He just staring at me. Then one of his buddies says, 'Ain't you the girl who likes it rough?' And I just rushed forward, stabbed Frank one two three four five times and he went down. Then one of his buddies started beating on me, and I'm crazy with the knife, maybe slice some of them up too, but then I take off. I look behind me once. They don't chase me because they're holding their buddy's blood into his body, but too much came out I guess." Deanne opens the paper again, starts crying. "I'm not crying for him, I'm not."

"It's okay to cry for him," Deb says.

"But I'm not. I'm fucking crying for me, okay?" She picks up the paper again and reads from it.

"Then they got the RCMP on me, can hear the sirens. They found me behind the Centre Mall, even still holding the knife and having a smoke on the stoop by the underground parking lot entrance. I'm real calm when the cop car pulls up by then. I tell them, 'Yeah, I did it, what the fuck you going to do?' They put me in Holding, then YK Juvie. Then YK Juvie transferred me up here to Jackfish Bay because they got too many other prostitutes from Yellowknife in there, and they said I was just causing trouble."

"And what's your plan for facing Frank's family tomorrow?"

"My plan is to turn to them when the judge says I can. Tell them I am sorry," Deanne says. She folds up the paper and I can see her hands are still trembling. "And I'm gonna tell that cop. You know the one who didn't believe me?"

"You gonna give him shit?" Megan says. She's dead serious when she says it, leaning forward and everything on her seat like she's watching some TV show drama go on. But we all start to laughing, can't help it, even Deb starts grinning. Deanne even lets out this shaky laugh.

"No," Deanne says. "I'm gonna thank him."

"What the fuck for?" says Megan. "If he believe you before, you wouldn't hafta kill that fucker."

"No. Not for the first time. But because, when they take me to Holding. That cop come up to my cell in the morning. Brung me coffee, says, 'I'm sorry, Deanne. I should've believed you.' And I knew he meant it. And he saw me, really saw me." Deanne puts her head down and the tears aren't coming hard and fast, but just slow dripping off her cheeks and dropping on her jeans. She rubs them in while we all sitting quiet.

Deb says, "Girls, you want to say something more to Deanne?" And Megan sits forward like she's gonna say something again but doesn't. I think we're all sitting in awe of Deanne, like she's our big sister or something, done something really hard and brave.

Later we're peeling the potatoes for chore time. Sherry's out buying groceries, doing the big run at Stanton's in Inuvik so we're alone in the kitchen. "We have to organize there, that's all I was saying to the girls in YK Juvie," Deanne says to me. "Like they aren't pimped out or anything, not like in Edmonton where you're giving all your cash to your dumbass boyfriend, they're spending your good, hard-earned money on fucking crack or meth or something, not giving you anything back. Yellowknife, we look out for one another. That's why no one said anything when the RCMP come asking for me on the street. But why bother hiding, Yellowknife's so small. At least I got three square meals here. Chance to get a job instead of hooking again once I get down there. You got family outside of Jackfish Bay?" Deanne says.

"No," I says. I don't want to talk about Tyler, fucker, bastard.

"So no one in Yellowknife once you go down?" Deanne says.

"No."

"I'll set you up with some names after your court case. You're bound to get transferred, most of the girls do after they're sixteen. And if I get that halfway house thing in Yellowknife, maybe I can come visit you too. There's some good girls down there in YK. My girlfriend, she used to dance at YK Inn? She knows some people still on the outside, come and visit you, maybe smuggle you in some weed for the bad times."

"I don't do none of that any more," I says.

"Maybe you will after you see it. YK facility not as nice as here. Some good people there, though. God, I miss Mary. I just can't handle only calling her three times a week. In YK we're allowed to have phone privileges every night."

I'm peeling the potatoes trying not to be jealous. Thinking it's Mary one week and BoDean the next week, but she's leaving soon and she got all that choice down there. Thinking maybe she got Mary or whoever down in YK, but she got me here. And here is now, today. Not Yellowknife. She's got these freckles on her cheeks that almost winking at me, like saying, try and peel me off, just try. My hands are shaking as I reach for another potato. Deanne just keeps talking on and my mind is thinking about her lips, I keep looking at them kind of sideways, so she doesn't see me looking at her, and I feel something swirling in my belly, like when I breastfeed Faith. She's got me back and forth, that Deanne. Sometimes I want to smack her for the shit she says—all trying to get better shit. Sometimes I can't believe how brave she is, what she says. But then I think I just want to kiss her, and maybe lie in bed with her, behind the locked doors, behind the doors when the electric lock snicks shut for the night, and the lights are low, just some beams coming in the little viewing window and we're warm under the quilts. She's lying there with me, and I am rubbing her freckles softly, then I kiss one and she giggles and takes my wrists, and holds them gently, kisses me, her lashes soft against my cheek, talking quiet to me so we don't wake up Faithy.

I concentrate on the cold potato, on the knife, take another potato up, and our hands brush against each other as she takes one too, and I look up at her and she is smiling at me and winks. I grin back, I feel like a little kid, but I want her to stroke my hair and hug me and hold me, and I blurt out, "I used to have long hair."

"Why'd you cut it?"

"I cut it some with an ulu that night, more when I was in the hospital, it was burned, the night we … the night I had Faith."

She's keeping her head down, because she knows the night I had Faith was the night of the Aurora Store. Even though I haven't said much of anything in Group yet.

"Why it got burned?"

"We … I been drinking. And Jimmy, he was lighting my smoke for me. Jimmy was playing with the lighter, putting it up close to my face and playing chicken, just fooling around. I was kind of low, like I was almost asleep. Then Keely says, 'What that smell?' and she screams at me, 'Trista, your hair,' and I was almost sleeping, didn't feel anything, and it was my hair burned right up one side, almost to my ear. It wasn't full out burning, just smouldering like an almost out fire on the Iceroad. So Keely gets some water and wets it, it stunk so bad, and Jimmy's laughing his ass off. So I just said, Fuck it, let's cut it off, Keely. So she went and got the Nanuk's ulu, she couldn't find any scissors, and I cut it. Didn't do a very good job, cut it better in the hospital after … the next day after Faith come out."

"Did you save some?" Deanne asks.

"Yeeah, just a little that wasn't too burnt. For Nanuk."

"Then it's not bad luck."

"Yeeah."

Deanne has her hand on my arm, and her hand is cold from the cold potatoes, and her nails are bitten down, some ragged around the nail bed, and she's got a ring on, with a pink stone. I think of the pink ring I got from the dentist's, and Mom sitting beside me, saying, "The blue one is nice." And I start bawling just like that. Deanne wipes her hands on the tea towel and comes around and Linda comes down from the workers' station. I am bawling, snot and tears running down my face, like a stupid fucking baby. Deanne just holds me and I let her. They give me tissues and I blow it out, and keep crying, feeling like my insides tearing out, worse than having Faith.

Some of the girls are over by the TV, sitting on the couch when I come out of my room later. I feel sleepy still, even though I slept for an hour and I still got that feeling like I been punched in the belly. Deanne's over there with them, and she's looking at me, waving me over. I don't want to sit with them. There's so much here, I want to just get out. Faith is up in the rolly crib at the workers' station, fussing, and Deb's up and walking, jiggling her, and there's the hall to Iso, then they got some other room behind there, then the door. I just want to run outside, no parky on, no shoes on, just run until I am numb from the cold, then go to sleep. There's only my room to go to, if I don't sit with them. They aren't laughing hard, but they're giggling in little voices. I want to smack them all, those girls, even Aimee, though she never done nothing to me I would of done worse and more to a blackfly. I know they done things too. I know they get crying and hiccupy. But they seem so calm, just sitting there. I can't even go to the kitchen, it's closed, or the classroom, closed. All these locked doors. Is it gonna be locked doors forever? What the court going to say. Me and Faithy, both inside locked rooms but not together. If I asked, Linda would let me go in my room again. But then the door snicks shut, and there's the three smoothed-down white shelves, the bed that smoothes into the floor, no hard edges anywhere. My clothes are on the shelves, nothing else. A book from the classroom. A bib for Faith when she drools. That's it. In my room at home at least I had some things. A picture of a baby seal on the wall, a photo of Mom when she was smiling at Keely, me taking the picture out at Jamboree one year, must've been me and Keely'd just turned five. That year I got the camera from Uncle Joe, and he was being nice and giving me presents just because. What do I have now in this place? These fake Christmas decorations like they're trying for some meaning here. The CBC's on and there's some music, like how they'd play at dances. What the fuck kind of first Christmas is here for my baby, what the hell kind of holy is gonna be good for Faithy in here?

five

When I was little around Christmas was when we were getting to do some drum-dancing and learned the dances from the elders. Nanuk, she'd enrol me in the classes out of the Ptarmigan Hall, and me and Keely'd go down and it would be all warm inside, done up like an old log house the Hall is, and then we set around and there'd be some talking and then we'd get down to learning how to dance. All the Snow Nanuks, some of the daduks, Lee's Auntie Mavis be there too, she was good at drum-dancing, like the Snow Nanuks could get it really going, even then, even they were old then, but spry.

Nanuk was always real quiet when I was little about my daddy being white, because she was embarrassed of me not having a daddy around, maybe made her ashamed of having her own kids without their father around, or even them being white. But Snow Nanuks didn't care, Snow Nanuks would say, "It's no difference, Trista, we all got the same colour blood pumping through our hearts, so you just never mind." And long ago on the whaling ships come up Arctic Sea, some Inuvialuit women worked sewing on the white whaling ships, had all colours of kids and no one made no never mind. Also Gwich'in mixing with Inuvialuit and both with whites. Lots of Inuvialuit kids were some light-coloured and then some are like real Asian-looking. Like we seen on the TV some show about Mongolia, and there's these workers out in the huts and some fishing they're doing, and farming, and they just look like some of the kids up Sachs way, real Asian-looking. Among us kids we could give two shits.

When you watch drum-dancing, the rhythm gets in you. The line of calm-faced drummers, the way they hold the drums on the side and tap at the same time. The drums look like a line of circle moons held up. I can feel the pound of Lee's feet through the floor as he dances beside his auntie Mavis and then I put my hands on the wooden floor of the Ptarmigan Hall, pounding goes up my arms. Keely watches the drum beaters and Lee, making her arms fly up and then down copying behind him like a baby bird, the fringes of Lee's caribou skin jacket almost touching the ground. Then Keely turns and puts her head on my knee because she's getting sleepy but I could watch the drum-dance forever, pretend we are all outside under the northern lights and calling them to dance their green-white arms and stamp their red-purple licks of feet with us.

Mom never told me who my dad was, and I don't remember no men who were special hanging around the house, except Richard, like just some of her friends I known since I was real little, and then some uncles. Nanuk didn't even know his last name, just that he worked the rigs up the Beaufort, come to Jackfish Bay and spend his cheques on the girls, and Mom was one of them. You get lonely in Jackfish Bay, why wouldn't you? Nanuk said they were doing the abortions at Inuvik Regional, but even though Mom was real young and shouldn't have been in the bar anyhow, she just been started going to the church again and even doing communion. That's what I couldn't figure when Nanuk told it, like she was getting all Catholic again, after she was pregnant. But people do some strange things.

The girls are chatting, can hear their voices go up and down like a song. The lady's on the windowsill again and I can hear the music the elders used to play in Ptarmigan Hall, the drums, not like pounding but light. Their faces calm. Me and Keely sitting on the floor watching the big kids dance, the tassels on their slippers flying.

The window's got spiderweb frost on it. It's really dry in Jackfish Bay and if we didn't have the Mackenzie River curling up alongside making us a small bay, this town would be a desert. But there's some snow trapped on the windowsill, and with the heat coming up from the floor, there's steam on the window, and I can see her face clear. I can trace it. The girls are playing cards, they're quiet for a change, and there's some music on, and the workers are talking softly about something I can't hear, just their voices have giggles in them and Deb has got the bottle's nipple in Faith's mouth finally and she takes it. I never noticed before that the lady's eyes are so black, and there's red rimmed around her eyelids like she been crying a long long time.

Her forehead is split today. Usually her head has just got her hair on it, like some curly hair, like she had just gone down to the hairdresser that day and asked for a bouncy curl perm and the hairdresser said, Okay, do you want a cut too? and the lady said, Yes, why not, it's payday, so then the hairdresser shampooed her hair and pulled a comb through it and said, My you got some thick hair, I might layer it for you, and the lady smiled, said, My grandkids got the same, we're lucky, my sister she's got such thin hair, and the lady smiled at herself in the mirror thinking she might go over to the Northmart after and buy some new Max Factor lipstick.

I am tracing her face thinking she really looks like some of the Snow Nanuks at the Ptarmigan Hall, they're laughing and smiling. Then Lee's dancing drum-dance and for a big guy he can sure make his arms go up and down almost touch the floor graceful. Lee grins at me and Keely and I hope at Snow Nanuks later he makes us some Eskimo doughnuts because even though we never gonna tell the Snow Nanuks, Lee makes them better than them, puts sugar on them, chocolate syrup sometimes. But the lady draws me with her eyes in the window and I am not at Ptarmigan Hall any more, just jail. I try not to look at the crack in her head full on because there's something black oozing out of it and I think it's blood, even though

I know blood is red, but in my head it's black, so black. Deb wheels Faith's rolly crib over to me and Faith is sleeping, finally she is sleeping, and I am so tired, and I keep tracing the lady's face. Wonder how soft her skin was, wonder who kissed the wrinkles that crinkled up from smiles and kisses she laid on her grandkids.

Faithy looks at me like that with her strange dark bluey eyes, not right on my face, then sometimes right at me, her brows crinkled, her fists push at my lips when I brush them against her. Deb says she's tracking some with her eyes and that's good, which she says means that Faithy is looking at me. I feel sad when she's looking at me, like she's thinking in her two-month-old head, Mommy, you better take care of me, knowing I can't. Maybe. On a day like today, haven't slept much all night, Faith neither, us up with her making hum noises and me half-awake with dreams, rocking her on my bed in the darkness. Then finally getting up and that small time of sun streaming through our dusty windows, and Linda's saying, Good, you done your chores, like she means it, and I'm on some line that says I'm good, and feel like going to fall off that line every second like them circus girls we seen on the TV, their feet curling around the tightrope. I'm feeding Faith. I'm talking with Deanne and jiggling Faith in my arms. I'm passing her to the workers and asking if I can go for a smoke. I'm smoking and holding that smoke like a grown woman, and nodding my head, and listening to the other girls out on smoke privilege with me. I'm here but don't want to be.

My hair, when I comb it in the wobbly mirror/not mirror they got for us, is pulled back, and I know I seen my face looking something like fresh and young. I wish too hard that it could be that easy. Brushing my hair back, new and clean for the next day.

I always loved my long hair. I could still smell the burn smell when Faith was pushing her way out of me.

"Breathe, Trista, don't hold your breath." Dr. Petterson, she's telling me, but there's a roaring in my ears and I am halfway gone, that headache crawling up my neck, the ache settled into my back, and I can feel Faith's head pushing out.

I see Faith with me and Keely out on the back hill, we're walking out on the land and we got Mom there and the Snow Nanuks. They all come to visit Faith on the tundra. I can see past her, walking, tottering in her parky, her hands out, but she can see, I know she can see because she bends down now and then to swipe at some snow the way little kids do, as if they can push it all, move it all from their feet. I can see beyond the river and the street downtown and the mud of the town of Jackfish Bay and the shrub and jackpines, and I float toward the blanket of rolling snow. The wind that is picking up the snow. It is nosing through the deep snowpack and just shy of a foot from where it lays seeds for spring under tundra grasses. I can see the wind playing with Faith, her face raised toward it, and Wind is stroking her cheek. It feels good to close my eyes and see this, I don't feel those worms in my belly when I think of them taking her away, all the stuff with the prison and the girls and Deanne and Linda and Deb and even Miss Sarah and Dr. Petterson, all the shit they tell me about, all floats away in this dream where Faith is walking, and moving and seeing across the snow.

"Are you cold there, child?" Mom says to Faith. And Faith knows her, knows this is her nanuk, come back from under the ice. I am standing back, watching them together, like we always been this way. Why couldn't we just always be this way?

Faith tries to talk to her, but now she can't find her voice in this tundra, it's like she's swimming under the snow, and the snowflakes are beating their iciness against her throat. I want to take her up and carry her, but she seems a long ways away now, and I wonder what Mom is going to say to her, do with her. Then Wind talks to her and Faith is smiling. Mom doesn't move, it's like she can hear it too, but is standing so so still, too still to hear really good.

"Is there much food?" Wind says, and I can see it fluffing out from under Mom's wolf's fur around her parky. Mom is humming as she separates the fur from the beaver. Now she is sitting on a log and we are all around a small fire and Faith is looking at her, this is her nanuk, now Faith knows her nanuk. I brought her out on the land and here is her nanuk, ready for her. I start to cry but they don't see my face covered by the trim of my parky, they don't see me, and they talk, they start to talk.

Faith finds her voice, it is a croak, and she answers Wind, "Yes. There is food. There is much food."

"I remember food," Wind says. "Not like here where I have to push and push myself at the seeds on the trees until I find something even close to what food was like out there. And then it does not taste the same. It is muted. Do you feel that way?" Wind asks.

"I don't know what food tastes like here."

"Hmm. Maybe because you are not of here. Permanently."

"What do you mean?" Faith asks. And Wind stretches under Mom, moves on the snow. And then it's like Mom is talking through Wind, I can see her mouth move, like it moved against my cheek when she'd kiss me, saying, "My little girl, what you been up to my little girl?" That smile she'd get in her voice when me and Keely been playing all day outside and our cheeks are ruddy and Mom's feeling good because we been getting some good northern air into us and getting some health from not being inside all cooped all day. I want to move from the log, and I can't move, but I see Mom go over to Faith and wrap her up. I close my eyes and I can feel her, and Faith, together, like I got the smells of them mingles all in there, Faith and me and her nanuk, my mom.

Mom nuzzles in to Faith's hood and pushes it back, musses her hair up, says, "All creatures and seasons come into one." Mom puts Faith down and then goes to clean the ulu off in the snow, as she pulls the beaver's fur and lays it on the snow. Wind nods his head at

Faith, lifts up her hood, grins at Mom with a sweeping breeze on her, and runs from us, toward the back hill lights. I can see the gusts of him in the lips of the snow he makes, Wind, always bringing old things. That's what the Snow Nanuks used to say, you could always count on Wind to bring you things. Now this, me and Faith and Mom.

Linda says that sometimes girls fall in love with other girls when they're confined or something, trying to make family. I don't say shit to her, but get a little scared, wondering how could she know that? She been watching me? But of course she been watching me, they're all watching me, and Deanne and the other girls, that's what them workers do, that's their job, how they getting their big government paycheque put right into their fat bank accounts. Deanne don't do nothing. Like she's not a hawk or nothing after me like that, though she seem some older than me. She got that girlfriend she keep talking about. She just come and sit with me and Faith in the TV room after we done in the classroom. I been giving Faithy her bottle and trying to whisper in her ear. I know what them doctors said, but sometimes I swear she move a little when I whisper in her ear, like she been hearing me.

Some days I feel happy so's I could touch that ceiling and then other days I can't stop thinking of Tyler and want to punch walls. And the days keep coming faster and less time with Faithy. Linda says, "Remember your breathing," and it's all I can do to go to my room and calm down. Or maybe I seen her with Faithy and she's been cooing at her or rocking her, and I know deep down she really loves Faith. Linda wants me to talk more about things, she says I'm too spacey only she doesn't say spacey she says detached. These walls, they're so white, and I inch around the chairs, and feel the legs of them, want to smash them through the windows. They got these wide windows that make it seem like we can see outside and it will make us better, not so stuck in here. When it's dark we don't see nothing but our own reflections. It makes me want to run through them. And the hallway. The hallway that ends in the cells on one side, then the little bathrooms, with the white stalls and white shower curtains, and then the classroom door that's always locked, even when we're locked in there and then the workers' station and the cameras, their TV screens that they look at, then the kitchen that is just one little room where Sherry is, and even though she smiles at me most days and she says, "How's it going, Trista, how's Faithy today?" And she comes over and takes Faith and Faith doesn't cry with her, and Sherry lets me make microwave popcorn when we've been good at night or the workers let us watch a movie, I still want to gash and scrape at these walls, scream them down to dust. Linda says if I keep not punching walls, if I'm learning the anger management, she's going to give me a present for Christmas, a reward of something her uncle made, and I want that reward bad, but sometimes, I'm in the shower and I don't have Faithy with me and I just want to punch into the tiles until my hands break.

Keely been coming around less. I didn't say, You're not allowed, but I'm thinking maybe she thinks she's got nothing more to say, maybe she thinks I only want to bug her for info about Tyler. On the phone she got all plans, talking about her school projects, talking about Christmas, what to get Tony for his present, her little brothers. Can't stop thinking about why she asked Jimmy over that night when she knew I was so fucked up over Tyler. Like she was a little bit happy Tyler was gone. Like she wanted me back with Jimmy, someone almost family, not some boy from down south like Tyler. Part of me knows Keely never do that on purpose, hurt me. Part of me knows too she hated me and Tyler's outside life, that life our friends seen us walking uptown and holding hands and not fighting outside the Northmart like her and Tony get into. I don't want to get smokes from her, feels like some bribe she giving me. Besides Deanne's been giving me some, and Deanne's so nice and says, "Whenever," when I ask her for one.

Keely's been trying to help me, and I love Keely like a sister. But she's outside there, walking with all them town people and doing school in the real class, taking care of her shit. I want to be out there, I want to be out of here.

Days like these I can't think about it, days like this one coming up Christmas, that lady looking at me, inside my head, and the Bitch is back from her training down YK but I don't know what she learned down there. She won't let me have phone privilege because she asked me to finish vacuuming but I was vacuuming then turned it off to go to the bathroom, but then forgot I was vacuuming and then she says, "Finish up what you were doing, Trista,"

"Okay I'm going," I says. But she gets into it with me and says, "Watch your tone."

"Okay!" I yell. And then she points to my room, which means she's not going to say it but it's a time-out and fuck her because I wasn't even doing anything and she treats me like I am two.

And even though I won't call Keely, or Auntie because I don't want to worry them, don't want to smash that excitement, that hope they got in their voices when they talk about the court case and trying to be upbeat about it all and how Faithy's gonna love her foster mom and it rips me inside but I still want to call someone, but this Bitch, I don't even give a shit what her name is, she doesn't even deserve a name, she won't let me have phone privilege because she is a bastard bitch whore all rolled into one.

Deanne walks by my room, whispers, "Careful, Trista, you keep pacing like that, they gonna put you in Iso," and I don't care, there's Deanne holding Faith, and seems like lately Faith seems settled with everybody in this stupid hole but me, all the times I take her and she's crying and fussing, and I don't want to go to Iso, but even at the workers' station can see that Bitch looking at me with her beady eyes and her fake hair-salon highlights like she's some flaming yellow witch come down to rain some hell on me.

"Trista. Do you need a PRN to calm yourself down?" Bitch worker says.

"Shouldn't be giving us drugs, just for that."

"What was that?" she says.

"We got to learn to cope, not with drugs," I says.

"Yes, but this is something the doctor left on order for you."

"Fucking doctor. Dr. Petterson? The fuck she know what I need?"

I start pacing again, scraping my fingernails down the wall and Deanne gets up and she's walking with me, and she's talking all low-like, "Hey, Trista, let me put Faithy down, what say we go have us a smoke, I got some tailor-mades that BoDean sent, what say? You got two more minutes on the timer, sit the fuck down and do out your time-out." And I sit as still as I can, and the timer rings and I request and go outside with her and that Bitch doesn't even nod at us, but Tracy, she comes out with us and I go get my parky and think good good good good good.

I can see the girls inside while I am smoking. Deanne lights up and passes a smoke to me. Tracy smokes too. I trace lines on the window, flick some snow off, pretend I am Window Lady looking in. That Bitch is holding Faith and she's rocking her like she owns her, and Faith is all mouth open and looking around in that faroff look she has.

"You work much with retarded kids?" I ask Tracy.

"Some," she says, "got a cousin who is slower."

"You think my baby's really fucked up?"

"She's got a chance, I think. Sometimes you can't tell till later, some get better, you know."

But she's got this down wind in her voice and I know she doesn't really believe it, and anyways she gets to be in on the assessments about Faith that they all tell me about but I don't really understand. The "cautious" findings and all that shit that says to me that Faith is more than fucked. Like the night she came out, she was doomed. And I know what I got to do. I smoke my cigarette and that Window Lady is lurking, I can't see her, but I can feel her and I know, I know Gus, God, Goddess, wherever, whatever the fuck you are, it's so fucking dark now, this December, I know what I got to do with my Faithy.

This is Deanne in Group, her fucking suck-up-get-better bullshit:

"So I was thinking about how I needed to call up my old girlfriend and tell her that our relationship is too abusive and too much like the old street life. So I can make more room for me and BoDean once I get down to YK, you know, to expand our relationship and get rid of the baggage."

And the workers are all nodding their heads like those bobbing sports dolls you see for Christmas at the Northmart and I can't stand her face, I want to smash it in and kiss it at the same time. It's like this when I can't think of Faith, like I am so inside my head and Deanne's. This is what Deanne looks like, when she's just sitting by the window or eating her lunch, she's got long long hair, and it's black, blacker than mine before it got all burned and I cut it. When she whips a look at you, first, it's hard and you think she's so mad at you, but then when you catch your breath and breathe a little she's smiling, and her smile melts like the ice on the road in June, slow-like, but then like a whoosh, it falls and the river underneath starts flowing blue.

I been writing her notes, I been writing some notes to her and when I pass her room to go in to my room to get Faithy a new diaper, I take the note and throw it on her bed, and sometimes she's sitting on her bed, reading some recovery book, and so I know she gets them, I know she reads them, and I know even the workers probably know, but I don't care I don't give a shit. How do they know? Never felt this way with Tyler, yes I did, yes I did, but what the fuck did that mean? I think that, especially when I'm holding Faith, I think that. Then I push it out of my head, because my court case is coming up in January and Christmas is coming and it's not any kind of Christmas we ever had and all them dreams we were having, me, him, Faith in our trailer, what happened to them?

They're gone, really, and then I see Deanne walking by my room, she's real tall and she's just so tough-glinty, like behind her black eyes there's something that's never going to break, and I need that. It makes my stomach go all up and down and we are sitting in the TV room and them workers are letting us watch some Romeo and Juliet because Miss Sarah said we needed to for class, and I am sitting near her and Linda has Faith up at the workers' station and I can hear them cooing at Faith, and then we are sitting so close, on the couch, me and Deanne, and we're not touching, but I can smell her hair, like she just washed it with some strawberry-smelling shampoo, and that smell better than the smell of the real fruit we get up when the Fruitman can make it on the ferry. Up summertime and walking through town with Keely, and feeling the sun on our faces, and not slipping around in the muck and mud. Everything's dry in Jackfish Bay and we got slushies in our hands and we're laughing and the sun is so hot, that July month when we get that one week of thirty-plus and it's so hot, and we can feel the sun soaking into our arms, and everyone is uptown and just watching everyone else.

And I smell Deanne's hair and I inch closer to her and I feel this flush and imagine her and me behind the school, and it's that killer July day and we can smell the grasses growing, like they're straining so hard to grow grow grow so fast cause they only going to have that one month, then it's getting cold again. And she's smelling so good, and I tug at her long black hair and she closes her eyes and we kiss, and her lips are so soft, it's like a little electric shock, like in winter when there's so much static if you turn out the lights and play the shock game, you can see these little sparks of blue. And I don't know care where Faith is and I don't know where Tyler is, and I know where Mom is, still in the hard cold permafrost, but I don't care 'cause I got someone and it's this girl, Deanne, and she is mine.

That Bitch worker come in again. We sitting on the couch and the workers turn on some DVD for us, something about drugs and rehab, but I wasn't really watching it. Holding Faith and then touching Deanne's hand. I got to talking to her again, and in my head, in my imaginings she says she and Mary now going to break up and she says she's just in it for me and Faith. I don't care if I believe her right now or nothing, I am just thinking for today.

Got her sliding her hand to me under Faith's quilt and it just feels right to sit like that and not think about nothing. The movie's got some nice scenes, like out somewhere where they got lots of trees that change those colours. Like our grasses out the back change when it's getting on spring and the snow's melted. But then the Bitch come in and say, "Deanne, no PDA." Deanne moves right away from me. I'm thinking, PDA, what the fuck is that? And Deanne mouths to me, No Public Displays of Affection. It's like we're in a jail down south from some stupid teenager TV show every time the Bitch come on. Aimee comes up to me and sits beside where Deanne left. "You can cut my hair?" she asks me.

"Yeeah," I says. "But tomorrow, when Linda gets in."

"They not giving you them shears today?" Aimee says.

"No way with the monster on."

She gets up and goes over to do more rug hooking. I'm thinking on putting Faith down in her crib, doing some more myself. We got so much rug hooking going on, Linda calls us the Happy Hookers and her and Deb laugh it up some. I know it's funny, what seeing Deanne setting there and she's got the Dumbo one covering her legs, it's the big one, you can put it up on a wall of a kid's room or something. And she's got her head bent down, all serious, and she's rug hooking. The Happy Hooker from Yellowknife. Deanne says to Linda, "Oh, you happy I'm hooking something. Don't give me no herpes, right, Linda?" And Linda laughs with her. Was Deb who brought them, boxes and boxes of them from the Tru Valu in Inuvik. Storekeeper donated them to us, for something to do. Deb and Linda and them other workers went in and had a meeting even, because we have to use these little eyehook things to hook the small pieces of yarn with, and were we going to hook each other's eyes out. Linda says to us, "You girls are a good group we got going here. Opening up, starting to act nicer to one another. We going to let you use those tools, but no putting eyes out, use your words." Megan nodded, me and Deanne of course we not doing nothing to each other even I get shit mad at her, then there's Aimee wouldn't say boo to a fawn it slapped her in the face.

Quiet before Christmas, seems like it's unreal, not even really Christmas like before when you're outside and all the decorations up Northmart. We got them here too, but not all that plastic shit. We're just rug hooking away. Deanne's already got her first one hanging in her room, they had to come and put special nails in it, because that was her Cinderella one and it was so damn heavy with yarn. It's a real beauty too, Cinderella when she's just looking in the mirror at herself with the pretty ballgown on and them little mice all around her, with some lace and ribbons going in and out her hair.

I go to put Faithy down and the Bitch got to come in and look, just to show she know I know she's looking. I try to ignore, like Linda says, "Why you think she pisses you off so much, Trista?" This is Group last time. I don't say nothing. I want to scream at Linda,

"She pisses everyone off, not just me." But I don't say shit because that's going to set Linda off like she thinks she's on a personal mission to find out just who that bitch is in your past and why she's renting your headspace so much. Sometimes a bitch worker is just a bitch worker, for fuck's sake.

I put Faith down and she's making that gurgling sound she does when she's just about to drop off. She's clutching at her blanket and I move it down some her sleeper otherwise she has it near over her head and all tangles in it when she sleeps. She's looking a little at me. I swear it. Sometimes I think she can see the shape of me, and I tell the doctor that when she comes, I tell Dr. Petterson, and the doctor looks a little glad to hear it. It's not much but it's what she's doing right now and she's not spitting up the formula so much any more, and I also swear it that she's getting fatter, like her little bum feels heavier to me when I'm cradling her and then lifting her up, Deanne says too. I pull the blanket away and lean in good and move my lips against her cheek, does she ever smell good, doesn't matter if she hasn't had a full on bath in the back sink, she smells so baby and new skin. Then I turn out the light in my room and go pick up my hook rug. I got Winnie-the-Pooh, the one where he's leaning back and he's got this big jar of honey that's almost empty at his feet, he's leaning back all fat and stuffed with honey, honey on his paws and all over his cheeks and there's bees going around. The bees were a bitch to do, they're so small. But I'm working on Winnie now and he's bigger and easier to do. Almost big enough for a rug, like to put over the baby out on the land. Faith starts to fussing. I go and bite a little at her cheeks, not hard, just enough that she's got a bit of my spit on her and she does her gurgling, jerks her fists up like she's trying to punch me out. I rub her belly and she calms some.

It's Friday and Linda's in and in a fine mood too, and that's awesome because we had that Bitch three days in a row and that makes us grumpy. We're all of us happy for Linda coming in, even

Deanne is up and joking some with them. I ask for the shears and Linda gives me the leather case with all the hairdressing tools in it without even asking me, or looking into my eyes.

"Aimee, you ready?" I ask.

"Yeeah."

"Come and set here, the light's better," I says.

"Okay."

"What you want? I can't do nothing fancy. Deb says there's not but three main haircuts, but maybe I know two. Layered and not layered."

"I want it all cut off."

"Like a bob?" I says.

"No. Cut it all, short, like a boy."

"You serious."

"Yeeah, sick of my hair. Dad used to love my hair, come home and put his hands in it, Mom still working and me and him in the living room. Fuck it. No more long hair."

I run my hands through her hair, then get the brush to make it right smooth. I'm thinking about her on her couch with her dad, only the couch got patterns like the one me and Mom used to have before Auntie sold it. They didn't need another couch like ours, when I moved in with Auntie and Nanuk. Richard's there and he's stroking my hair. I got that clasp in, the one I got in kindergarten, the one with the two red apples hanging off it. Every time he pushes his hands through my hair, it tugs at that clasp and it's like it hurts and I want to tell him, but I don't want him to stop. I'm wishing Mom would stay at work all night, so she can't come in and then get me off to bed, and then Mom and Richard are setting on the couch all night.

I get the shears out and I start cutting on one side Aimee's head, her long hair coming down. She's mixed like me but her hair doesn't show it, she's got dark brown almost black hair like roasted chestnuts

Nanuk put in the stove for Christmas. But as I cut it, I see lots of light bits in it, light brown underneath and some golden stuff too like the sun decided to just come out from under it. As I get closer and closer to her face though it starts to lighten up more, picking up a nice golden to her face that looked so sickly when her hair was long. Deanne goes and get the broom, we're not saying much. Even Megan comes in and doesn't say anything because it's a big deal and we don't say shit when a big deal's going on. Aimee's face, when I go in front and start to layer out her bangs, she's getting younger and younger. It's still her same old thin Aimee face, but she's smiling and she looks so little. Like we're seeing that little kid inside her, all her hair been covering that kid up. She's got these nice dark eyebrows that are shaped. When I sweep her bangs to one side to check and see if they're even, she looks at me, and then I suddenly feel like I am looking into someone much much older, just the eyes. I move to the sides and even them out more. A short cut is just like a long layer. You just got to make sure the layers are even in the layering, like they don't got bits that stick out none. When I am done, I use the brush to get at the little bits. It's fast, and I hold the mirror up to her. She doesn't grin, but I know she's got it in her eyes that she likes it.

"Thanks, Trista. It feels so light on my neck. Let's go out for a smoke, I owe you one," Aimee says.

"Yeeah, let me pack up and I'll be out."

I clean up all the tools, flick the bits of hair off the shears, and brush down the table. Deanne's sweeping up the floor and Megan says, "Lookit all that hair, we could sell it to a wig store or something." I shake out the towels in the sink and get those last bits of hair into the trash, put the towels in the wash, and zip up the leather tool case, give it back to Linda. "She looks good, Trista. Those haircutting magazines Sherry brought in for you helping any?"

"Some. She wanted short, that's easy. Used to give the boys short before I came in."

We're in the living room and Aimee is hooking a rug, Deanne's writing a letter and Megan is on the computer in the corner playing Spider Solitaire, because Deb is on and she lets us do shit like that because she doesn't think it's going to rot our brains just for one night to be normal. Not like we can get on the internet. Sometimes in the classroom Miss Sarah lets us on it, to do some research about Anne Frank or maybe we're looking up the Mackenzie Delta, that was cool that one time because I swear I could see some polar bear in Sachs, but Deanne just goes, That's ice coming away from the shore, too damn big to be polar bears, you goof. And it's like Deb knows what's going on between us. Most times we're not allowed in other girls' rooms. Deanne finishes her letter and comes and helps me put Faithy down in her crib and then Deanne pulls me in to her room because she's showing me her hookrug, the one that's done with the Bambi on it. It's good, lots of blues around it in different blue colours and then it's got the little thing in the middle, brown and big-eyed. It would be good for the baby's bed, we got someplace else to go, out of here. I run my hands over it, and it's warm and nubbly and Deanne come up behind me and presses me against it. I let her, she goes, "Wouldn't mind putting you on that rug, lick you up some." And I start to shiver, she's running her hands up my side. I know we only been in there a few minutes but thinking on Deb catching us as Deanne puts her tongue on my neck. I want to but it makes me think of the future, where they gonna put me for my crime, how long it's gonna be. Deanne's got her older girlfriends in YK too, what she gonna do with me and a baby? And then Tyler, the shit, the stank-ass whiteboy running out on us. Who the fuck cares? Don't want no great white fucking hope saving my ass anyways. Like Linda says, "Why you keep thinking that Tyler is going to come up and take you out of here, Trista? Jackfish Bay is your home, will always be your home. You can go away but you can't take it out of you. How you going to deal with it?"

Deal with it? By going, by fucking leaving, by getting out of here. But I can't think about that and Deanne's got her mouth on mine, she's pulled me around and she's really into it. I'm liking it, it feels so good to be kissed, but it's like I am standing above us, like I am bigger somehow and watching all this with giant's eyes. I can see me, and Deanne's hands in my hair and she kisses good, her tongue flickering in and out. And me slowly into it back at her. I can see Deanne wants to push me on the bed and I want to go with her, my legs start to move and it's like we are joined at the belly. But then I move and she looks at me.

"What?" she says.

Who's the great white hope, I got any hope with this girl too? I got to start thinking forward like Linda says. But why should I listen to her anyways, what she got going on too. That Linda, she just working up here some stupid job with fucked-up girls and then she got her own girl at the high school in Inuvik, doesn't even live with her, lives in the residence for the school kids who have parents out in the communities. Like our little school Jackfish Bay not good enough for her. Deanne is kissing me and I can see us in a little apartment in YK and Faith is in her own room with lots of blue about, she likes blue if she could see it more, I know she'd like some blue. Deanne's making little sounds. I want to close my eyes and go there, but I keep thinking about Deb, and Deanne hears someone coming and we break apart.

"Girls. Come out into the living room," Deb says and I know she knows but she doesn't say anything.

Later Deanne's on the phone and I'm wondering why Deb's letting her on phone privilege so long. I pick up Faith and bring her into my room, thinking that the workers can think I'm going to have a nap, sometimes me and Faith do that before dinner. But I can't think. I close my door and hear the snick automatically shut, even though it isn't till bedchecks that they really lock us in. Faith is sleeping. It's when she sleeps that she looks almost normal and I can almost believe everything's going to work out for her. She's going to find a good family, with a real mom and even a dad, and maybe an older sister who does right by her and even can talk some stories to her, she's less than quarter, like me, she's only an eighth Inuvialuit, and how lost them stories going to be to her? All the things she's got shutting her off. I try to cheer myself up a little, I really do, but I can still hear Deanne's voice. I try to think of me and Deanne in a camp tent we made together up Husky Lakes a stretch. And we're outside in the long sun, past 2 a.m., and the fire's going and we're telling each other about some stories when we were little, or maybe she's got some stories about her Dene people and we're not talking nothing about Yellowknife or her fucking guys, or her kissing Mary or her even leaning over and kissing me, just us, under the midnight sun.

Like the elders are saying we can all make the good times again. We have to work at it together to bring the Snow Nanuks back and listen to them. That maybe out on the land we can do better. And after Mom died and then Auntie was out a lot, down at the bar, because you drink up some pain. Then Richard too starts to ignore me and then I'm out the backfield with Keely. Me and Keely go over with the boys at Nanuks and I try not to think about how we were over there at the Snow Nanuks, try not to think about how long ago we were over there almost every day. We're supposed to be in school most days and most days we are. But we spend a lot of nights at the Snow Nanuks. Most times we play, they got all these board games up on the shelf with the torn covers half the time we don't know how to play them, just making it up.

"No, Keely, you got to match up the dots, like the twos have to go with the threes," I says.

"But that don't give you enough, then what you do?"

Me and Keely at her mom's right before I went in, I got my belly out in front of me and Tyler gone and I just spend that week before Jimmy in some kind of froze-up place. I try to turn to the boys, watch them wrestle and fight, watch them chortle or giggle over some stupid TV show, some stupid thing that Elmo says and I can't believe they can still find that funny, Keely's brothers. Yeeah, they still got that like innocence in their big black eyes. I can see it when I wipe their faces, tell them the candy going to rot their teeth and they'd be young men of twenty with their teeth falling out, and they gets these big eyes, looks at me, "For reals? Going to hurt like at the dentist forever?" Then they run and brush them teeth so hard I figure they got long long teeth gleaming through their gums like the teeth of the dogs on the dogteam—meat-eating teeth that can rip and tear at raw flesh, some muskrat or beaver their sled-driver caught down by the Gwich'in camp.

But back then, even froze, somewhere inside there was Faith rolling about and maybe even telling me, even after Tyler gone, that I can do it too. Before Jimmy, before fucking it up again. Why didn't we stay at the Snow Nanuks, me and Keely, why we go running out to the bars?

"You did what all the kids were doing, Trista."

"What?" I say.

It's Deb beside me in Group and that fucks me up some because I am in my head. Deb's face is like the Snow Nanuks, the one who had the long hair she twisted up and had in a bun. Deb's younger but got eyes like her.

"I don't want to leave Jackfish Bay. I want Keely to come to YK, maybe come live with me, Faith come later too."

"Keely can visit you. She has to grow too, Trista," Deb says.

"Some family."

Keely and me are working at the Northmart, I got Faith in my belly maybe four, five months. Some days it's sweet with Tyler. Some days I know he's in his head and is drugging and drinking too much and I think he got this look in his eye that says he's going, but I fucking ignore that, I fucking push that out of my head. We get off the Northmart at 6 p.m.

We're standing over by the jewellery section and some people from the bar, they smiling at us. Sometimes it's real hard to work that section of the Northmart, especially on a Sunday when the liquor store is closed and you get some of the old people in, buying the hairspray. Donnie, the shift manager, he says, "Okay, but only let them have four." He's from Newfoundland and I guess he knows that shit there too. I don't want to give it to them, but the way they're pushing the bottles across the counter toward me, and they're looking down at my nametag, and they says, "Yeeah, Trista, knew you when you were no higher than a jackrabbit, at your mom's knee." But then their eyes get some clouds in them and I know then they remember I don't got Mom any more and for a minute there they were forgetting, the hairspray on their mind, but they don't forget once they look at me. I look like her that much now.

And this one woman, she's smiling and some of her teeth I can see just got filled by the dentist, all shiny with that fake white, and her tongue is flicking out, and we just pretend. We pretend she's going home to fix her hair. Roll her long long grey hair up in some spongy pink rollers she bought last week, pin them, and ask her husband: "Ya see any strands I'm missing in the back, honey?" and he says, "No, darlin', and chee, you're looking good tonight," and she's blushing like she's fourteen again, and she's looking at herself in the mirror and she feels good, don't she, she feels good because they're going out tonight to see their young ones, and maybe play some of the TV bingo, and laugh some over some old jokes and remembering and then maybe go bundle up in their parkys, get the little ones in their snowboots and all warmed up in their gear and maybe take a Ski-Doo ride after dinner, what go see if they can scare up some foxes in the side bush just few minutes short of town. But they're not going to.

This old one. Her hands are shaking as she hands me the twenty-dollar bill, she's shaking and she can't wait to get home to pour the hairspray into a glass and add some ice and Coke and pretend it's Jack Daniels or Jim Bean, and drink it down while her kids' kids are playing the Nintendo they brought over, because they hate talking to Nanuk when she's drunk, they hate talking to their hairspray-drinking Nanuk, so she stays in the kitchen and smokes and hides the hairspray bottles and counts her coins out till tomorrow and tells herself, "Morning come and I can get me a real nice drink."

But there's Keely and me, we're off shift. Sometimes Keely, when it goes bad with Tyler and me, she's saying, "You can come live with us." I know that, I do know that but me and Tyler when he's talking the good shit, we got little Faith coming. But I do save for smokes, though Keely's always saying, "Why don't you roll some more with me?" But I'm only saving for Tyler, I don't smoke much of his, I'm quitting soon, I swear I am. It doesn't look good for the little kids around to see me smoking and I'm getting bigger in the belly now, they can see and I watch them, just looking what all us adults are doing, gets this line up near their brows like we all some strange creatures they're trying so hard to figure out. And we are.

I pull off my Northmart vest and I grab Keely. "Want to go over see we get a good DVD?" I say to her, and all is good, it's Tuesday night and I don't care what Tyler's getting up to, if he's going to freak out I'm not coming home to him, but going home with Keely, my family.

"You'll have that, honey," Deb says to me. "Sometimes you have to leave before you can really come back home."

Tuesday, and time is going faster, it's some days now, only some days now, and I try to breastfeed Faith but Linda says, "Trista. She won't take it any more." And I just hold her I want to hold her every second I can. And Deanne, she's looking at me, we're eating some pie that Sherry made. We don't get much time to just sit, with Group, and school, and work training, and Faith at me for more formula, and she's starting her crying early and I just want to sit with Deanne and eat this pie. Sherry's making all different kinds so we have them for like a special Christmas week of pies. It's a weird kind, I didn't eat much pie growing up, maybe Auntie brought some ice cream up from the Northmart when it was getting almost old and she'd scoop that bit off that had the freezer burnt on it. Most times we only had the ice cream right as the ice broke up on the Mackenzie, that time sometimes a month or longer when we don't got the Fruitman coming up, the road too mushy for his rig, or the ferries aren't running down McPherson way. Then all the milk and lettuce and oranges get bought up, and what doesn't is priced up, until it's almost gone bad. Then Auntie goes in and buy the cheese with the blue shit on it, and the ice cream that's getting old, the milk with that layer you got to strain off, but it doesn't smell bad, just got to get the stuff off then it tastes fine.

Deanne, sometimes she's pushing her hair back from her face and her mouth is moving around the fork that's got the pie on it, the lemon meringue, Sherry called it, we seen her mixing up the egg whites and making it all peaks with the egg beater, and Deanne's talking about … something, maybe BoDean or Mary, or some Yellowknife fun thing she's remembering. But I can't hear her really, it's like I got an ice ball whacked in my head, how you'd come out from the school and someone's yelling, "Ptarmigan!" and they whack you with a hard ice ball, and your head is whoozing while you just ignore them and grab your smokes, stand a little to the side, 'cause if you look up at them they gonna get you again, yeeah.

"Trista, you want more pie?" Deanne says.

"No."

"You thinking big things?"

"No." But I am, I am, I want to scream at her, Come with me, I'm gonna take her and we're gonna get out of here. Please, Deanne, come with me and we can go out on the land and just live there like old times, like the Snow Nanuks done long ago, won't you come with me please?

"Come on, we gotta do these dishes before Group," Deanne says. She squeezes my hand as she gets up with the plates, and I want to start crying, it's that fierce and sudden and I feel like some newborn arctic Wind, just inching blind around the den.

It's Linda and me talking, just one on one in the corner of Iso they use when no one is fucked up, just for some private time. Linda's doing some shrink talk, but I'm not letting her know it's not gonna work. I got plans now.

"You wanna tell me about it?"

"What's that?

"You and Deanne?" Linda says.

And I got this fearball coming up my throat, tasting like puke. I guess my eyes go all round and trying for innocent, 'cause then she says to me: "Trista, anyone can see, not time to be embarrassed about it. But you have to talk about it. Do you think it's realistic?"

"Maybe." What's realistic, what's realistic, bitch. But then I think, Linda's not a bitch, Linda's not like that other worker who comes in here try to rile me up and get me going. Linda, she's the one who knows when I'm calling Tyler, and how long and when he's not calling me, and it's been a long long time, can't hardly remember our place and why.

"Trista, she's with someone else. And she's also not from here. She doesn't live like you," Linda says.

Live like me? Like not hurting someone who didn't do us no harm? Kicking the shit out of Mavis. And even she's been there when I was buying licorice sticks since I was little. Mavis who'd give us some extra five-cent candies, even we got no money to pay her back later, Mavis at the Aurora Store who'd chuck us under the chin, say, "Chee, you're growing big, getting pretty, your hair nice and thick and long." That's Mavis Gibson who comes to my window, that Window Lady.

And, Linda, you're thinking I'm not like Deanne, got no violence in my life like Deanne got, some street in me like Deanne got. What I got now? I don't got shit, but a fucked-up baby, and a court case I don't have a fucked chance of getting out of. Soon I got no fucked-up baby, no messed-up retarded-forever baby, who can't look straight at me when she cries, who can't hear me when I sing some songs Mom taught me, not to her, not to my Faithy. And then they're taking her away, and then, if all I got is Deanne, and all we got is kissing a little while we're out on smoke break, and just after school when they let us on bathroom break, then right before bedchecks before my door snicks closed and locks me and Faithy in, then that's what I fucking got, that's all I fucking got. I don't care if it's unrealistic. Plans and plans and plans.

"Trista. You talking about this, or holding it all in?"

"Talk about what?"

Deanne's on the phone again talking to all her YK friends about Christmas and making it sound like she's gonna have some huge feast party when she down there and she done all her court case and she went for sentencing today and got time to do in YK and why is she all thinking it's just fine now? Just leave? Just fucking pack up and leave? Aimee's talking quietly at Megan while they're hooking some rugs. This is after school, after Miss Sarah trying to get us to do more math. I can't think math straight in my head, and Faith is crying, can hear her all the way at the workers' station, imagine Linda's got her and she's pacing up and down the hall to calm her some. Faith been like that for days now. Like she's restless and wants me to fucking play with her all the time, look at her, feed her, cuddle her. And Mavis at the window is saying something. It's all nonsense to me, but it's like her mouth is open and screaming at me and them words are coming out, but they aren't English or Inuvialuktun, or any words I can figure on. But it's hard to juggle Faith and try to get that bottle nipple in her mouth, ignore Mavis at the window, then see Deanne get up and ask for more phone privilege. She's on there right now.

Deanne's on the phone I can hear her laughing. She showed me a picture of BoDean, and BoDean looks like some fucking guy, wearing a Mac jacket and short hair, and smoking and looks like she's trying to be a rig-pig or something, and Deanne's in the picture too, and she's laughing. She's at the phone, laughing like that now, I can see her and she's twisting the phone cord in her hands, and pushing her hair back away from her eyes, like she does when she is happy.

Can't you hear me? I don't want you to leave. Don't go. But Deanne just keeps talking and I look down at Faith and think, Me and you, me and you, me and you now.

Daduk, when he was home from camp for Christmas week. Daduk come over and sit on the couch just Uh-yeeah-ing, smiling at me, he lost his teeth long before, and he's got to chew that caribou drymeat to shit, but Auntie, she cooks some fresh meat nice and slow so he can gum through it, he's laughing all the way. Daduk'd eat, then talk about going up Husky Lakes with the dogsleds when he was a boy. They'd even make some icehouses, even though the NWT put up sheds there even when he was little. But his dad teach him how to cut ice in the squares, build it up and in, nice and tight, with a furnace hole at the top. They'd go in, him and his little brothers, bring in some good seal skins, their beaver and caribou moccasins, get all cozy inside and talk stories. This is after Christmas dinner, after, when Auntie's maybe gone out, and Nanuk's sitting smoking and watching the CBC, sad because the town decided no bingo on Christmas nights. Daduk just set there, get to laughing about the little games, his eyes going up so I can't even see them any more, all lost in wrinkles.

"Trista, the snow. Was like it smelled different then. Not this dirty shit smell you got here in Jackfish Bay, near can smell the stink of the oil and the shit them military put in the Mackenzie a way's back. This snow, up Husky Lakes, was like smelling some holy arctic bear kick up white chocolate, pure and fresh. Me and my little brothers, we got our furs against that packed icehouse snow, laughing about some Wind we chased, breath so white, it blinds streaks against the snow. Even sun up, we're laughing till four in the morning, little Wills telling stories of Wind, how Wind come up in his dreams, pull him down to the Lakes and dunks him in once, two three times. Little Wills, he had some story in him, he did. He tells how Wind just wrestling him under the cold lake water, growling at him, 'Now, Wills, you gonna come up in the world and stop chasing after me with your slingshot and rocks. You leave my breeze alone, not anything for you to have.' And Wills is all sputtering that lake water, spitting out at Wind, 'Never you mind, Wind, I after you till the day I'm hanging your white breath off my new slidey dogsled, mighty Wills, that's what they gonna call me, Wind hunter!' Wind is screaming at him, the way Arctic Winds can when they're good and mean, you don't hear that much up here, but of a day when the lights are bright and just so, and they're out on the snow hunting up some new seeds to scatter, and they look up at the sun, knowing they look so good, thinking they even better than Wolf or Bear or Caribou, well, right then, you hear the Arctic Wind call, and that's Wills got him screaming like that now.

"That time, up in the icehouse Husky Lakes, Wills maybe seven, but he's got the story strong in him, and we're all silent, thinking about that Wind scream. Then Davey, who's maybe a year older than

Wills, but always got to best him, Davey asks, 'Where's that Wind breath now, Wills? Yeeah, you full of shit, you don't got no Wind breath.' Davey, always trying to kill the stories. Wills sits up some. 'That breath, buried out near these Lakes, something sacred that breath. Have to give it back to the land Wind lives.' And we looking back and forth between them. Me thinking, I got brothers wiser than shit, and I lie myself back, real tired, can hear the adults up a stretch laughing, they got the bottle out already. And me and my brothers, we know then's a good time to stay in the icehouse, let them laugh and curse it all off some hours, so we lie ourselves back and sleep."

I whisper into Faithy's ear, "Stories and stories I gonna tell you, little girl. Me and you all wrapped up in snow, safe and warm and tucked in."

Been a long time since Daduk come round Auntie's and talked the stories. Sometimes he go off from Nanuk, live up by himself past the backfield aways in his old cabin. Seems right before Mom died, he's round a lot, and talking to us, and laying off the bottle even. But now, all's I seen him is around the Icebox Bar, with his old friends. Playing like those adults he used to talk about, all's they got is the bottle between them and a lot of shit talk. But Daduk, when I first come in here, he come around, once. He come around and give me some smokes he rolled himself, tell me: "Trista, you don't got to go round fucking things up. So get it good now." And even I know what he said, I think it's long over, some days I don't got any hope for no one. All's I seen are Daduk's sad eyes looking at me like he knows he's talking hopeful shit, and me and Faith, we got nothing.

"Trista?"

"Yeeah."

"You need to engage with Faith more. You seem listless these days. You want to talk about the good news about her placement and what Dr. Petterson said about her brain scan?" Deb says.

"Tell us," Megan says. Aimee's beside her, looking at me with her big eyes, that haircut I give her making her look so different. Even Deanne's grinning at me like some monkey.

"Maybe," I says. "Maybe she's gonna be okay."

"What about her hearing," Aimee says quietly.

"Not good," I says.

"She will probably always be deaf, Trista. But there's lots of things that the doctors can do now. When she's older," Deb says.

"Yeeah."

"I'm making her a hookrug, Trista, for her Christmas present, just for her," Aimee says.

All them Christmases, like they're running into one, and I don't even have that many to remember. The only one I remember of Mom, maybe a month or two before she died. How she liked to spend one whole paycheque on all just Christmas stuff, walking around the Northmart for going on an hour, even though we know everything in that store front and centre. I'm up in the cart, and Keely's with us, she's standing at the end and making mouth faces at me, pulling cookies and shit off the shelves, Mom's just laughing at her. And we're not rushed, like we usually are in the Northmart, in and running out, trying to get shit home before everyone in town shopping here after work.

"You girls want I should get some spaghetti for the night after Christmas? Something easy to make when we're all tired?" Mom asks.

"Yeeah," I says. "That kind." And I'm pointing and Keely grabs it, dropping it next to me.

"We're gonna have the best time, the good times, Daduk's coming, and your nanuk's bringing all her good friends," Mom says.

Or maybe she doesn't. Maybe I can't remember that. Maybe I just remember me and Keely going into Northmart stoned out of our minds on some crazy weed that Tony's brought up from YK, and we're just wandering around the Northmart, first the TV section, and then the manager kicks us out for sitting on the couches, because who knows some day, who knows what fucking day, someone's going to come in with their bingo or rig or welfare money and buy a twenty-seven-inch TV, and us townies better the fuck move on and not sit all stoned on his couches. Then we walk up to the cafeteria and order shitty fat-covered fries and wait for them, sitting in the little seats and there's some elders but we don't look at them because they're always looking at us with sad eyes, like they don't know anything about the weed we been smoking but they can smell the "don't cares" in the way we slouch at the table, they wonder at us, if their friends have got to us under the covers when we supposed to be little and safe and sleeping, and they're drunk and fucked up and wanting. Then we get our fries and eat them all globby with gravy because we are so hungry suddenly, we have the munchies and we pretend we're at the coffee shop in YK and we're cool like those kids living down there, who smoke weed and have money to go to the Boston Pizza or the coffee shop, but all we're doing is pretending in this shit-ass dirty fucking Jackfish Bay. Then Keely gets up, says, Gotta go home and babysit. Auntie working up the grocery section, and Nanuk's gone, and I don't want to go home to the quiet house.

When you're on the Iceroad in winter, it is dark. You can't see the blue hard ice under you, the cracks and the fissures that sometimes you bump into, you could get a flat and not know it until you're in the snowbank.

There are rig trucks coming up and down, some of their headlights beamed at you, and when you're driving you can't help but look right into them. Even when you seen them, sitting in the back seat with Keely, and you're maybe four years old, maybe just going on five, and driving to Tuk to see some people, because your Mom said, "Get in," and it's dark and you don't want to go to Tuk, you want to stay home and it's late, but she says, "Get in," and so you get your blankets, because it's not a long ride, but some nights it could be real long and you want things to hold on to when you fall asleep in the car.

The northern lights, they're coming down at you, on the car, and you're little, wondering if this is it, will this be the last time you seeing Jackfish Bay, and is Mom going to drive right off of Tuk and into the Arctic Sea? Keely says she heard they find cars, just off in the ocean, lost on the ocean ice, lost the road path and gone, and don't even find them until break up, and then there's a car full of dead people washing to shore.

Mom's not talking to us, in the dark of the car, she's putting on lipstick and mascara, her left arm on the steering wheel. I am watching her but she can't see me, and I think she is beautiful, she is so pretty, she's whispering, "Fuck," when she jabs her eye with the mascara brush, then wipes it away and tries to put some more on.

The northern lights are like streaks of slime that Keely and I'd play with, some weird shit we got at the Northmart, you put it in your hands and it'd slide out, you couldn't hold on to it, then it'd go into the snow and we'd kick at it, bury it.

The drive is long this time, but then, quickly, we're up the riverbank and in Tuk and on the town streets, you can see the lights on in people's houses but that's all, little bits of warmness. Mom stops at a house and we pile out, Keely and I grab our blankets, and then Mom brings us into this room, says, "Go to sleep." And there's no TV or nothing, just a picture on the wall of a big dead polar bear lying on his side, a blob of red in his side, and a hunter standing over it with a spear in his hand. She's gone and I sleep, huddled up to Keely, because there's a heater but it's not on and we're cold. Then later Keely is way past sleeping long, and I wake up to some noise, have the fuzzies in my eyes, the door opens. A man stands there. He's tall, with some light coming up behind him from the hallway. He's got a beard and it's got orange glints in it. "Which one is she?" he says. And Mom comes up beside him, points at me. They seen me watching them. But the man doesn't say any more. Just looks right at me, his eyes something warm in them. Then he closes the door.

Can't remember the way back that time, can't remember coming home to Jackfish Bay or dropping off Keely, or even Mom in the mirror.

"Trista. Give her to me, rest your arms," Linda says.

"No. No, I gotta calm her, I can calm her. Just let us be. I can make her stop, see? I put the hare's tail against her face and it helps, she calming down, just give her some time, let us be."

Snow Nanuk is singing, cutting the sinews from the caribou skin, and wrapping the beaver pelts up, rolling them together with the muskrat furs.

"What are they for, Nanuk?" I says.

"For the Inuvik Jamboree and we got to get ready. We can make all our clothes and moccasins and mukluks, and parkys for our families, so they are nice and warm in the winter, and we can bring the rest to Jamboree, so that other families who don't make the crafts, they can also be warm."

"What's Jamboree?"

And the minute I ask it, I can see it again, like Nanuk up and put that thought inside my head for me, out on the ice, the Ski-Doos and the trucks lined up on the snowy banks, the kids running about, and the Ski-Doos in the middle of the Iceroad, screaming past and kicking up the fine layer of snow on the road. The booming of the speaker, "That's a win for Derek Ford!" And the boy comes up on his Ski-Doo, gets off, and accepts the trophy, he is grinning, and the photographer from the newspaper takes his picture. The Nanuks are in their Mother Hubbard parkys, red, green, and blue, some with the flowers on them, some with little designs like animals, they are holding hot cups of boiled tea that Auntie makes, in the tent, over the big big cookstove. I go into the tent, and Auntie says, "There's my girl, did you catch a hare's tail yet?" And she gives me a cup of hot chocolate.

The booming of the loudspeaker again and all the kids are running down to see the harpoon toss. "Keely, c'mon!" I scream but it's just to hear myself because she's right there beside me. I run with them, seeing at their legs pumping, arms, and the hot chocolate spills on the snow, brown and rich, Keely is beside me, laughs at me. Grabs up my cup of hot chocolate and drinks from it, her mouth a chocolate smile.

"Hurry, Trista," she says, "we gonna miss the toss, Ralph Finder gonna go first and he's the champ." She takes my gloved hand and we run together, and she doesn't run as fast as I know she can, because Keely was always the one who was the fastest at any racing the Snow Nanuks made us do, get some energy off the burn they says to us, c'mon run it off, little ones. I don't look at Keely, but I love her for it, watch her feet pound on the packed snow, the glints of blue from the Iceroad far under it, my tongue out to catch the tiny flakes coming down from the sky, mixing with my breath.

Later, I'm alone and wandering the tables with all the beaded slippers, parkys, mukluks, and clothing on them, the rows of jewellery, touching the necklaces, and the Nanuks don't say, "Get your grubby hands offa them, little one," They just letting me touching the stuff they made. "You know what that's made of, Trista?" I look up into a face I don't know, can't think of who it is, but then know. It is Nanuk Marjorie, one of my Snow Nanuks. "It's made from the woolly mammoth tusks from long ago, they were like elephants, see the picture? The pendant is made from mammoth ivory, and it's very very old. You can touch it." I hold the necklace. It's like my ulu necklace, but this one is shaped like a little muskox, I put my fingers over it and remember Snow Nanuks knitting with the muskoxen underfur, the qivviat. And while I hold it in my palm, I can imagine the huge woolly mammoth creatures, snuffling and moving very slowly, maybe with their friends the muskoxen over the tundra, their big heads of hair crusted with snow and ice, their bodies huddled together and warm. "One day, when you are bigger, I'll teach you to carve," Nanuk Marjorie says. "Mostly it's the daduks who carved, before. But my daduk taught me, and one day, when your fingers are a little bigger and you can hold the instruments right, I'll teach you and Keely. Then you can make some things for jamboree too, save some Christmas money."

The muskox carving is smooth against my fingers, and I lay the necklace down. Keely's yelling at me, from the Iceroad: "Trista, c'mon, let's go see the dogsledding teams!"

The Snow Nanuks are sitting around the fire, it is dark as I wake up, and I'm in Nanuk's arms. "That was a long sleep, Trista, do you feel better?" And I nod, thinking, How I been sick, what I been sick from? And I'm glad I don't see no Richard sniffing around, but worried too, like where is he and how come he's not around. I wipe the sleep out of my eyes. I feel Nanuk stroking my hair, the best feeling this side of having Nanuk singing while she's working, soft. It's long again, my hair, I feel Nanuk's fingers sliding through it, and as I sit up, I can feel it sway against my neck.

"We're going to go on a little drive, Trista, c'mon and help me get packed up," Nanuk says.

I walk off the snow, and I'm in Nanuk's house, the old one, where Mom used to live. I can see the caribou on the plains picture, the oil painting of the old daduk with the pipe in his mouth, the kitchen and the light blue fridge, and the bathroom with the yellow walls and the mirror that has a tiny crack on the left side. These are all the things I know about the house, when we were there before me and Mom moved to our own house and then Richard moved in. Even the carpet, the way the dirt left some foot trails in the front hallway and all the shoes, all the kids shoes and adults boots, the parkys in the closet, all that wolverine lining. I'm snuffling my face into the smell of the coats. I can smell these people, long gone, all of them, these smells, I think. Nanuk's in my room, and I can see my little self, mouth open and breathing heavy with the kind of dry air winter sleep breathing. "Don't wake her up, Trista, she's still just little," Nanuk says, she's saying it to big me and we're looking at that kid, who looks a little like my Faithy.

Nanuk whispers, "Trista, stop dawdling, get a move on and help me." Nanuk gives me an armload of parkys, and puts two plastic bags of moccasins in my hands. I go out to the car, put the stuff in the trunk, and go back for more. We go in and out of the house, emptying my closet of the handicrafts, the clothes, and the boxes filled with jewellery. I wonder where all this stuff comes from, can't remember Nanuk making all this stuff. Nanuk says, "Okay, that's it," and we get into the car.

It is very dark on the Iceroad, but warm inside the car.

"Tuk Jamboree's a good one, Trista. They'll buy lots of stuff from us, I hope. Good this year too because now me and the other ladies, we been working hard on making the crafts, the clothes," Nanuk says. "You can't tell anyone we went to Tuk, they think, well they all think I'm still driving there, getting money from your daddy. You can't tell your mother. She don't trust that I'm not taking money from him for you. Even though he come down from them rigs and offered. My girl, so stubborn. But she's right, we not taking any more money from him, going to earn on our own now, Trista."

I am almost falling asleep, my head in Nanuk's lap, and Nanuk's got one hand on the steering wheel, one hand stroking my hair.

"He's not a bad man, your father. Don't ever think that, Trista. Them men, they make them out to be all bad, going out on the rigs, leaving their women pregnant, having to fend for themselves in town, never hearing from them. But your daddy? Just like he couldn't ever be tied to any town. Even I could seen that once your mother bring him home. He's happiest up on that platform on the Beaufort, bundled up in his minus eighty down parka, got his snowboots on, just one big black thing on that platform, the huge oil piston sliding up and down, the wind near breaking off his face. He can't be out there long, what with the frostbite'll get you in three minutes. Inside, I can see him, Trista, just like when Daduk went up there too, when he's young. Inside watching TV with the other men, sitting writing them letters to your mother, all of them filled with these wishes: 'When I get off this time, what say you and me go down California? I hear they got them waves that'll slap you silly if you don't watch, warm and fresh.' Then he gets to Tuk, calls your mother, yeeah she went there, went to see him near every time.

"But last time, when she brought you girls, when she brought you and Keely, you was only four. And he damned couldn't even talk to you. Tell you who you are. You remember that? Your mother, when you were asleep, led him in and said, 'This girl. This girl is ours.' And later he held you, kissed you, put you back down in bed. But he left again for the rigs and your mother was all mad about that, what she been expecting, him to hold you up to the sky and say come and be forever? But I don't blame him. He's got that Beaufort Sea in his veins like all them boys. He'd be fit to be tied he ever have to live in town and make family. And he works hard, and he loved your mother hard, even if only for a time, and no one could have ever faulted him for that."

I rock Faith's crib, I rock the crib and she's sleeping, she's finally sleeping. I take up her things, her little socks. Put them on her. Don't get cold, baby. Don't you worry, baby. Mumma's gonna make it all right. River's gonna run, Faithy, River's got to run.

I'm little and down by the river again. But the Iceroad is almost gone. The ice is shifting and I can hear it cracking. People are in their cars, maybe four or five trucks lining the riverbank. They are watching Break Up. The ice starts cracking, sounds like a rifle shot and I hold my gloved hands to my ears. It is silent, and then another crack, a shifting and movement underneath the ice, like something ancient woke up. Then the ice starts to move, and I laugh as the trucks beep their horns, people come out of the warm insides and whoop and yell, there's Auntie, and there's Nanuk and Daduk and there's Keely's mom and they're waving me over. "Come see it, Trista, it's moving. It's spring, it's here!"

The big blocks of the former road start to move, and spin past me, and suddenly there is the grey-blue of the Mackenzie River again. I know I am supposed to remember it. But this is like the first time I seen it. That long long winter of ice, moving. Deep and blue and moving past me, the arctic terns start to lift and dip, hover over the ice and logs and diving to see if any fish fry dare poke their heads out of the cold water.

The breeze comes up and lifts my hair. I kneel down on the spongy riverbank and take water into my mouth, because it is June and spring, and the ice is gone, long time swimming in chunks to the Arctic Sea, and the river water is cold and biting, but slick and smooth on my tongue.

There's my daduk, and many other daduks, and they are not in the bar, they are out fishing, the sun is on their faces, that cool sun, when it shines almost all night, the dusk comes, and the daduks are out in the night on the river, when the wind has died down, and there's Daduk, he's waving at me. "C'mon, Trista," and I know the water is cold, but I duck into it and dive down and when I come up to the bow of Daduk's boat, he pulls me out and the calm wind makes me dry, my parky is warm in the boat.

"You must be very quiet, little girl, the fish don't like the talking too much." Daduk grins at me, gives me some feathers to wind around the flies, the hooks. "Make those tighter for me, Trista," Daduk whispers and casts out.

I wind the feathers around and around the hooks, ask Daduk, "What fish will come?"

"Oh, maybe some inconnu, some burbot, gonna fry up some good northern pike and smoke it too, in the smokehouse. You ever been to the smokehouse, girl?"

"No."

"Come summer, all kinds of smells there, once the whitefish start giving us their bounty, come July, come August, smells so good up in that smokehouse. Enough smoked fish to last until next summer and then some. Got Johnny and his crew, them boys, they set up their nets and haul in something good. Me, I'm just one of those that likes to cast out single. Feel that wind?"

"Yes, Daduk."

"That wind? Comes all the way from the North Pole, then shifts, come from west, where there are fishermen casting off the atolls, praying to their gods for some fish so they can keep their people safe and fed. Down that Pacific, they got people who been fishing for centuries, you can read about them, Trista, read about them in that library sometime. Then you go farther down that wind, there's the people in Australia, they call them aboriginals too, funny, uh? That word? Means 'not original'? But down there in Australia, they're the original people, like us."

"Not like me, Daduk. Like you, but not like me."

"Oh, Trista. Don't you worry about that now. It's all the same blood. You and me. Just some stories are different. Some thinking is different. It matters. To know where you come from. But it matters more where you belong."

The boat pushes out into the centre of Mackenzie River, and I'm suddenly on the riverbank, watching Daduk go far out, I can see his boat dance in the waves, a kind of jaunty happy filled with light. My eyes are up to the sun, my face turns to it, and I think at the big of it, this sun that seems to go on forever, but still I can hear the faint crying, that keening wail coming from my baby back at the jail, and I know I got to go, see the Snow Nanuks in my mind's eye, "Do not stay long, Trista, for you will be swallowed." And even though they are nowhere near here, and not seen, even I want to swim in the river and rock in the boat with Daduk all summer, I hear their words and start walking away from the river, up the small hill. As I cross, I put my hands up to my eyes from the glare of the sun against the glare of the dirty snowpile, left over from June, and in that instant I'm in Mom's arms, and I can't hear the baby crying any more. I'm watching Mom, who is rocking me. I try to talk to Mom with my eyes, but Mom can't see me, not yet. And I look at that river again, but it's not flowing. It's hard and frozen. Dark.

"Little girl, little girl. You can't forget me, little girl," I whisper into Faithy's ear. "Don't forget me even when that other mom is holding you, feeding you, changing you, loving you. Don't forget you have me. I waiting here for you. Gonna take you out of there and go and get us our own place. Our own food and heat and clothes and couch and things. You gonna have everything. From me, little girl.

Remember me." Faithy wriggles in her sleep, her mouth open, and I blow against her cheek like Wind kissing Daduk's boat.

Never gonna leave you. Never gonna go away. They can't take you away from me.

Mom's crash isn't sudden. In my mind's eye, I can see it coming, the large fissure that took an hour to build up, to stop Mom's car. Then she is falling, into the hole of it, the valley, the ravine it made as the crack rose up, bringing the river ice with it. Her hands are off the steering wheel, and I rise up, see Mom smile at me. "This is it, Trista?" she asks and closes her eyes. I put my fingers up to Mom's face. She's so still. I put my fingers to the corner of Mom's mouth, kiss that soft sweet place, whisper, "Yes."

"Trista."

"Yeeah."

"Trista," says Deanne.

"Yeeah, what the fuck?"

"We going over for work experience today. Greenhouse. Linda told me to tell you."

She's standing in my doorway and I think I slept through the breakfast and I am all messed up because why they let me sleep through the breakfast. I hate missing meals because then I don't get to say hey to Sherry.

"What the fuck you doing in my room?"

"Just telling you," Deanne says. "Get ready."

I don't even look over there but pull my shirt over my T-shirt I wear for pyjamas, then pull my jeans on. Faith isn't in her crib, they must've taken her to the workers' station. I go to the washrooms and there's Megan and Aimee already waiting.

"We gonna start more Elder Hospital today too, no school in the afternoon," Aimee says. She's putting on some cream and it makes her face white.

"How come?"

"They thinking you get the transition after your court case. Linda told us in Group, remember? Maybe me too, maybe I get to go down to YK. Maybe I want to work in a hospital when I get out, maybe even with little babies," says Aimee.

"What stuff? What transition?" I says.

Lee's driving the van again but I am not going to look at him, don't look at him and we get in the van and been so long since I was out, even not going out for smokes much since my head's been a mess, can't sleep. The van is cold and we got ourselves bundled up, but it's hard to get used to even being outside. Deanne doesn't sit near me and she should get the fuck away. I lean against the window. Don't know why they still got me on this work training, on any work training here, I don't have the court case resolved yet and maybe they going to put me away for a long time, gonna take my baby away soon, fuck it's coming it's coming, why the fuck they want some fucked-up girl learning shit from the Greenhouse I don't know.

Lee's got us out of the van and into the Greenhouse. It's warm inside and smells good. Things are planted, just starting to peek out under the plastic wrap we put on them to get them warm and cooking underneath the dirt. You can see the marigolds making a break around the back of the beds, and little sticks for them to lean against. We get in there and today there's even some people working quietly on their plots, the planted lettuce and carrots, peas and kale, lots of greenery, putting their seed pictures up so they know what's gonna come up where. One lady's got this blinking baby Jesus and Mother Mary on her shirt and I keep looking at it, thinking it's baby Jesus' birthday soon, never been to church that much with Nanuk or Auntie but sometimes Catholic church camp in summers with

Keely, good free food and sometimes games. But then that talk about letting baby Jesus into your heart, how he can take all that away you let him in and how you go to heaven if you're good but sometimes if you're bad you don't go to hell, like if you're bad hurt yourself, commit suicide like that you go to this other place and if the babies don't get dunked then they die and they go too. He made it sound like a floaty place, kind of airy and there but not there. But then when Keely asks the priest: "You think Singer can come to heaven too, or he going to that floaty place?"

"Who is Singer?" he says. And I says, "He's the dog who come around to all our places to get food. Someone left him when they moved down south last summer."

"Well, he wouldn't go anywhere," the priest says and I don't have to look at Keely to know she's pissed like me. We run home that night and tell Nanuk and Nanuk's got her hands in her little seed tray, shifting the dirt around to plant some herbs for the kitchen window. Nanuk says, "You got your God right here in this here earth, girls. The plants grow then give way to other plants then they help the others grow so they never really dead. Making sacred, this earth, that's the dirt, snow, river, what all you got around you. Making sacred means sacrifice, same thing."

I know I am not supposed to but I go to the end of the planting bed, the part we got finished at the Greenhouse and lift up the plastic wrap, sniff at the soil. Makes me think on the months that are going to come.

We're driving in the van home and the kids standing around the store, and how they are smoking, calling out to the van, "Whooo hooo, crazy girl van!" I imagine the wildflowers that are hardy, coming out the sides of the road, still dirty snow lining the paths, June in Jackfish Bay. Back then, before all the thinking I did, I'm thinking of Tyler, how he could just be out there, just out there with those boys, and Tony and Keely too, smoking and yelling at the van.

Like we did when we were younger, not even knowing what that meant, crazy girl van, thinking it was the nut job girls up there. Older than us. Not from around our town. I think of them pictures of Faith's two-month birthday that Deb took, there she was, eyes open, this little little baby. And she didn't look anything like me, maybe some around the eyes like Tyler, just vacant eyes, and a soft faraway look in them, tiny hands. And there's me, holding her in the picture, and I'm smiling, nobody can see I'm ripped apart inside, it's coming out of my eyes like glass shards.

We pass the old school. Lots of the high school kids go down the hall there, to pick up their sisters and brothers, bring them back home to plop in front of the TV until Mom comes home from work, make them some Pizza Pops, and maybe play some PlayStation with them. Me and Keely picking up her brothers, but we stand outside Ms. Epstein's class, she was our grade four teacher too. Ms. Epstein come up to me, hugged me, my belly big under my parky and she knows and I know and she don't say much about that. That was the greatest thing about Ms. Epstein, she was the kind of person who could just hug you, wasn't scared of you getting bigger, or looking mean.

"And so what's Trista going to do?" Ms. Epstein said, and she could say that in a way, use your name as if you not there, like this was the story of your life and you and Ms. Epstein were sitting in the reading corner, with all the cushions around, just you and her, and she really wanted to know. We're passing the school and I'm thinking about that, thinking about telling her.

"Don't know. Maybe. Maybe help some people."

"What about the elders?"

"Yeeah. Maybe, like when the worker came in, said they needed some kids to help, with the elders maybe."

I trace my fingers on the little desktop, feeling the top of the desk, that desk that I remember me and Keely colouring on, making the white spruce trees, the snow, the cars driving on the Iceroad. Seems long time ago, since we were little.

Lee starts humming and he turns on the radio, we drive up along the river and I got my head pressed against the side window. I want to be driving out of here. Get my baby and drive the fuck out of here.

I can see my body laid out that night Keely told Jimmy to come over, I'm drunk and on the couch and rubbing my hands on my belly. Like a long spruce branch that needs straightening, like one me and Keely had to go get for Richard when he was mad at us for not bringing in the cordwood in time, and the fire died down. He didn't whip hard, just one tap on the back of my legs. Just I felt bad, he worked so hard, and Mom gone two, three months, he missing her and not looking at me like he used to on the couch and I'm not maybe his good girlfriend any more, then I'm not remembering my chores. I can see that spruce branch laid out, and me stretched beside it. And that night, the ulu I cut my burned hair with wedged in the couch and I rolled over it when I woke up, but it didn't cut me. Rubbing my eyes, seeing Jimmy wake up too, he's on the floor, and I got drunk mouth. "You want to get some smokes?" he says to me. Keely sleeping on the mattress in the corner.

"Yeeah," I says.

"Do a line."

"I got Faith," I says.

"You got fuck all," Jimmy says.

I go over to the coffee table and he's laying out the coke and I snort it up. I touch the carpet and it's got that same feel like the Snow Nanuk's place, and then I am laughing at him. Keely wakes up. "Where you guys going? Don't go."

"C'mon, silly, let's get smokes," Jimmy says. And I am off gone with him.

Linda comes in the classroom and tells me to come out to the workers' station and I think something's wrong with Faithy but she tells me to go into the visiting room and Keely's standing there.

"Hey," she says.

"Hey. What you doing here? They let you?" I says looking back at Linda, but she's left us alone.

"I called, just asked if I could ..." She's pulling her zipper up and down nervously. "Trista, I wanted to come. You know, see you, before they move Faith."

"It's not gonna happen yet, it won't happen yet. There's still time," I says and I want to get out of here I have homework and shit to do and why she coming on a weekday it just fucks me up.

"I wanted to tell you," she says and when she looks up at me she stops pulling at that stupid zipper and she's crying, oh don't cry, Keely. "Just ... if they put her in that foster home in Inuvik. Like Linda says. I can go see her for you, Trista. It won't take long to skidoo over there or me and your auntie can go together in the car and make sure ..."

"What? Make sure what they not beating her or anything?" I says.

"No. It's gonna be a good home, Trista."

"I don't give a fuck you gonna go over there, who cares what you're gonna do?" I says and I want her to get the fuck out of here.

Keely comes up to me and tries to hug me, but I feel wooden like I am being held by some tree doll I don't know. But she won't let go and I hear her whisper in my ear, "Trista, we gonna look out for her, don't worry, okay?" And I start to shiver like I'm standing outside in the snow with no snowboots on and the door is locked and can't get in. She won't let go of me, keeps saying, "Okay, okay ..." until I push my nose into her parky, breathe deep the smell of her cigarette smoke with her perfume, the wool and the wet wolf fur around the trim of her hood tickling my face. Keely hugs me tight and I pull away.

"Yeeah, Keely. Be nice if you can visit her for me. She's your family too." And I know the words are making her tears dry up, and we sit for a bit and talk about some kids from school and she feels better, swiping at her nose and smiling at me, but I still feel that wall inside gone up strong bricks to keep those thoughts of tomorrow or the next day away. Linda comes in to tell Keely it's time and Keely hugs me again quick and I sleepwalk through the next day.

The little vines in my belly moving around and around. Then we're in the van again. Not the Greenhouse any more. It's a different day. It's coming faster and faster and faster and I want to be with my Faithy. Deanne's up front and Deb is driving today. I am missing time and I don't know where the fuck my head is at. It's maybe after lunch, and I am tired. Megan's not shutting up, talking to Tracy about some shit about the hospital.

"Maybe I can go and help in the cafeteria too, just for starters."

"There's lots of places. They got to hire a certain amount for the job program, for retraining or, like you girls, to get into a career path," Deb says.

I got this taste in my mouth like the Jack and Cokes we had that night before we went out for smokes. Can taste Jimmy's mouth on mine.

Deb's talking to Janet, she used to work with us down the Northmart and now she's at the hospital. "Here's your smock, a hospital uniform I got from one of the older workers. You can use it now, Trista." I don't look up at her much but she's smiling at me anyways and I wonder what the fuck she got to smile about don't she know about me, don't she know I am some fucked-up girl.

"This'll fit you. Judy says she just grew out of it after her first baby." It's light green, and starched, and so clean. When I put it on in the changing room, Megan is still chattering away and giving me a headache.

"Time for a bath, Nanuk." And the patients, the elders, the women, in the bathtub, sliding down under the bubbles and giggling as the workers put in the rubber ducks and plastic boats. Deanne's over in some other room and I get to assist with a bath without her around, it's just me and Aimee. I think the toys are kind of mean. Maybe this woman, this woman who has eight kids, she don't want a plastic boat in there. But Tracy says, "You see, they love them toys."

"C'mon, Nanuk, you want a bath?"

And Nanuk Marjorie, Patricia, Donna, they all giggle, their spit sliding down their mouth. Tracy rolls Nanuk Marjorie's chair to the big bathtub, and I start filling the bath with warm water, Tracy goes to the toy bag, throws in plastic boats, and Nanuk Marjorie starts to move her old claw-like hands, "You want the red boat?" Tracy says. And Nanuk Marjorie giggles. "You some good girls," she says.

"Nanuk's husband, he was my friend's uncle, you know the Ford family?" Tracy asks me. I nod.

"They had a good many fishing boats. Caught some coney your time, right, Nanuk?" And Nanuk Marjorie moans, chortles, then moans again, like it's hard for her mouth to move around the words sometimes. "Yeeah, your husband flew them nets out on the Mackenzie River. Don't I know it, used to be my daduk would come home with such a haul, gone out with your husband on a trip. You fed us all up good, didn't you?" I like how Tracy can do that, talk to them that way.

Nanuk Marjorie rests back, like she can see the past. When we put her in the warm bath, she suddenly gets floaty and moves around like she could walk right out of there, like she's a fish waiting for her husband to catch her.

"It's like their bodies, they remember, get some baby in them again," Tracy says. I rub the washcloth up and down Nanuk's body,

Nanuk closing her eyes with the softness of it. This wrinkle and this, this will be me one day, I think, Me, old, and all this life. And as I move the washcloth over Nanuk's body, Nanuk sinks in deeper, lets the bubbles float all around her neck. I think this been a good way to get old. I bend down and smell Nanuk Marjorie's cheek, let my lips rest there, and Nanuk giggles again. And I put Mavis out of my head, I don't think about Mavis and why they letting me be kind to my nanuks again.

We're driving home and Deanne's not saying much and I don't look at her nothing anyways. My hands are all pruney from washing nanuks and I think I'm going to ask Linda if maybe maybe next time I bring in my haircutting stuff and maybe they let me cut some hair for the nanuks. We were up and talking with the other nurses on their break just like we was on a break too, like real workers. But we're inside this crazy girl van again and there's them kids, outside the Icebox Bar, John's got a beer in his hand, and them other boys, and I seen Tony behind them. I move my head from the window, the steam from my mouth clouding it up.

"You're my little bird, baby, you gonna see. Gonna see what summer can do to this town. Oh there's the garbage and the shit piled up, but we're gonna clean that all up. When the pussywillows come out, soft fuzz like your hair. When the shorebirds come out, the warblers, arctic terns, ducks all taking fast to the river. Wait Faithy, I'm gonna show you."

six

"Hey, when you get here?" Deanne says. We're piling out of the van and there's this old lady come up and hug Deanne and I don't like how she's taken to hugging her, don't like it one bit. They go in together and I can't hear them. We get inside and taking off our parkys and they must've gone in the visiting room because I can't see where Deanne went.

"Wanna just ask if we can smoke, Trista?" says Megan.

"We just took our parkys off," I says.

"So."

"No, I gotta go," I says.

"Where you got to go in a hurry?" Megan says and her face is scrunched up, but I ignore her and move past the workers' station, go into the living room. But Deanne's in her room with the door propped open and there's that lady helping her put all Deanne's shit into a big black suitcase I never seen before.

"Trista, come take Faith," Deb says, rolling the rolly crib over to me.

"No," I says.

"She needs a feeding," Deb says.

"Where Deanne going?"

"She's transferring down."

"Who the fuck is that messing with her stuff?" I say, but I know it's not nobody gonna do her any harm and I can fucking figure out who it is, some lady helping her get her shit together and go but Deb says, "Deanne's transferring down today and Mrs. Barker's her social worker. She's going down with her on the plane."

"I don't fucking care," I says but I can't stop standing there, by the couch, just willing Deanne to look at me, why won't she look at me? She told me it was going to be next week and why is it today and why didn't nobody tell me? Deb rolls the rolly crib and picks Faith up and holds her out to me. "Sit here and try to feed her," she says. So I sit but I can't concentrate, then Deanne comes out and she's grinning, the bitch, why she grinning like that and she says, "So this is it, we'll see you when you get down," and Megan runs up to her and hugs her and then Deanne goes and hugs Aimee and Linda goes about and hugs her too and gives her something and then Deanne's hugging Deb but Sherry's not there because she's on break and not back until later and I'm thinking, How the fuck can she leave without saying bye to Sherry, the bitch, and then she's coming over and leaning into me and hugging me and I say, "Why you going now?" and she says, "What do you mean?" and I say, "You said next week." But then Deanne holds me and whispers, "It is next week, Trista. Today's the day. It's gonna be okay, I'm gonna call you." And she kisses my cheek and says some more shit but I don't hear her, my head is pounding and my cheeks are flaming red just sweating too and she kisses Faith at the top of her head and I just want to fucking punch the bitch, how can she not tell me this lady coming today and fucking taking her right like that?

"Trista? I see you when you get down," Deanne says.

"Yeeah."

"Okay then."

"Yeeah. Okay." And they're leaving out of the living room and Deb goes in to Deanne's room and starts stripping the bed. Aimee moves over to me and sits beside me but she doesn't say nothing, just moves the blanket on me and I look at her, try to say something but it's all I can do to just breathe.

When you walk on the Iceroad, you know you can walk on forever. You could walk all the way to the Arctic Sea and get lost up there. Maybe so lost even the angatkut never find you. So lost you are stone cold and there's no cache around to feed you, no family to bring you into their iglut, no one to whisper to you, You're safe, you're safe here. Then when the Iceroad starts to mush up, you slide under and fall, float under there with the sleeping coney and jackfish, the top of the world.

Fucking leave. Fucking go.

Me and Faithy.

Don't touch my baby. No one's gonna hurt you, baby, no one's gonna take you.

Then I see him at the door. He's older, but he still has the orangey beard. My daddy. He doesn't say anything, but I know, I know he's come for me and Faith and he's going to take us down south away from this shit.

Then I see Mom. She's not looking at me. It is dark and night and I can see that Iceroad out my window. I'm not gonna put you in the crib, baby, stop crying, baby, shhh shhh shhh.

I close my eyes and I am on my hands and knees. "What is this?" And I hear Mom from afar, "Trista." There is no Richard around and there are no boyfriends around. I can't smell any men around, just me and Mumma and me and Mumma and the carpet is rough. And I try to crawl up to the window, the little wisp of breeze coming in, trying to see Mumma, but then someone catches me around my belly, "Not there, Trista, come closer to the stove, it's warmer." And it's Mom and Mom puts her face against mine and rubs there, and I giggle, can feel the funny bubbles of sound coming up against my mouth and out. Mom, Mummy, Mumma puts me in the high chair, and there is food, it is different from the milk, and I know then why Wind misses it, this food, this sticky good between my fingers, the banana, the hard crunch of the oatmeal, and the bottle milk, the bottle milk is there, and I try to make sound, try to move it past my mouth, and Mumma hears me, and it is then that I hear her, very clearly, "What are you saying, Trista, can you say Mumma? Can you, my girl?"

And I open my mouth and talk, but it comes out funny and I flail my arms in front of me, and I see my fingers and can suck them, and they taste of the caribou meat that the Snow Nanuks cook, strips above the fire. And I lean against the high chair, trying to see, "Where is Nanuk?" Mumma brings a book, and I try to open it, this book, these words, I can hear them, and it's about a bunny that runs and runs and runs. Mumma is reading to me and there is happy in her voice, I slide my palms against Mumma's face and Mumma smiles, says, "You like the bunny story." Then there is the bath, the white big basin and the warm water and I am sleepy, and the washcloth runs back and forth on my skin, soothes, and I am sleeping, Mumma singing, Mumma humming, and I sleep. How do I remember this? In this dream-like place, with the white walls and the baby is sleeping now, the baby is sleeping. All these dreams, thoughts, and memories come and wash over me like all them tears I never cried for Mom, all the times I wanted to go down to the Iceroad and pound on it and scream and make some big fire to thaw it up, make the old Mackenzie give my mother back.

Make that river break up. Give me the summer back, see the river, Faithy, see it run so fast? See the flowers, look at the flowers.

Summers, we kids mostly stayed around uptown. But one time me and Keely's had enough of walking up and down Main Street, seeing the same kids and going into the hardware store and looking at the old dusty toys, then walking into the drugstore and buying a bag of chips, then eating them and sitting in front of the bank, looking at what someone had carved new into the wood side of the walls. But this one day, we packed up the picnic blanket from Keely's mom's, and we went to my house and grabbed some old Cheez Whiz from the back of the fridge and a loaf of bread that had more in it than some of the other bags on the kitchen counter.

The fireweed was out on the back hill, and we walked up Tullinqit Road for it seemed forever. Here, you can't get lost because the only road opened is the Dempster and the Airport Road, and both are opposite the back hill. Here, if you walked forever you'd just run into one of the tiny runoffs that come off the Mackenzie, or maybe, if you could of walked far enough and you had a Ski-Doo with the snow on the ground, and you had some jerry cans of gas with you, maybe you could go as far as Hodgins Lake, or even Husky Lakes. Keely, it's like she wanted to walk all the way to the Beaufort.

But we're only nine years old this one summer and we didn't get far before we laid our blanket out on the south side of the fireweed and sit down. I'm on my belly and making some chains out of the wildflowers. In school, Ms. Epstein, she's teaching us about the flowers. We got some of the names from the elders, when we go about Ptarmigan Hall, but it's easy to forget. Ms. Epstein, she's all about making us sing songs to remember the names. She gets the elders to come in and tell us some of the old stories.

One time my nanuk come in. She's wearing her mukluks and it's dark come on, maybe December before Christmas. She's talking slow-like and I know she's a little nervous, because she's got her head down. But she's laughing a lot, she likes to laugh, my nanuk. And the kids, they all know her, seen her in the Old Time Dances, jiggling right fast and keeping up with the best of them, or even doing some drum-dancing with the littler kids. We all know each other. But in school it's different. Like the teacher makes us listen more, like we're something out of a book, not just Nanuk who lives at my house and boils her tea in the mornings and just sets and sews some and waits for Maisie Ford to come over for the TV bingo after dinner. But some old lady who got some good stories to tell. In the teacher's eyes, it's like we listen more, she makes us.

So Nanuk brings some Eskimo doughnuts to our grade four class, and the kids all come about because they know from the Jamborees that she makes some of the best, except that one year when she didn't make nothing, no sewing, no doughnuts, not even boiled tea or did any crafts, the year Mom crashed on the Iceroad and we were in sitting quiet for the year, remembering her. But Nanuk's got her blue parky on, the one's my favourite, with the little blue daisies and she's taken up some wildflowers, some cranberry blooms and put them fresh in her buttonholes. She starts telling us about the bumblebee, the egotak, how when she was little and they were all out on the land, spring and the Break Up already two weeks in, her daduk and dad gone fishing for some grayling or char near the Lakes. How her brother had the breathing problems and he was always coughing and sneezing, like he was sucking his air through an arctic tern feather, it was that hard to breathe. How they was setting around the wildflowers and fleabane, just watching them bumblebees, kids could of set real quiet just then, not like us all sugared up on the pop and candy, she says. And then that little egotak bee just set right on her little brother, that is my Uncle Davey, and just set there and he's almost trembling, but looking right at it. It didn't sting him none, or even leave the little yellow pollen it got up and collected on its feet, just set there awhile and then flew off, kind of zigzagging away into the brush. That night, Nanuk said, that night Davey wasn't getting to wheezing at all. He slept still and proper and wasn't thrashing up against their bed blankets or whining to Mom about water, or coughing strange. And he never done that no more, that egotak just takes that sickness away.

I think of Deanne singing. How the last few days before she left she was singing, humming, easy happy she got around her. "I'll come visit you, Trista. Or you might see me if you go to YK."

Keely is singing some song she learned in church, what we go to when no one is up and we're bored on a Sunday, the Igloo Catholic Church. She's singing about God, and got the whole world, and I'm thinking of that little egotak, making myself a wildflower chain.

Please don't take the baby away. First Deanne, then Faithy, then Trista. Where you gonna put them all when you taking them away? Not the baby.

We just need to give her some formula, hon.

Give her back, give her to me.

I fall asleep again but when I wake up, it's like it's my room at home when Mom was still alive, not like it was before when Richard was there for a little bit, before Auntie came and got me and brought me to her and Nanuk and Daduk's. But I wake up and see the pictures I made in kindergarten, those pictures with all the colours they got in them. I feel my long hair, keep it long because Richard likes it long like that. I know I'm in here and it's not that late, because the light's still on, but it can be late and maybe I don't even know it. I'm touching my hair and I'm thinking about Richard, I'm saying, "Richie, Richie, gonna take me up the back hill." And I'm smoothing my hair, making it nice for him like I used to. But it's like I can see the big girl me too, that swirling feeling in my belly when he'd do that, take me up in the truck and park and then tickle me some and I get all sleepy.

I'm still wondering on it when Mom comes in and she leans on the doorframe, "There you are, get up now, sleepy-head, you'll be late for school," And I'm grinning at Mom but can't get the words out. Mom, don't go. She grins some back at me, but she's going. I walk to the closet and there are clothes. There are pants and dresses and some are blue, and I like that blue, that's a Nanuk blue, like my parky, and I put on the clothes, feel the soft shirt against my arms, the hair on my legs raises up some, and I'm not thinking on Richard no more, just thinking of Nanuks and wondering maybe me and Keely get some time after kindergarten, go get babysit by the Snow Nanuks, what they can talk stories inside our heads.

Mom calls, "Trista, hurry now, we don't want to be late, or the teacher'll have your hide." And I'm sitting there very very still on the bed in Iso now, and then it blips out again, I can see Mom's face so clearly, the smooth skin on her cheek, her ear, I can almost touch her.

Mom's got my hand hold tight and we're walking. The sky's dark still, and the light's gone from the sky because the sun is sleeping behind the earth. There are lots of kids walking on the road, and they are quiet, their heads down against the cold, their parkys lined with wolf and wolverine fur. They clomp on the snow, and I can hear the squeak of it as their boots lift. I think of Wind, how Snow Nanuk wants me to, not thinking about that Wind in so long, neither Richard, how come now I got all this swirling thinking inside my head. Now Faith gone, should been thinking about her, should been remembering her and her little soft head and alls I'm thinking on is stupid Wind and stupid Snow Nanuks, and the fucks for? I'm dizzy and I'm dizzy, and I'm still just walking with Mom. It is quiet and still, just cold, so cold and no wind on my face. There are big steps to the school and I stop in front of them, don't know what to do, and Mom says, "What? C'mon, Trista. I have to get to work, hon." Then we climb the steps and walk into the school, the classroom. There are the other children, some of them, I can see their wide smiles and remember some from the Snow Nanuks' place. Some are running up to me and this one, this one with short black hair and a red red ribbon that she lets me touch, says, "C'mere, Trista, hurry, get your stuff put away, it's music first." I don't see Mom leave, but take off my parky, and sit with the other girl, where's Keely? And then Teacher comes in. She's got a guitar and she sits, says, "Okay, class, you know this one," starts to play it and we start up to sing. Their voices all lilt up and I think I never heard anything so beautiful, like inside Snow Nanuks' place. And I don't ever want to leave this place, this school, the warm dark, the lights winking at me from outside this music. And I don't see Mom leave, don't think about Mom again, why can't I see her, remember her more?

Linda says, "Who wants to start?"

The RCMP didn't even have to show me those pictures of the murdered woman. When they laid them out on the table in the squad room, I could see Lee guarding outside in the hall, looking in at us.

The pictures of the Aurora Store were laid out in colour in the squad room, but I remember them in black and white in my head. The cash register, and she's got the cleaning trolley out because it was late and she was almost locking up. The brooms and the toilet brushes, and the Pine Sol, and the Northmart brand tub scrubbing powder. In the squad room the RCMP is showing me these pictures. My belly is pulsing, empty of my baby, my baby they got in the incubator up in the hospital. Lee's looking in. Was his auntie that was murdered. That's in them pictures. Just cleaning that night. Just doing her graveyard shift at the Aurora Store, minding her own fucking business. Was Lee's Auntie Mavis, and he's staring right at me. His eyes saying to me, What the fuck, Trista? What you doing with Jimmy on some dark northern night in the Aurora Store, stealing smokes?

I know it's bad for Faith, for the breast milk I'm gonna give her, I want to go back to her, please let me go back to her and don't make me see this, don't make me feel this evil stuff come up inside my throat and we're not really allowed to smoke, but the RCMP let's me smoke, and look at them pictures. They got Jimmy already shipped to Yellowknife Juvie. The RCMP come for me at Inuvik

Regional the minute I was cleared by Dr. Petterson. She didn't want to let me go because she told them I just gave birth, the bruises Jimmy laid on me throbbing. But she has to say I'm okay, let them take me. The RCMP asking me, that one officer who known me, asking me, "Why, Trista? We know you been a good girl since you been pregnant. Haven't seen hide nor hair of you in here. Why you done this, Trista?" Then Lee staring at me through the glass. And I tell them. I tell them.

Me and Jimmy was cold. We had run out of smokes. You're always cold in Jackfish Bay, who don't know that? What you got to wear anyway? Some shit-ass thin crap coat from the Northmart they put on sale and it still costs you a hundred bucks and so thin, you walking to school or home and the wind blowing ice right through face numb and dark so dark. We wanted smokes. "You got money for smokes, Trista?" Jimmy's saying at me. "No." Another long fucking cold night without no smokes, and crying from fighting with stupid fucking Tyler who is gone, where the fuck? Me and Tyler had been fighting, one of our fights, but things been going so good between him and me. But he was worrying more and more about Faith, how Dr. Petterson been saying she's not moving as much as she should in my belly, maybe we have to get early to Inuvik Regional, maybe she will come out a preemie, two months early.

It serves me right it serves me right.

Where's the baby?

Who is looking after the baby?

I don't know if it's night or day. The room is dark and the crib is empty.

Mom's at work at the Northmart. Richard and me are watching something on TV and I am just glad Mom is finally gone because she hogs Richard all the time.

"But you know you are my only girl," Richard says.

"Yeeah. Tell Mom I'm your only girl."

"I can't tell her. She would be hurt. You don't want to hurt your mom, right?"

"No," I says.

"So then. We take our time when we got our time. That's what it was like with Romeo and Juliet. They didn't have lots of time. They had their families. Didn't understand."

"How you know all this stuff?"

"I read me some," Richard says.

It's that part that I know I'm putting my old self into the thing. Because I don't really remember him saying that. I don't think. It's like we're studying something in the classroom. Like Romeo and Juliet. I'll remember something like seeing the movie on TV. Not the old one that Miss Sarah showed us, but then she showed us some bits of the newer one with the gang shooting at the gas station, and then it's like I can remember it on the TV. I got the crocheted blanket set up. Then I go get some popcorn. I know how to make the popcorn because we got this button on the nuker called "popcorn" and all you have to do is press it. It seems like it knows exactly when to stop it so the bag is perfect. So I take the bag out of the wrapper. It's that kind that Richard really likes, the kettle corn kind. "Sweet and salty, just like my Trista-kins," he says. Mom lets me put it in the cart when we're shopping around the Northmart. It's the first thing I put in that I know he likes because it's in the first aisle with all the crackers, chips, and candies. I like those Goodies, the licorice kinds. No one likes those, not even Keely, and that's why I like them some too. Because then they're kind of only mine. First time I took them over to Snow Nanuks' and they setting around, says, "Trista, what you got there." And I give Snow Nanuk one, a purple one, and she tries to chew it but her teeth don't work good so she spits it out in her hand. "Eeeuck." And she giggles. I put it in the trash for her and then get her a tissue. She lets me wash the Goodies spit off her hand. She's got lines that go all the way to her wrist it seems, and I like rubbing there. I throw the tissue away and go back to her and she cuddles me up to her like I am a good girl. She smells like wolf and she's got some leather smell round her too, also smells of bread and her hands are rough. She just lets me sit up with her and she's rocking a little.

Like that with Richard too. But with him like I got a livewire going through me. Like when I was little and I put that fork into the electric socket behind the Christmas lights just to see I could get some more Christmas lights to come out of there. Gave me a little spark through my whole body like I was the Christmas lights all of them for a minute, a second. That's what sitting with Richard's like. He tickles me and then tickles some more. Under the crochet blanket. He's my boyfriend and no one says it's different and when I grow up and leave the house, get my own up the street, Richard's going to come live with me, not Mom any more, he said.

It doesn't matter what we're watching. I remember lots of it. There were some weird things on TV then. I loved the shows that were kind of like Japanese, Richard said. There was this Jack and the Beanstalk one, and his face was strange. It wasn't a white face. But Richard said the eyes were too big for Japanese too. Richard said the Japanese animation made the characters kind of Japanese and kind of white. So their eyes looked like ours. Richard is Inuvialuit, more than me but he doesn't say it. He always says "like us" and then I feel like that's like me too. Because we're together. The babies we gonna have? They're gonna be full Inuvialuit then. Richard says we can take them up hunting.

"A girl or?" I ask.

"How 'bout a girl and a boy," Richard says.

"Yeeah. Twins. That look the same."

"But if they're girl and boy they won't look the exact same like girl and girl can look," Richard says.

"Why."

"Because it's the difference between fraternal and identical. You can only be identical if you are the same sex." He was always knowing all this stuff. He read lots of books. I can see them there in Mom's house, all lined up. Thick books too. When we wasn't watching the TV, he was reading and telling me things. "The polar icecap is melting."

"Yeeah. Teacher said it too. We got to make a picture and send to YK. Send to the poly-tit-sions, Miss said."

"That's a good idea. She sounds like a good teacher."

"Yeeah, she's the best, even let's me in when I am late."

"Why're you late?"

"When Mom isn't on time."

"Yeeah, your mom, not me. I always get you to school on time, right, Trista? Got to get you educated."

Yeeah. And he did. He shopped too, when Mom was too tired from work. He cleaned the house. Even put on the yellow gloves and cleaned the bathroom, the toilet. Let me come and dry up the dishes when he done cleaning them with the dish soap water. His hands under the hot water, got all pruney and felt different when we'd sit together later and tickle. He was a good boyfriend. The best boyfriend.

"But he wasn't your boyfriend," Linda says.

"What?"

"He wasn't your boyfriend, Trista. You were seven, eight maybe when he left you, your auntie says. Seven-year-olds don't have thirty-year-old boyfriends," Linda says.

"Yeeah."

I let her think I know what she's talking about. My head hurts and Aimee's looking at me strange. Why can't it go back to last month when I knew what the fuck was going on? Give me my baby back. Give me something to hold. Where's my mother gone, where is me, where is my Faithy? I think about the crocheted blanket and I can almost feel it under my fingers. Then I look down and it's just my jeans.

This is them all in the living room, they got the baby and they're passing it around. Like I made them something and now they think it's theirs. It doesn't feel a part of me any more. Maybe that baby is not my Faithy.

"Why don't you hold her, Trista, just for a bit," Aimee says, moving the blue blanket from that baby's face. She jiggles it next to me but I turn away.

Them girls. Megan's got the baby now. I know she's not trying to make me mad. I can see the baby's foot sticking out and I think its toenails got to be trimmed. Megan's got her mouth on its fingers. It's not crying or nothing. They shouldn't let them have that baby here in this jail. Don't they know this here is a jail for fucked-up girls who do bad things. Don't they know that baby isn't safe? Crazy girls.

Nanuk Marjorie dies. It's Christmas Eve Day but we're on the work training at the Elder Hospital just for the afternoon to give out some presents we knitted to the elders and Tracy says we are going to help make Nanuk Marjorie clean for her family to come in soon. Nanuk Marjorie, who could tell you stories of the camps, when she was a little girl and come home summers from the residential school. How happy she was to run and run and not have the Edmonton city smells clogging up her lungs. Nanuk Marjorie, even I remember she lived up at the Snow Nanuks' when she was too alone in her other house and her kids grown. Nanuk Marjorie said, "You gotta take all these lost kids up if you can."

The Snow Nanuks didn't have no husbands round, Nanuk Marjorie had lost hers to the city, he'd gone down to work in YK, never came back. But she didn't worry. I wonder how the Snow

Nanuks had caribou stew on every time we kids came by and were hungry. Those boys could eat the house down. But they always had the biscuits and bread and Eskimo doughnuts out for us, some little treats.

Nanuk Marjorie the first person I ever seen dead, besides Mavis. She died in her sleep, Tracy says, her face unlined and it was like a smile was on her lips, like she knew. The nurses lift the sheet from her bed, with Nanuk in it, put her body dry, in one of the tubs. They start sponging her, and I smell shit. "It's when they die. Every muscle relaxes, nothing holds in," Tracy says.

And I pick up a sponge and start on Nanuk's toes, while the nurses clean her up. "Just like a little little baby," I says. As I make the water slide over Nanuk's toes, her feet, it's like how Nanuk gone back to being tiny again, this cycle, finished. I don't want to cry. But right then the nurses cut Nanuk's nightgown from her and I see her breasts. They got brown spots on them, and the nipples wrinkled. I imagine all the babies who put their lips there, and then I sponge Nanuk's ankles, let the warm soapy water slide over her legs, and the tears come.

We're in the van again and I seem to be lost in my head. Wondering why I can't get that baby back from that crying fussing screaming place she goes to when I hold her, how long they keeping me coming and going and working and not working. Makes me think of that tiny spot of spring in June when there's no snow to hold them kids back from playing in the fields, every kids are out. Every corner of the town lit up like it's two o'clock, and all the kids safe, energy like mosquitoes biting them in the night, the light of the Arctic sun. Where is my Faith? Where is my little girl, she been growed some now. Will she ever go out playing with those kids in the 11 p.m. night light, running around them bases pumping her strong legs and laughing up at the Arctic sky?

I say to Linda when we get back, "Nanuk Marjorie died." And the minute I say it, I want to take it back, don't want to share with her this sadness, this feeling of things finished. But she smiles at me. "You remember telling me about going to the house when you were little. She is a Snow Nanuk, Trista. She is your Snow Nanuk."

And I remember, lots of kids crowded on the carpet, Nanuk in the kitchen talking with the other ladies and having tea. The TV wasn't on, just some old-time dance songs on the CBC. I can see Keely flipping me a card, that card with the big water on it, the Niagara Falls cards, I can't imagine how much. I remember wanting to go there.

Linda doesn't hug me, just pulls me a little close. Leans in "Missing you, Trista, talking with you," she says. "You coming out of that place you been in?" She tugs at my parky a little, I forgot to take it off after I come in from the van, like that wind coming up off the river, feels like almost spring and Break Up but it's not it's a fooling wind like we get sometimes right before Christmas. "We got Christmas dinner tonight," Linda says. "You okay?"

"Where's Faithy?"

"Right here." And she pulls Faith's rolly crib out from behind the workers' station. I move real slow to take her up, feels like I am wading through sludge, and walk to my room.

"Trista?" Linda says.

"Yeeah. I'm just ... I just gonna put my stuff away ... change my clothes," I says.

I take the smock off, put on another shirt. I look at Faith sleeping, and she's got the blue blanket against her cheek and she's drooling a little clear spit coming out from her. I can hear her breathing. I stroke her cheek and she stirs, opens her eyes, blinking at me.

"It's gonna be okay, little girl," I says to her. I put my parky back on and wrap Faith in her fleece. I stick stuff into my backpack even though I don't have a wallet or nothing, where's my fucking wallet? No matter. Put the backpack on and bundle Faithy up inside my parky. "There, little girl. You snug up?" Walk to the door.

"Trista," Aimee says, looking up from her homework she's already got spread out.

"Hey," Megan says, jumping up from her chair. "Faithy awake?"

But I don't stop to let her see, I don't got time to let her see. Walk past the workers' station and through the visiting room doorway and there's the back door, the back door just got to open the thing and I am out of here. But it's locked, it's fucking locked. I know I can open it. I know I got the key to the trailer right here, the key's right here. Then Linda's behind me. "Open the door for me, Linda," I says.

"Where you going?"

"You know where. Open the fucking door."

"Why don't you come back in? We can talk some, get you fed some before talking about where you're going," she says.

"There's no fucking time, Linda, open the door."

Then she's got her hand on my arm and I twist away from her. "Don't fucking touch me!" I scream but I didn't mean to. Just why won't she let me out? And I got my back to the door, can feel the backpack pushed against my back and Faithy's starting to fuss in her almost cry and I jiggle her, fast, up and down up and down.

"Trista, focus. We have to get her out now. You're dilated but don't push until I tell you," Dr. Petterson says.

But I want to push, I have to push and my belly is aching for me to push my legs open and there's so much pain against my back and that fucking Jimmy why he been kicking me and the inside my legs trembling so and what's dilated am I gonna die, is she gonna die and

"Trista, give her to me. Let's sit down a minute," Linda says and reaches for Faith. And like that it all comes out in a rush and I feel like my legs gonna go out from under me.

"No, no you can't take her."

"We're going to give you some steroids for her lungs," Dr. Petterson says and the nurse is pumping into my arm with the blood pressure thing and pressing a needle into my tube and why are her lungs gonna need this and oooooh it comes again that wave that makes me lose my breath. "Hold on, Trista, wait for it to pass, breathe." And the nurse looks into my eyes and says, "Look right at me and follow my breathing, deep breath in," and I try to do it like she does I look into her eyes so deep I can even see the red veins there and who is she and oooooh it fucking hurts so bad, my Faithy, keep her in there she's too little she's needs more time.

And I am twisting away from Linda and I climb up on the chair and it's not high but Linda looks far far away my head is swimming my head is pounding and Faith starts to scream and I'm holding her I hold her tight and her face is red, it's purple almost and I feel the chair start to move or maybe it's me and I fall, Linda's there, Deb's there, Megan and Aimee, where's Deanne, that bitch? but they can't catch me, they don't catch me and I fall from the chair but then run into the corner. "Fucking let me out, let me out!" and there's the window and there's the door and it's fucking locked and I know there's no way out and Faith is screaming. "Oh baby, oh baby, please, Faithy," and there's no fucking way out. "Just let me leave, Linda, let me go," and I slide down the wall and little Faithy won't stop crying and I'm trying to kiss her but her fists are jerky and angry in my face and her face is wet and so is mine and I bury my face into her blue blanket. "Give her to me, honey," I hear Linda say. "Give her to me, let her go, honey," and I'm saying, "No, no, don't take her," but she's screaming so hard, the baby, the baby's coming.

"Okay, Trista, this is it, I want you to push when you feel it come on again, push as hard as you can, sit up more, come on now, look at me," but then they all start moving around and Dr. Petterson telling something to that one nurse and I push and push but "Stop!" Dr. Petterson says and she's making me lie back and I can't stop I can't stop my back fucking kills my back is hurting and them nurses running around more now, the panic on their faces and words words flying around Faith preemie pre-eclapmsia magnesium epidural everyone stressing around the room my cunt ripping apart my head shooting pain sparks inside my eyes Dr. Petterson not looking at me but between my legs then the other doctor come in that other doctor I seen in the ultrasound room and he's telling me he so far away voice gonna put a long needle in my back why do I need a long needle and suddenly the pain drops I can't feel anything a seed splitting its flower that tiny flower gonna stretch up and grow or wither and die still gonna get born live or die live or die. Faith.

"She's crowning," Dr. Petterson says. I imagine a little girl with a princess crown on her, one of them what is it? Tiaras. A long pink dress like them ones they got at the Northmart. A little girl, a little girl. I can hear Mom say, "My little girl. What a good girl you gonna be when you're all grown up."

And I feel Linda's hands wrap around her and my face is aching my breasts my hands are aching arms fingers but I let Linda take her and my head aches with Faithy's cries and I'm alone.

Snow Nanuks say, "C'mere, little Shorebird, come here little Ptarmigan. Why you going uptown walking. Why you not here with us long times. I got some work I want you to do for me. Come skin some caribou hide with me. Here's my old ulu, it's old, but it's sharp. Ready. Just for you, little girl. Come on up here and let me show you."

I hear Tyler's tattoo gun and think, Fuck you, Tyler, and all your shit talk and who wants me anyways, you're right who wants a fuck-up like me. Stupid fucked-up dumbass quarter-blood 'sko girl who wants to kiss girls all day under the midnight fucking sun thinking her life is some fucking perfect if she only had a new beginning if only she coulda been one of Daduk's brothers able to talk story or hunt good or make some money and stay off the bottle and the drugs and the fucked-up boys away from her uncles and able to take care of her kid she born and not kick and kick some woman being kind to her since she was a little one.

I hum. There's that song about the bee that she likes, the song of the egotak I made up just for her, for when we get to go out and lay in the fireweed and brush, for when she gets some wildflowers on her head and she laughs and laughs when the petals fly on her cheeks, for when we're outside, and the river is running to the sea, and the air is still and quiet and you can feel the whole world belongs just to this moment. For then. I hear them breathing, these people.

"Trista?" Linda helps me up. She leads me past the workers' station. Deb is holding the baby. The baby's got these hiccupy cries. Like she's almost done crying. I don't look at the other girls, but even with my eyes down I feel them around me. Linda takes off my backpack. Unzips my parky. Eases my arms out of it. Pulls back my covers. Sits me on the bed. Takes my shoes off. Wipes my face with her palms. "Sleep now, baby," she says.

I'm dreaming, got to be, can see the Snow Nanuks, I can see them running, they are never running when I'm on the tundra, just moving all slow and lumbering, got all their parkys on and their sacks, but I see them running now. It's spring, and fireweed and red lichen are on the tundra, tiny wildflowers waving their little stems up, saying, Lookit me, lookit me. I'm trying to chase the Snow Nanuks, and they are rolling in the wildflowers, their bellies going up and down because they are giggling so hard. I land on one and we tumble together in the grass, and I put my face up to Snow Nanuk and breathe some in, that good clean smell of soap, and old stretchy skin. I rub my face in Snow Nanuk's cheek, and Snow Nanuk laughs and laughs, holds me tight.

Where's Faithy? "Where's Faith?" I wake up and can't see her she's not in her crib where did they take her did they take her away oh please don't take her why is she gone again and I see my blue pen I see it over by the shelf and I scrape it down again and again on my arms and the bell sounds and Linda runs in and grabs the pen from me I don't care I don't care and I scrape my nails down my face, my Faith and then she's got my hands behind my back and drags me to Iso and I pound and pound and pound the wall.

Later the bell sounds and the door snicks open. "Trista? We're going to keep you in Iso for awhile. Until the meds take effect, to give you some down time." She moving my chin up, making me open my eyes. "We can monitor you better in here. Linda will come in and stay with you," Dr. Petterson says.

And she leaves.

Seems I don't wake for a long time, seems I got this dream place where I see Faith running, she's running in the snow. And Keely is there with her little brothers. We're going somewhere, I have a bag slung around my shoulder and we're going up the back hill behind town, maybe we're going on a picnic? We don't got the Ski-Doos, just walking, but real slow, and Faith is running ahead of me, and I don't have to call her back because I can see Adam running after her. He's got long long legs, and Keely's seeing that I'm watching him, and she says something to me, I can't make it out, but there's a smile in her voice. I'm just feeling a hole fill up inside, watching Adam and Faith together, like me and Keely and Lee long ago. He's caught up to her now, and he's bent over her a little, showing her something in the snow, and she turns and she's laughing a big wide chortle, and she's got a ptarmigan baby in her hands, Adam is cupping around the sides so the baby doesn't fall from her, and she's giggling. "It tickles," she says, and her voice is loud and clear as the wind, and she lifts up her arms and drops the baby away, and it drops for what seems like a long time but only seconds, and then it shakes its wings out and flies a stretch, plops in the snow.

Iso. Iso. Isolation. There's a window here. No Mavis talking to me at the window.

They bring in food. One time Linda, who I seen dropping the tray off, she stays for a long time. She strokes my hair and I am sleeping funny, on the floor. "I'm going home tonight, little girl. Got your present you gave me last week under the tree. Can't wait to open it. You think about happy Christmas now, think about future times, Trista. I got something for you too, will come see you tomorrow. You're going to get through this," she says.

Another time I ask Deb, "How long am I going to be in here?"

"It's only been a few hours, Trista. We want you to try to get some sleep."

I think about Linda opening up the picture I made her of me and Faith. Us standing on the Iceroad with the first sunrise behind us like I imagine for January 4. Wrapped up good and tight in our parkys. The fireworks from Sunrise shooting up way beyond the sun's rays. The orange of the first light of the year reflected on the Iceroad, lighting up our faces.

This is how you are a good mother. You pick up your baby when she is crying. You don't squeeze her hand no matter how hard you want to because that's not going to stop her crying.

We're so cold, we just wanted smokes.

You have to rock her. Then if that doesn't work, you have to check her diaper and even if you seen it's a little wet, you have to change it. It don't matter if you don't got clean ones or on the outside you can't afford to buy them. In jail there's lots of clean diapers for Faithy.

The blood and the cash register.

You put her on the bed, and push all the books away and the pen away and the journal away. You put her on the bed, and lay a mat out under her little bum.

Mavis is looking behind her left shoulder. "What you kids want so late? I'm closing. You got money for them smokes?"

Then you unsnap the jumper, and pull it up, be careful of her belly button. It's just swollen because it's got a little hernia, Dr. Petterson says. It'll be small soon, don't touch it or try to poke it in. Untape the diaper, then have that washcloth handy, then get that other diaper ready.

And Jimmy grabs the store shelf, all the smokes flying down. Why's he doing that?

That diaper should be right beside you because if you have to go get a new one, she might roll off, and fuck she's too retarded already, you wanna make her more stupid, can't you do anything right?

Jimmy's screaming, "Don't tell me what to do, you fucker. Had enough of people telling me what to do." And he pushes her.

This is how you are a good mother. When all that is done and her bum is clean and dry and she's still wailing in your ear, and you're rocking her gentle, and you seen the worker coming to the window of your door, the noise of the electric lock snicks softly and the worker lets herself in and wants your baby, fear you can't take the crying.

And I'm behind him, behind him and kicking and kicking her and screaming. Not thinking, not thinking they gonna get me for it.

The worker says, "C'mere to me, Faithy," and the worker is holding her arms out to the baby, you don't let the baby go, no you don't because you are a good mother, and you're the only one can breastfeed her and comfort her.

They gonna take away my baby and get me for it good for a long long time.

But you give Faith over to the worker anyway because your milk's not coming out proper anyhow. You give her up because she can't be in this jail for bad girls any more. Not with fuck-ups. Not with murderers.

I know she's dead. I know because her eyes are glassing like the frost on the windows of the Aurora Store. Jimmy is stuffing packs of smokes into his pockets, wiping at his snotty nose. I keep kicking her harder and harder. Until Jimmy's grabbing at my arm. "They're coming," and we're running down the back stairs, but there's a guy who's seen us, he's yelling, he's in the store now and seen her on the floor, and we're running up the main road, my breath ice ice ice and my belly so big, "Fuck you, Trista, look what you made me do, you dumb fuck," and he pushes me in the road and starts to pound at my stomach and we can hear the sirens and the RCMP come for us, then I'm down on the ground and the tires skidding in the snow, Jimmy face before they pull him off me, red and spitting. "You fucker, Trista, why the fuck you get me all riled again, why the fuck we drinking that shit, why the fuck you always wanna get me in trouble?" And I don't say nothing to him, just let him beat me and Faith inside me.

"She was already dead when you kicked her, Trista," Linda says.

The baby's crib is empty. They took her to the foster home and I don't know what's gonna happen to me. I think they took that baby away because that baby is no one's baby. No one good. And I am so tired. Linda's here and she's got my head in her lap and I am feeling too little, not my big self, not my mother self. When I dare look up at Linda, it's like seeing her through ice eyes, I been crying so hard it's hard to see her. But she's got this look in her eyes, like she's got this look that says she loves me, and I wonder how she can get that in there. Feels like we been in here forever, and I can smell that closed-in smell you get from sleeping too long, the crustiness of my eyes and my mouth feels gummy and dry. "But I kicked the shit out of her. I did that to her."

"Yes. You did. And that was wrong. But she was dead after Jimmy pushed her. She hit her head. You have to know the reality of the crime. You can't carry this forever."

I am breathing and I imagine Faith breathing, is she alive? My little girl I wanted for so long and how she came out that night, to kicking and screaming and me fucked up out of my mind and Jimmy's dead-sounding voice: "Come on Trista, run, they're coming," and she's coming, my Faithy is coming into this world of violence I laid out for her.

Linda leaves a book on the floor. It says, My Name Is Masak. It says, on the back, that it's about a girl who grew up and was in the residential school, from when she was little to about my age. It says she was from Aklavik, not far from here and still on the Mackenzie River. It says it's about how she was called Masak, then she was called Alice. Then she changed her name back to Masak. But I feel like I don't have no old ways in me. I have Inuvialuit, but I got the white rig-pig in me, that orange-bearded man in me who stood at that doorway and didn't even want to come in and hold or hug or touch his own kid when she's awake enough to feel it right. I'm that kid lying there, squinting in the crack of the open doorway, wondering what they're thinking, maybe, why did we make her, what is she here for, look how she fucks everything up.

Mavis is talking again. She doesn't seem so mad, she just calmly looking at me. Now she is beyond the window. Now she isn't at the window, she just ups and walks in and sets herself down on the chair here in Iso. I'm laying on the bed, looking up at her. Linda in taking my tray maybe some time ago, she says, "Trista, you don't eat, we have to put you in hospital, put needles in your arm. Come see here, the pottery cup I got my uncle to make you. See it has little scissors on it. Got to think forward, baby. Eat this bread, least drink your tea." And I do, I am drinking my tea. It's the only thing I can drink, and it doesn't taste like Nanuk's good sweet Red Rose boiled tea. However much I want to make it so, it doesn't.

"I was going to get my hair cut that day," Mavis says. "Was getting ready for my little grandbaby's first birthday. You know Jenna?"

"Jenna Ford?" I says. "She Maisie Ford's niece?"

"Yeeah. She's the one," Mavis says.

"You want tea?"

I hold the cup up to her and she drinks from it. I think maybe it's going to go sliding all over the floor because I figure she's a ghost spirit, but it slides right in and disappears within her.

"My hair was too long, wanted it some short and styled," Mavis says.

"You want I cut it nice for you, Nanuk?" I says.

"Yeeah. You do that for me, girl. Be good to have it cut nice, Trista," she says.

"What are you thinking about?" Linda says.

"Hope maybe. Maybe I got some hope," I says.

"Tell me."

I sit up and look at her, this woman who has been here for me. Trying to help me fill that hollow cold I been fighting with inside me. And I tell her.

I see this. I see this. For Faith, and for me. I know it might not happen but it's something that I got to see. To make me move forward. A life with my Faithy. A life I can get for me and her, so that I still know I hurt Mavis. I know her name and I know she's gone now. Maybe she's forgiven me? I don't know if she's forgiven me. But I got to be taking that part inside myself and saying I'm going to be the one who is walking those steps going to crunch in that snow and keep putting the feet forward. I can't think of doing it sometimes. Getting more job skills and real world. Maybe take some hairdressing course down YK when I get out. Maybe it's not like real jail time but rehab and getting better, and making progress. I get tired thinking about all Linda and Deb been trying to do to get me better. Makes me tired and thinking I don't know much. Which I don't. But I know some things. I have my Faithy. Maybe she's in that foster home in Inuvik and maybe it might be some time before I can come back and visit her proper. But in my head I have her, and I am holding her and she is ah ah ah in my face. Her eyes roam around my face and she's drooling, grinning some and not fussing. She's looking up at me and I can believe what them doctors say that she might only have some mental retardation, or maybe time will tell and not at all, that she will get through it, her brain will adapt. She's never gonna hear. But she might be able to go to school normal like with other kids, hear with her eyes, talk with her fingers, get some ear operation, lots of things.

Me and Keely, me and all the kids we were some lucky when we were little. We had our Snow Nanuks, raised us up best they could. They still around, watching, waiting to see if I come back to them. They here up north, watching over me no matter where I am.

That's some thing. That's one great big some thing. And I dream. I think on my little girl. What she might be. Will she get out of there, that world she got inside her. This dream I got of her? Goes like this:

Faith is packing a big black suitcase, and there's the picture that Ms. Epstein gave her, on her birthday, even though Ms. Epstein teaches the little kids now, and Faith doesn't have her as a teacher any more. It is a picture made by an artist up Holman way, now they call it Ulukhaktok, and Ms. Epstein got it at the Christmas Craft Sale. On the back it says, To Faith, who will read up a storm in Yellowknife.

My Faith is trying not to cry, because she is a big girl now, she really is, she's just turned twelve and the school down south Yellowknife, they've given some scholarships to some northern kids, and she's going down to that school. I was scared to let her go, asked Nanuk, "Isn't it like the residential schools, sending our kids away?" And Nanuk shook her head. "No, not when she's living with a Dene family. She needs to read good down there. And we've been teaching her the ways. She won't lose herself."

Faith's friend from school will come too, and she and Faithy will live with a real nice Dene family, and that family has a girl just one year older than them. That girl likes to sew and do some caribou tufting and since I have taught Faith, Faith can show the new girl just how. How you have to be patient and gentle and pick good strong threads, and stick to just a few colours at a time so as not to overwhelm the artwork, that's what Nanuk says and she knows, because Nanuk's doing good with her art, just sold lots of caribou tufting works and even might go in a gallery in Edmonton, or as far as Toronto, to represent some northern artists. And me with my hairdressing shop doing good, all the ladies go to me, I know how to cut their thick hair just right, even some of the men say so, go to me instead of the barbershop.

"Don't worry, I'll come visit you," I says to my Faithy.

"I know you will," Faith says.

And I know Faith believes it, and I think it's not that that makes her sad. It's leaving this place, this house, this north. She knows that Yellowknife is still north, but it's a big town, with lots of people, almost twenty thousand, and no Mackenzie River.

"You'll be back in time for Ice Break Up," I says, because I know Faith feels worried.

"Will you come down then, and get me?"

"No, you can fly up on your own. And we'll be right at the airport, picking you up, hugging you. Think of all the books, Faithy."

I know she knows, and that's what makes her pack a little faster, thinking about the books, all the books she has read in the little Jackfish Bay Library, nearly gone through them all, as Ms. Epstein would say. Because my little girl just knows how to read them. She read them fast, not any trouble like some of them other kids have with reading, like even I had with reading. Not my girl, she good at reading. Was a time when we all thought she was retarded. Was a time when the doctors said, No, Trista, your girl Faithy not ever going to do the other things normal kids can do. Them were those bad times. With all that happened and Jimmy and the Aurora Store. But it's gonna be different, they seen what Faithy can do. She come out of it. Slowly she grew. Faith and all those books lined up on the walls of the big library in Yellowknife, just waiting, breathing to be opened and give her something new.

"You'll be needing this." I put the ulu necklace around her.

"But, Mom, you can't give me this," Faith says.

"Yes, I can. It's for your new beginning now, Faith."

I got the handcuffs on my arms. I didn't kill Mavis, I still got to go to court with Jimmy. I got aggravated assault for what we did. All this time, me talking to Mavis, me thinking I was the one who killed her. Linda says, No. They put you in here because of your alcohol and drug history. They put you in here for aggravated assault, because you were there, and you kicked her. But you didn't kill her, Trista. Jimmy pushed her hard. She cracked her head and died. Why do you think he did that? Why were you there, Trista? Why did he push her? You were doing so good, and then you get mixed up with Jimmy again.

They don't know. They don't know how Jimmy just moved so. Coked up and fucked up. Made Mavis get out of the way for the smokes. Pushed her and then her head go down on the counter, bad. Just moved her and was mad. Just wanting to be safe and little again at the Snow Nanuks' house and now I'm bad and fucked up. That how you can be doing so good and trying hard then things fuck up for that one moment and you never get it right again.

They put me in the van, and we're going to the courthouse up Mackenzie Road in Inuvik. I get there and through some doors and there is Jimmy. He's in a grey jumpsuit with Corrections YK written on the back. He sees me, and his head is shaved. I can see a scar near his ear. He smiles at me. Just a little. I don't think I figured on seeing him smile. I smile back a little, what else can I do. But his eyes are sad. He knows we're in for the long haul and I guess I do too.

I recognize lots of the town people, sitting in the jury box. And Mavis's kids and other town people sitting in the audience. The judge says many things, but I still can't really hear her, my ears are still not working good, but I hear her say, Do you understand? And I say, Yes, ma'am. Then we sit down, everyone does, and there's so much talk that's got no sound. People come up to the box and talk, and their mouths move. I don't look behind me. I know Mavis's daughter is sitting behind there. All I can hear is her silent weeping, it's like the tears are sliding down my back. She's got a light pink dress on, and the red lipstick, just like I dreamed Mavis told me in Iso. And how Mavis don't like that combo, but she loves her daughter. Then it's time Jimmy says something. It's like someone turned the sound up because I can hear him, just him. He turns, his head down, and apologizes to Mavis's family. His eyes don't rise to them. I want to think he's a fucking coward, but I know him, I know how messed up he is. How he feels.

Then it's me. I get up, and I turn and I look right into Mavis's daughter's eyes. They're so brown and lined with red, and I expect them to be hard and cold and mean, but they're just crinkled around with sad wrinkles. I think on all that Mavis was for me, and I look at her kin. I say, "I'm sorry. I could say this for a million times the rest of my days. Still you wouldn't know how much."

There's lots of talk, with the lawyers, with the judge. This is after, after Mavis's family goes, and they meet with me in the conference room at the facility. Linda is making me talk about the plan in Group. How I can go to YK and serve my time out there. It's three years. How I will be nineteen when I get out and the YK place will put me in a good halfway house where I can go to school and get my training in something, maybe even cut hair. Visit Faith in the foster home. And come and live in Inuvik, maybe even get my baby back, just me and her. She smiles when she says it, Linda. She been here for me, so many times. I want to believe her. I want to have that hope inside.

I hear in Calgary there's Chinooks, in Edmonton all spring nice then bam comes a snowstorm hits between the eyes and says, "You thought summer was coming but it's not. You're gonna be fucked with snow for another week."

In the Mackenzie Delta, most years we start making bets on Ice Break Up. Even Northmart gets into it. Maybe put June 6,

10:20 a.m. down on the ticket and someone'll win a big twenty-seven-inch flat-screen TV with a satellite box. Or maybe the Snow Nanuks try to keep the gambling out of it and make us kids a big cookout by the Mackenzie River on the chance it'll happen in the afternoon. But there's this breeze. Cold Arctic air coming down from the Beaufort Sea one day and then suddenly the next this warm wind. Going past your cheek like some lost Nanuk giving you baby kisses before passing on. There's a hush too, sitting down by the river.

Sitting on top of Lee's red pickup truck, passing each other the Thermos of coffee to keep ourselves awake, I imagine me holding Faithy and Lee's keeping us laughing with his made-up Johnny Cash songs. "No I swears," he says. "This one is not made up. 'So it farts farts farts, like a ring of turds, a ring of turds, going south south south, that ring o' turds, that ring o' turds.'"

Keely's whispering, "No way, Lee," and giggling. Lined up there with the other trucks, the blue of the 11 p.m. sky cuts at the short treeline, then the white of the ice on the water. Little bumps on it, places where it's gone mushy then frozen again in ripples, the rigs have been off it for some months now and it's not smooth like in the dark of winter. The hush. Even the mossies and black flies seem lazy or asleep and we don't have to pull our hoodies around our faces to keep them out. The Break Up can happen anywhere, along McPherson, maybe even Aklavik, southwest of us at Jackfish Bay, or even north and near the mouth of the Arctic Sea. Then Lee stops singing.

"Hey," he says. And we all point our faces northward. It's a faint cracking at first. Like the creak of a big ol' daduk setting down in his favourite chair. Then a huge thunderclap sound and a roar goes up from all of us, horns honking, people jumping out of their cars, kids jumping on their bikes to tell others. We're all jumped up, Lee's standing in front of the truck, me and Faithy and Keely jump to the bed of the truck.

"Shh," Lee says and, "there." He points to the north and we see it. The white and grey and black ice chunks bunching up against each other like it's a huge muskrat under there working with an even bigger beaver and they're both working like stink to make the biggest dam. Then the rush and it's out. And the river's blue and rushing, tree branches, hunks of ice suddenly moving and that place that was a road, that was something we could run, jump, skidoo, drive across is gone, fast flowing, moving to its own go-away place.

Faith is gurgling and her fists move against my cheeks as she fights against my chest, clamouring to be held closer. She's blinking, she's looking at me, and I see inside the blue of her eyes the rush of the Mackenzie River, the push of the Arctic Sea ice forcing the current south instead of polar north, mossies, terns, blackflies and jaegers, gulls, shorebirds dipping madly in the river, wildflowers of all colours growing intense under the twenty-four-hour Arctic sunshine. We all fall to hugging and whooping and Lee grabs us one by one and helps us off the truck. I hold up Faith to him and kiss his grizzled cheek as he sets me down and grins. "Looks like that old river's got somewhere to go again, hey, Trista."

And I see my Faithy rubbing her fingers over the smooth ulu necklace, feeling the warm from the mammoth ivory. And she can almost see them, the muskoxen moving safely north, turning their ice-encrusted heads to her. For her good luck, her goodness. For her forever north.

ACKNOWLEDGMENTS

To my friends and family for their support.

To Jolene D. and Maja H.: Your strength is my constant touchstone.

Much of this novel was started in creative writing classes at the UBC MFA program and the Banff Writing Studio 2006. A million thanks to my fellow students and teachers in both programs.

To my agent, Denise Bukowski, for guidance far beyond expectations. Thank you to the exceptional editors at Penguin Canada: Nicole Winstanley, Barbara Berson, and Harmony Ho for incredible comments and support. Thank you to the marvellous magician copy editor, Heather Sangster. I've discovered that it takes a posse to write a book, and mine is tireless and compassionate in all the right places.

A Penguin Readers Guide

Having Faith in the Polar Girls' Prison

To download a Teaching Guide by Cathleen With, go to www.penguin.ca/PolarGirlsTeachingGuide

ABOUT THE BOOK

Set against the stark and haunting landscape of Canada's far North, *Having Faith in the Polar Girls' Prison* is the heart-rending story of fifteen-year-old Trista. Confined to the prison in small-town Jackfish Bay while awaiting trial, Trista chronicles the events of her life before the birth of her not-quite-healthy baby daughter, Faith, in a mesmerizing stream-of-consciousness narrative.

In a story that spans several weeks, Trista details life in the detention facility, including Group sessions with the other three inmates (also young girls from northern communities); her developing crush on Deanne, a fellow inmate; visits from her best friend, Keely; appointments with Dr. Pettersen, who periodically checks on Faith's progress; and talks with the social workers, who try to draw out her story.

Throughout the narrative, Trista gives glimpses of life before prison, when she was still with Tyler. In their trailer they build a world in which a hopeful future is possible. It's a safe world where the two of them will live with Faith, far away from the sexual abuse, drunkenness, and poverty that Trista has known all her life.

After several disagreements with Trista, Tyler decides to go down to Yellowknife to earn money to open up his own tattoo parlour—a dream he's always had. Trista is devastated, and doesn't hear from him for weeks. Then one fateful night Keely calls Trista about meeting up with Jimmy, an old boyfriend. Lonely, bored, and upset with Tyler, Trista agrees to the meeting, and together they take a trip to the Aurora Store, with tragic consequences.

As Trista tries to make sense of what happened that night and to deal with her complicity in the events that led to her incarceration, she struggles to accept that Faith may have fetal alcohol syndrome and will soon be taken away from her to be placed in foster care. All the while, she hangs on to memories of what was good—the love and protection of the Snow Nanuks, the traditions and stories of her community, Keely's friendship, and Mom when she was still alive.

With heartfelt compassion, rare insight, and a compelling new voice, debut novelist Cathleen With explores the themes of loss and love, heartbreak and suffering, and the possibility of forgiveness. With lends light to the hardships of the teenage girls and clash of cultures in this remote region that has never before been represented in literature. ■

Q: Why did you choose to write about the girls of Canada's far North?

After teaching overseas for many years, I decided I wanted to come back to Canada. I found a job in Inuvik, Northwest Territories. Many teachers had talked about how rough the job was, but I loved it: the almost instant closeness with the students and staff, the small-town feel. Early on I was struck by how difficult it was for the young girls—and boys—living in such a small town. With often excellent activities for youth going on, and good social and band services, I wondered why. Many kids were caught up in drinking and drugs, or getting pregnant or contracting STIs at a young age.

Though we had several books to study in class by amazing Northern authors—specifically Robert Alexie, Richard Van Camp, and Alice French, who wrote *My Name Is Masak*—many of the girls wanted stories about their lives now, specific to the Mackenzie Delta and their age group. I've been writing since I was young, so I started writing short stories for them, and it grew into a novel. ■

Q: Jackfish Bay is a fictional town. How closely does it resemble the northern towns you lived and worked in?

There is a very close resemblance between Jackfish Bay and Inuvik, though I set the story outside of Inuvik because I wanted to show how many people there, whether Inuvialuit, Gwich'in, or white, in families or in the social services, educational, or hospital systems, are concerned about the kids in their town and are helping them stay off drugs and alcohol. I also wanted to show how easy it is for young people to be influenced by their peer group and lose or forget their sometimes excellent upbringing—their Snow Nanuks. Many kids I knew were trying so hard to do better—to stay in school and to not get drunk every weekend. But it was difficult for them. The scenery of Jackfish Bay is the Mackenzie Delta—the beauty of the people and the land. ■

Q: Were sudden infant death syndrome (SIDS) and fetal alcohol syndrome (FAS) common among the girls you worked with up north? How did the girls deal with these tragedies?

Yes, both SIDS and FAS were prevalent causes of death or affliction for the babies of the young girls I worked with, and I should stress that even some girls who were not drinking and "being good" during their pregnancies could have their baby die of SIDS later on. Researchers have been looking into teenage pregnancies and SIDS deaths, and there have been studies suggesting that some teenagers have premature babies whose lungs are not developed. Two of my best students—girls who worked hard at not using drugs or drinking to cope with their problems—have lost their babies to SIDS. They are my heroes because of the mature ways they dealt with death. I know I could not have coped at their age the way they did. One of the girls had just lost her baby when I started teaching up north. It's easy as a teacher to get depressed there during the winters: the darkness, and seeing some kids fight their own demons. But seeing her come to class every day, trying to live after suffering such an intense loss—it gave me hope. Sometimes the girls will get pregnant as soon as they can after a SIDS death, but this girl waited until she was older. And I can happily say that today she is the proud mother of a healthy baby girl, and she's working and taking classes in her spare time.

FAS is also quite common, as many girls and boys are drinking or using drugs and having unsafe sex. The cycle of FASD (fetal alcohol spectrum disorder) is all over the North: kids with FAS having babies with FAS. It is very difficult to have been born addicted to drugs or alcohol and then not get into using and becoming addicted when you're a teenager. Also, kids with FAS have a difficult time in school, as they often have learning disabilities and behavioural challenges, so they often drop out early and work in jobs that don't pay them a living wage. It is then easy to get depressed and start drinking—starting the cycle all over again. ■

Q: Why did you choose to write using a stream-of-consciousness narrative voice?

When I write, I hear voices first. It's like a play going on inside my head. I hear the characters speaking to each other, then I "see" where they are and the conflicts they get into. I felt very close to Trista, and could feel her yearnings for a better life with Faith. I think her confusion, thoughts, and dreams could only have been told in the first-person, stream-of-consciousness voice because I wanted the reader to feel with her, grow with her, and know what it was like to be her: trapped and confused but suffused with love for her baby and the North. ■

Q: Good role models for Trista are few and far between, especially male ones. It seems that Lee is the only positive male influence on Trista. Even Tyler isn't entirely positive because he abandoned Trista and her baby. Why did you choose to portray the male characters this way?

It was difficult because from what I had seen working with the girls, the stories I'd heard, most of the male influences were either absent or abusive. But Trista does have her Daduk, she does have Lee, who is like a strong big brother to her. And though Tyler has his faults, he was trying to make a life for them and got caught up in his drug use. I wanted to show how hard it is for the girls who are sometimes left behind. The boys they're in relationships with are also confused—and very young—and it's easy for them to run away. It's often the mothers or the grandmothers of the pregnant young girls who look after the girls. Not everyone experiences the abuse like Trista did, but I hate to say that in my research it wasn't exactly unusual. And not just confined to the North. In the end, this was Trista's story, and although it's fiction, I didn't want to shy away from the drug use, drinking, and abuse that are pandemic in many communities. ■

Q: The girls are enrolled in several community programs—gardening, working in the nursing home. These programs have a positive effect on the girls. In what ways do they ready them for society?

I wanted the girls to connect with some things they may have forgotten. With the snow on the ground from September to June, it's easy to forget that connection with growth and nature, the cycles of flowers and plants and the fruit they bear to sustain us. Caring for and washing the elders connects Trista with the family and community she lost while living her dreams with Tyler in the trailer. Though these girls have committed crimes and must spend time rehabilitating in the juvenile detention facility (or prison, as they call it), I think programs like these help them realize they are still compassionate and can develop skills to be worthwhile to the communities they live in. ■

Q: You titled this book *Having Faith in the Polar Girls' Prison*. Does Trista succeed in having faith, considering her "desperate hope to manufacture a fairy-tale perfect family," as one reviewer says? Is there a measure of hope despite the bleakness of the subject matter?

There is no fairy-tale ending in this book, that's for sure. I think if I had written something fluffy and flowery in the end I would have been dishonouring the kids I knew up north by belittling their struggles. I think Trista comes to the place where she realizes that the dreams she and Tyler had had big holes in them. But remembering her Snow Nanuks, the good and bad of what she and Keely had gone through as kids, and her love of Faith, she comes to believe and hope that her dreams of family, connection with the land she lives in, and wishes for her baby's future can come true. ■

Q: What happens to Faith at the end of the book? Does she have a hopeful future, the way Trista had envisioned?

I didn't write about whether Faith actually got into the special foster-care home or what happens to her at the end of the book. I left that open because I want the reader to journey with Trista to their own conclusions. Will Trista be able to get Faith back after her time in the facility is up? Will she be a good mother to a child who will probably have many difficulties in life? Has the Polar Girls' Prison given Trista enough help and hope to mother Faith? These are questions open for discussion. I, for one, have seen that river run again after such a long long winter, and hope that one day you will also go up to the Mackenzie Delta to see that beauty. I guess I'm saying that I have faith. ■

Q: Your interest seems to be focused on at-risk youth and their stories. What will your next book be about?

In my youth and my travels I've been lucky to meet people who have struggled against seemingly insurmountable odds to live lives of grace and beauty. My friends, the students I've taught and people I've met in the different countries I've lived in, have helped me get through my own troubles and appreciate life. I lived in Cambodia several years ago and worked in an orphanage that was helping children exit the sex trade. My next book will be about Angkor Wat and the children who live and work around the temples. ■

DISCUSSION QUESTIONS

1. The mother-daughter relationship is one that is missing in this novel. How is Trista's mother portrayed? In what ways does pregnancy become a way of "saving" or making things better?
2. Why do you think Tyler left? What does he represent for Trista? How much of Tyler is wishful thinking, and how important are the wishes (setting up the tattoo parlour, haircutting, etc.) to keeping the hope alive?
3. How is the prison both a place of imprisonment and a place of safety?
4. Is Keely a good friend? In what ways is she responsible for what happened that night at the Aurora Store?
5. How much does family history matter? Is Trista doomed to repeat the mistakes of her mother and grandmother and, to a larger extent, her community?
6. Trista and the other girls are described as "the babies who having the babies up north." Is it fair for workers from the South to come and try to understand the problems of the North when they didn't grow up there themselves?
7. How are the Snow Nanuks a maternal influence in Trista's life? How about Auntie or Nanuk? Linda and Deb?
8. Storytelling and traditions seem to be the antidote to trouble-making. Discuss the elements of native culture and how they play a role in Trista's development.
9. Discuss the symbolism of the Iceroad and the Ice Break Up.